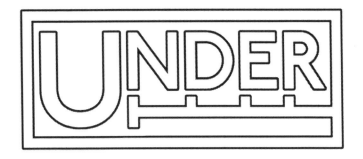

# DAVID WAILING

This book is a work of fiction but makes reference to real people, events and locations. For more information, see Author's Notes at the back of the book.

Many thanks to Tug Wilson, Kath Middleton, Julie Stacey, Manab Roy, Steve Opsblum, Eileen Gilbey, Rosemary Green, Ann Voysey, Paul Tilling, District Dave's London Underground Forum, Guerrilla Exploring, London Transport Museum, Subterranea Britannica and Underground History. For full acknowledgements and bibliography, see Author's Notes.

Visit the Amazon Kindle Bookstore for more novels by David Wailing in eBook format.

Contact the author at **www.davidwailing.com**

The short story **Signal Failure** was previously published as a standalone eBook and acts as a prelude to **Under**.

# Signal Failure

Saturday 25th March 2017

3.47am

Emily was jolted out of half-sleep by a beeping sound. She looked up to see the train's doors slide open with a clank and a grinding of steel. On the other side were the yellow-tiled walls of a London Underground station.

Still only at Knightsbridge? Bloody hell, this is taking forever!

She forced herself to sit upright, grabbing her handbag before it slipped off her lap. A quick look at her phone to check the time, then she flung it back into the handbag with a sigh. A few passengers walked off the train but she stayed in her seat.

An automated female voice rang through the train cars: *"This is a Piccadilly Line service to Heathrow Terminals 1, 2, 3 and 5. The next station is South Kensington. Change for the District and Circle Lines. Alight for the museums and Royal Albert Hall."* The same message scrolled across the electronic displays in letters composed of bright orange dots.

There was more beeping before the curved grey doors rumbled shut. With a gentle jolt, the Tube train started moving again. She watched the station pass by outside the windows, faster and faster: people, posters, signs, chairs, barriers, then tunnel-blackness. It sped on beneath west London, carrying Emily

1

toward her home and her bed. God, she wanted her bed.

She was more than a little tired, because she was more than a little drunk. Surprised, actually, at how woozy she felt. Normally she could handle much more than the amount she'd put away earlier.

It had been a twenty-first birthday party, at a bar round the back of Covent Garden. Emily hadn't seen Dhwani since their schooldays in Golders Green, but any opportunity for a night out in the West End was worth taking. She'd had a good time, but eventually realised that the barman with the broad shoulders wasn't that interested after all, so said her goodbyes and staggered toward Leicester Square Station.

At least Emily could get a train home, without throwing money away on minicabs and Uber. Since the Night Tube started running last year, she had the freedom to go anywhere, on the weekends at least. That Oyster card in her back pocket had been given a proper spanking.

Not that the Night Tube was much better than in the daytime. How long has she been on this sodding train, she wondered? Half an hour? It's crawled along since Leicester Square and sat on every platform for ages, even stopped in the tunnels a few times.

She squinted up at the wide map of the Piccadilly Line, as if she didn't already know it was ten more stops till Boston Manor. Or Boredom Manor, as she always called it. Depressing to think how far away she lived from all the good bits of London. "Zone 4?!" she remembered saying. "They're still on coal out there, aren't they?" But it meant the house she rented with

Kay and Alicia was just about affordable, and it was easy to get to their university in nearby Brentford.

Ugh, don't start thinking about uni... the coursework she still hadn't handed in, the big exams round the corner. At least this was her final year, although what she would actually do with a degree in Broadcast Journalism, she had no clue. One thing she did know was she needed a decent job to stay in London. No way was she living anywhere else, London's nightlife was where she belonged!

All right, it was true: going to uni had turned her into a bit of a party animal. But, Emily told herself – and anyone else who suggested having more quiet nights in – she'd earned it. She was forced to grow up fast when their family split in half, years ago. She had only been twelve when she had to look after a suddenly fragile mother. But ever since Mum moved out of London and down to the coast with her great-aunt, Emily had been catching up on the good times. Even if it did lead to being stuck on the bloody Underground.

Bored, tired and light-headed, she glanced around the inside of the car. Strip-lights, adverts, air vents, patterned seat covers, blue and yellow handrails. Nothing worth looking at. The colourful warning signs were as unremarkable to her Londoner's eyes as grey clouds in the sky. *Priority area for baggage. Items trapped in the doors cause delays. Please keep feet off seats.*

She supposed it was no different to travelling on the pavements and roads above ground. Wherever you went, there were signs, announcements, flashing lights and beeping noises telling you what to do. Go here, don't go there, do this, don't do that, no entry this way, exit that way. They were absolutely every-where.

Funny, she'd never thought about that before. No need to think in London, it told you what you needed to know.

Some people clearly resented this, judging by the way Tube signs were occasionally defaced. On a nearby door, someone had scratched out a few letters of the yellow sticker saying *Obstructing the doors can be dangerous*, which now read *Obstructing the doors can   anger us*. Comic genius, she thought sourly.

The people were even less remarkable. Night Tubes tended to be busy around 2am, but at this time of night it wasn't even half-full. Three beautiful black women with heels and handbags, laughing about their night out. A noisy quartet of well-dressed teenagers, boys in shirts and girls in skirts. A guy in a loose chequered overshirt with rolled-up sleeves, asleep with both arms folded. An Asian couple – maybe Korean? – sitting quietly, hunched over their phones. An overweight Arab man in glasses doing the same with a tablet, earphones plugged in as he watched a movie.

And there was Emily, in her best jeans and white blouse and long belted coat, bored of her own reflection in the opposite window. Blonde hair fell over her face as she rested her head against the glass panel beside the seat, wishing it was her pillow. She felt the vibration of the train as it slowed to a stop.

*"Good evening, ladies and gentlemen."* Oh, here we go. Emily let out a tut-sigh, along with everyone else,

4

as once again the driver's voice came over the crackly PA system. He sounded young, with a faint Irish accent.

*"Our apologies for the slow running of the service tonight. This is due to an earlier signal failure on the Piccadilly Line. Repair work is underway and we should be on the move shortly. Thank you for your patience."*

God, signal failure again? That was always their excuse. More than once, Emily wondered if that was a code of some kind, hiding the fact that every single part of the Tube was falling to bits. Or maybe the bulbs just kept burning out. Nothing worked without those red and green lights – trains, cars, people, all the same. Red and green, stop and go. No need to think in London, it told you what you needed to know…

Next thing she knew, the train jerked back into motion. Did she doze off there for a second?

She scrubbed her face with both hands, trying to wake herself up. How come she felt so glassy and detached when normally she could drink her mates under the table? Christ – did someone spike her vodka and coke? She did leave her glass for a minute when she went to the loo. Stupid! That might explain why she felt so out of it. Or maybe I'm just getting old, she thought. Coming up to her own twenty-first birthday in a few weeks. Surely she wasn't turning into a lightweight already…

She stared through the window. There were rows of cables all bunched together on the tunnel wall, mostly grey but one red and one green, plus two thin copper wires. They all lazily drifted from left to right as the train edged along. Then suddenly she was looking at a wall. Not the curved tunnel wall but flat brickwork, so dark it was barely visible. A minute later, the cables were back again.

Squinting at the wall squeezed a memory out of some crevice in her brain. Her dad's voice, talking about... what did he call them... ghost stations? Old Tube stops that weren't used any more, so trains just went right through. Maybe one of them was behind that wall.

Why did Dad tell me that? And why did Mum stop him, leading to some kind of argument? There were always arguments. Emily pinched the bridge of her nose, not even sure it was a proper memory. She might well have read about ghost stations in the Metro or the Londonist website, somewhere like that.

She felt the train turning, with a harsh metallic squeal from its wheels. Quite a sharp turn judging by the way the car ahead veered to the left, showing her all the people on its right bank of seats. The fingernails-on-blackboard screech dragged on for a while, making her wince, and then faded as the train once again slowed to a halt. The sound of electric motors – a constant background hum that you only became aware of when it stopped – stopped. It would start up again when the train was ready to proceed.

More tut-sighs filled the silence. The rowdy teenagers jeered and complained, then went back to flirting and laughing. A couple of the others glanced up and pulled a face.

Her gaze wandered back to the scrolling dot matrix display. Another of the million signs by which London guided the ebb and flow of its people.

*This is a Piccadilly Line service to*
*Heathrow Terminals 1, 2, 3 and 5*
*The next station is Shroud Lane*
*Please mind the gap between the train*
*and the platform*

She blinked. Hang on. What did that just say? Shroud Lane? That's not right, it's South Ken next stop! London Underground have cocked everything up tonight.

While staring at the electronic sign and waiting for it to go by again, Emily tried to remember where Shroud Lane was. Somewhere west, she reckoned, one of those obscure stations on the upper left of the Tube map, or was she thinking of Hanger Lane? Or perhaps Rayners Lane, what line was that on?

The display remained blank, and the train remained still, and she remained tired. Emily glanced back down the length of the car, wishing those kids would pipe down a bit. Then she might be able to nod off, for the next ten stops at least.

With a sudden mechanical whoosh that made Emily jump, the train's doors slid open.

All along one side…

*"Shit!"*

…then all along the other.

She snapped awake, staring at the doors. All were wide open, every one! And on the other side was…

Nothing. Only the bare interior of the tunnel, lined with cables and coated in grime.

The same reaction sparked through the other passengers, who all looked alarmed. The teenagers loudly freaked out: What the fuck man, oh my days, Jesus what's going on? The man in the chequered overshirt was up on his feet, glaring at the nearest doorway. The three women grasped each other as if the train were in freefall.

Emily turned to face the car ahead and saw the same thing had happened there, with similar shocked faces. It looked like every single door had opened.

The entire train.

The *wrongness* of what she was seeing felt like a punch to the eyes. This never happened. The doors weren't meant to open inside the tunnels, ever! Travelling on the Tube was like being in a solid bubble, but now the bubble had broken, and the gaping spaces made her feel abruptly vulnerable...

The Arab man said "Knew this train was knackered."

This triggered a wave of laughter. The Koreans held up their phones to take pictures of the open doors, as did two teenagers. "Driver's pissed!" shouted one of the lads. "Oi mate, you pressed the wrong button!"

Emily forced a breath through the knot in her chest, then made herself relax back into her seat. It probably was something as simple as that. She'd read that TfL had to hire a load of new part-time staff to run the Night Tube. The driver whose voice they heard was probably just as exhausted as his passengers. Any second now, he'd realise his mistake and flick the switch to close all the doors again.

Her head turned back and forth, looking at the rows of open spaces. Something about them gave her the shivers. Like those dreams everyone has, of walking out of the house and forgetting their clothes. She felt bare.

It struck Emily just how closely the tunnel squeezed in on the train from all sides, almost pressing against its metal skin. If it had completely broken down, were they all supposed to exit that way? Is that why the doors had opened? She couldn't imagine all these people trying to get out through that narrow space.

Or anyone getting in.

No idea where that thought came from. She caught her breath. The thought of there being people in the tunnels, climbing into the train from the outside…

Surely the driver would make an announcement and explain. Surely the doors would close again.

Aaaany second now.

"For God's sake," muttered Emily. She stood up, going dizzy from a rush of blood to the head. A stale breeze wafted through the open doorway in front of her. She felt a clutch of vertigo. There were only a few inches between the ridged steel lip of the train floor and a drop into darkness, but you'd think it was the edge of a cliff, the way it made her feel. Get a grip!

She found the nearest emergency alarm, flipped up the panel and pulled the red lever inside. A small screen lit up with the words *Driver Aware* and it gave off a steady, regular beep. She leaned close to the speaker grille. "Can you hear me?"

"Tell him the doors are open!" called one of the

three women in a shrill voice.

Emily felt stupid, wondering how to phrase the completely obvious. "Um, don't know if you know this, but all the doors have come open? Hello?"

The alarm beep stopped –

– the lights blinked off –

– the entire train went black.

Screams in the darkness. Proper screams. Emily might have been one of them but her throat felt choked tight.

She spun round, staring into nothingness. All the strip-lights had gone off at once. Not just in this car but the ones ahead and behind too.

She reached out, grabbing one of the handrails. Oh God, she can't see a thing, what… and then she realised there was a small rectangle of light outlining the shape of the Arab man, still in his seat. From the tablet perched on his lap.

Over the screaming and shouting, Emily bellowed "Your phones! Get your phones out!"

Her hand clawed inside her handbag, finding her own smartphone. The sight of the familiar icons on its screen calmed her a little. With a tap she switched on its camera light, pushing back the blackness. Similar beams from other people's phones started spiralling madly, reflecting off the windows.

The panic died down as everyone realised they could now see each other, but every passenger – except the Arab man who still had his earphones in – was on their feet. The silent train echoed with voices: Oh my God, oh my God, what's happening, it's terrorists got to be terrorists, get the lights back on, oh Christ it's terrorists it's got to be, we need to get out, what the fuck's going on...

This isn't happening, Emily thought and almost said aloud. It can't be happening. This just doesn't happen, not here, not on the Tube!

She felt as terrified as the others but mixed in with the floating glassiness of being drunk. Her whole body was tense, heart pounding, eyes huge, yet there was a feeling of being detached from this somehow.

The emergency alarm panel was no longer lit up. She aimed her phone's light at the open doorway beside her. The metal ribs of the tunnel glimmered dully, layered with soot. And there was something else – an oblong lamp fixed to the wall, dirty and unlit. A once-heard fact from long ago popped into her head.

"It's a power cut!" she shouted, startling herself.

The hubbub from the others dipped as they all turned her way, making her suddenly feel like a schoolteacher. Power cut, they babbled, what's wrong with the power, how d'you know?

"The lights in the tunnel are off, look." She tilted her phone's beam at the dead lamp. "They're meant to come on if the track current stops. That means there's been a bigger power failure somewhere. Might have affected the whole line?"

Her words settled upon them all like a comforting blanket. Power failures were understood, they were only ever temporary, the power would be back on soon, this had happened once or twice on Tube trains before. Emily told herself all this even as the other

11

passengers parroted the same thing to each other.

They clustered together in the centre spaces. She watched a couple of them stab at their phones as if they might miraculously get a signal down here, dozens of metres below ground. The constantly moving lights made bulky shadows of their bodies, and their faces into glowing masks. The open doors on both sides yawned wide. Instinctively, they all backed away from them.

Emily felt it too. The shaky sense of being exposed.

One of the silhouettes walked toward her – the guy in the chequered overshirt. He winced as she aimed her light in his eyes, then downwards apologetically. He was tall with cropped dark hair and a sort of baby-face, but his eyes were serious.

"If it is a power cut," he asked in a low voice with a Polish accent, "why do the doors open first?"

She opened her mouth as if to answer him, knowing she didn't have a clue.

They both spun as they heard a thumping noise, accompanied by shouts and demands to open the door, hey, you in there, open the door!

She realised where this came from. "The driver's cabin!"

The Polish man stepped past her to the interconnecting door. In the dark, she could just about make out the warning signs plastered on it: *Danger, risk of death if used when train is moving. Emergency use only.* He yanked the handle down and pulled it open, then did the same to the door on the other side and stepped through.

Emily took a breath and made herself follow him, stepping across the gap between one car and the next. She didn't look down. For a second, the breeze of air from the open tunnel whispered across her skin.

There were only five passengers in the first car. Sitting down were a stocky ruddy-faced man with both hands wrapped around a handrail, and a pale goth girl with her knees drawn up to her chest. They stared warily at the open doorways. The other three people were at the far end: two men in suits and a woman in a silvery dress, punching and kicking the door to the front cabin, yelling for the driver to open up, what's going on, turn the power back on, what the hell are you doing, let us in!

They calmed down as the Polish guy approached and said a few quiet words to them. Emily ran her phone-light up and down the sealed white door with its own colourful labels: *Door alarmed. Keep clear. £80 penalty fare or prosecution.* Its handle was behind a glass panel lined with green metal, and above it were more signs: *No admittance. Break glass for emergency access only.*

The Polish man looked at her, as if asking permission, and she nodded, as if giving it. He lifted one leg and kicked his solid worker's boot right at the door, loudly shattering the panel. His hands didn't seem bothered by the shards of glass that they swept out, before he gripped the lever within, twisted and pulled.

"Push!" Emily told him. It seemed obvious the door wouldn't open out into the passenger area, couldn't he see that?

He pushed. But nothing happened. Cords stood out in his neck as he yanked back and forth, forearm muscles bunched. The door stayed closed.

"Has he locked it from the inside?" wondered Emily aloud. "Or maybe the door's just broken."

"Or the driver might be sick."

Emily turned at this new voice. Her phone's light shone on a slim, mixed-race man about her height, wearing a leather jacket, colourful t-shirt and black jeans. She hadn't seen him before, so he must have walked through more than one car to get there.

"He might have had a stroke or a fit, he could need help. I'm a nurse," he added.

"That might explain it," she agreed. "There's some kind of dead-man's handle on these trains, isn't there? Like, if he lets go, because he's unconscious or something, the train stops?" She wasn't sure how she knew about that.

The Polish man shook his head. "I think it is electric. You know? Electric shock in here." He rapped his knuckles on the door. "Shorted out the train, knocked out the driver. That's why he's not talking."

She nodded. "That makes sense. If something's blown up in there, it could have electrocuted him."

"Christ, if that's true then we need to get to him *now*. He might need CPR." The nurse pulled off his leather jacket and slid his phone into his back pocket.

Emily realised what he was thinking. "You're going outside the train?"

A few of the other passengers reacted to this. Outside! You can't do that! You can't go out there. If

14

the train starts up you'll get crushed! Jesus, that's crazy. Let's just stay put, all right, someone will come help us –

"He might be dead by then," the nurse told them.

The Polish man walked to the right side of the car. He peered around the rubber-lined lip of the open door, looking ahead. "I can go."

"No way you'll fit through there, man. You need a skinny boy like me." Big grin. "And I'm a nurse. I said that, right?"

Emily gave him a worried look. "Just be careful."

"Okay, skinny," smiled the Polish man. "I'll help you." He gripped one of the nurse's arms, holding him up while he edged around the doorway.

He went in facing the tunnel, using the cables as handholds while his feet probed downwards. He sank about half a metre before he could stand on the lower part of the curved wall. Slowly, the nurse side-stepped along the narrow fissure between train and tunnel.

He was outside.

Emily and the others watched him through the windows, his back dragging against the glass, bunching up his t-shirt. The Polish guy stayed near the door and aimed his phone-light so the nurse could see where he was treading. It was such a bizarre sight, watching someone squashed up against the window like a human-sized bug.

She couldn't resist saying it. "Mind the gap."

"Smartarse," came the nurse's muffled voice through the glass. A nervous giggle from the others.

As they watched him inch his way toward the front, Emily realised she was sweating. Without movement, the air in the train had become stifling. She took off her long coat and handbag and threw both on a seat, keeping her phone in her hand.

The nurse disappeared from view as he clambered alongside the front cabin. All they could see were glimmers from his own phone-light sparkling through the front window. "Can you get inside?" Emily called. "What can you – "

"He's gone!"

"What?"

"The driver's gone. The door at the front's open, I can see it through the window. He must've got out and left!"

The Polish man looked at her, eyebrows raised. "So, this was all deliberate."

The suited men and the woman in silver all started talking at once, jabbering about terrorists and madness and being trapped, until Emily shushed them with a swiping gesture.

"Go inside the cabin," she told the nurse. She had no idea what had happened to the driver, whether he was on drugs or had a claustrophobia attack or what. All she knew was that getting into the cabin was the next logical step. "See if you can find the radio, it might still be working. Or you might even be able to turn the lights back on."

"Yes ma'am!"

"Smartarse," she replied.

"Oh."

"What?"

No answer. Goosebumps tingled along her arms.

*"What!"*

His shouts were dulled by distance. "I can see something. In the tunnel."

"The driver? Is he there?"

"No, something on the tracks."

There was a twist to the Polish guy's smooth features. He looked nervous. Why was he suddenly nervous? "A train? Another train?"

"I dunno, it…"

Silence.

"Hello?" Damn, she wished she knew the nurse's name. "What's happening?"

"It's moving. I think, uh… I think it's a train but it's…"

Silence.

Emily swallowed. Now she was nervous too. Really nervous. Shivery icicles were dripping inside her body.

But why? If it was another train then it had probably been sent back to rescue them. That's what her brain said. Her heart was saying *let me out*. Her legs were saying *let me run*. Her skin was saying *let me off*.

Slow seconds dragged by before the nurse's voice came again. "Shit."

Then "Oh shit. Oh shit."

Then "Oh God oh God oh God oh God oh God oh God oh God…"

The woman in silver was squealing, face crumpled, as her phone slipped from shaking hands. The two men grabbed her, shouting and swearing as they all backed away from the cabin. The stocky guy and goth girl were also running, scrambling through the interconnecting door to the car behind.

Emily grabbed a handrail to anchor herself, to stop herself joining them, every nerve in her body pushing her to *run!* The Polish guy was still by the door. He stared through the gap where the nurse had crawled, gulping for air as if drowning.

She made herself lean close to the window nearest to the cabin. "What can you see?" Her voice was high, edging toward a scream. "Are you okay? *What can you see!*"

Nothing but silence.

Nothing but her own heartbeats and breathing and…

…and a sort of absence of noise, like a vacuum sucking at her ears.

Emily found herself bolting back down the walkway, the Polish man right behind, seats and handrails and windows all appearing as flashes in the jerking light-beam from her phone, gaping black archways on either side waiting to pull her out, and she banged her elbows and knees going through the interconnecting door into the second car, where over a dozen passengers were clustered together at the far end, a mass of shapes and faces and noise.

She stumbled to a stop before them, panting for breath. Her body was shivering so much she collapsed onto a seat. All around her people were talking, crying, moaning, shouting.

The Polish man stared back the way they had come. He pointed with an unsteady hand. "What… what…"

She held up her own hand, as if to say *Not now. Not yet. Can't talk about it.*

Still gasping, she made herself look at the front of the car. So thick with shadows she could barely make out the two open doors between it and the next.

She wanted to see the nurse come walking through them. With his big smile and colourful t-shirt. Just saunter in and ask what the fuss was all about, that the rescue train had arrived and the fire brigade were here or something, something normal like that…

The doors hung open, absolute blackness beyond.

The Polish man dropped into the seat beside her. His round, smooth face was as pale as milk, even in the dark. He had the bluest eyes she'd ever seen, but they were frightened eyes, as frightened as her own.

She felt him grab her arm. "We need, we need to, to get out," he stuttered. "Get off this train. Now."

Another wave of detachment crashed over Emily, making her feel like she was floating, like none of this could be happening. But still her skin crawled, her stomach churned, her body agreed with him, *get off this train now!*

"What do we do?" A new face was shoved into hers – one of the four teenagers, the lad who'd said the driver was pissed. Despite his flawless haircut and immaculate clothes, he looked like a terrified child. "What do we do!"

Emily tried to take a deep breath, straining hot air through her throat. She touched the Polish guy's hand and he let go, allowing her to stand up. Her legs wobbled and she clutched a handrail. She had no idea what she was about to say.

"We need to get off this train." Her voice was lost in the gabble from the others. "Everyone, listen... guys..."

*"Listen!"* roared the Polish man. The others quietened, save for a couple who kept sobbing.

"We all need to go to the back of the train," said Emily, realising as she spoke that she did actually have an idea. "There's an old station behind us. We just went past it. We can get off the train and walk back to it – "

Get off the train, no chance, I'm not going out there, no way, no fucking way, there's something out there, don't go near the doors!

"Look, if we just get to that station then we can wait there for someone to come, it's not far, we just – "

I ain't going in that tunnel man, it's an attack, oh God I knew this would happen to me, I don't wanna die down here, shut up, we're dead, we're not getting out, shut up!

"Just go." She felt the Polish man's grip on her arm again, propelling her through the crowd. Together they pushed past the shadowy bodies.

They moved backward along the length of the train, passing through another set of interconnecting doors. The end of the car was at a sharp angle to the next, since the whole train was still stuck in the middle of a curved tunnel. Inside, it was the same:

total blackness, doors wide open on each side, passengers chattering and panicking in the dark, lit only by the glow from their phones. She was vaguely aware that some people were following them but this wasn't the time to look back. The Polish man held onto her, and sometimes she held onto him, as the two of them hurried to the back of the train.

In the third car, they passed through a cloud of voices:

Can't you hear it, they're under the train, you can hear them scratching around, there's something moving under us, it's just mice, they can smell food, oh God it's rats, they're gonna get up here, the rats are gonna climb up and they're gonna get in...

And the fourth:

I think there's people out there, I saw a face, don't be stupid, you can't have, I swear there were faces, didn't you see the eyes looking in, they're out there, I saw their fingers pull open the doors, they can just walk right in and get us and...

And the fifth:

I can smell gas, I think the train's burning, don't be crazy, I saw smoke, can't you see the smoke, it's gas, poison gas, knockout gas, we're under attack, they're gonna gas us and then they can come in and do stuff to us...

Emily gritted her teeth and tried to block them out. *Just keep going.*

The sight of another sealed cabin door told her they'd reached the last car, since all Tube trains had driver cabs at both ends. The few passengers here all had the same anxious expression, but they didn't

21

seem as scared as the others. Instead they asked what was going on, why the train had stopped, what was all the shouting about, was anyone coming to help.

All she could tell them was "The driver's gone. We're getting off the train, you need to come with us." What else could she say? She still had no idea what had just happened.

Ignoring their questions, Emily tried to remember where the platform had been at Knightsbridge. She pointed to what was now the left side of the train, facing backward. "We need to get out this way."

As before, the Polish man leaned through the open doors and peered ahead. "Okay. Let's go." He gripped the cables on the wall and lowered himself down.

"Don't! You'll get electric shock!" cried a female voice. The four teenagers were clustered nearby: the Asian girl who had spoken, a blonde girl, and the two dark-haired boys.

"It's okay," Emily told her, "the power's off, remember?"

"Yeah but might come back on any time, innit!" said one of the lads.

"Stay on the left." Emily was surprised to see the overweight Arab man walk up behind the kids. His glasses were askew and he was panting hard, but still had his earphones in and his tablet under one arm, as if he planned to continue watching his movie as soon as this was over. "The live rail's in the middle. The one near this end isn't electrified."

Hearing this, the Polish man gave him a thumbs-up and stepped down. They watched him sink past the floor of the train, sliding between it and the tunnel wall. He stopped and held up his hand. Emily pocketed her phone then reached out to take it. His callused fingers felt rough on her palm, but the firm grip was steadying. She also held onto the cables with her other hand and stepped off the edge. Her shoes – she never wore high heels, thank God – balanced awkwardly on the sloped lower part of the tunnel. There was barely enough space to squeeze through. Dirt-coated iron struts brushed her face and the train's hull pressed against her backside. But it was only a metre or so before they emerged behind the red-painted cabin section.

Emily tapped her phone back on and swept its light around. She stood with her feet either side of a smooth metal rail – *not* electrified, she had to remind herself. There were three more rails on the right, two mounted on pale ceramic posts. She guessed those would turn her into burnt toast if she touched them. The circular tunnel disappeared into blackness ahead.

Her skin tingled again, with some new sensation that wasn't easy to name. She shouldn't be down here, on the rails. To be actually standing *inside* an Underground tunnel...

She looked to the roof. London was up there. Its weight, its centuries, bearing down on her.

The noises from the others distracted her. She helped the four teenagers scramble out, rushing as fast as they could. Then came the Arab man, who somehow wrenched his bulk through the gap, although it left his shirt torn and the skin beneath badly grazed. It looked like a few more were following behind him.

"Come on." The Polish man took her hand again. Emily followed him, walking with the rail between her feet in a slightly bow-legged way, trying not to trip on the raised tracks beneath it. Their phone-lights swept ahead, picking out the circular iron ribs of the tunnel above, the rails below, the dead oblong lamps along the sides.

She heard others following, full of nerves. Once again, she felt a bit like a teacher. A teacher leading a class of scared little kids on a school trip. Through a minefield. The image brought a jagged bubble of laughter that she swallowed down.

Holding onto her guide, Emily trod on through the dark… actually *walking* through the Tubes… and soon realised she could see a lot better. The tunnel up ahead was bathed in a hazy beige light. This made everyone move faster. As they did, the curve straightened out and they could see the tunnel stretch a long way into the distance.

Behind her, the teenagers' voices rang louder. Where are we going, I can't walk like this, where's this station, you said there was a station here, why don't we go back, just keep moving!

She bumped into the Polish guy's back as he stopped. Following his gaze, she noticed the ceiling had become a high, rounded arch. The tunnel was still curved on the right but the left was a flat, grey brick wall. It was about three metres tall, reaching to the domed ceiling but not meeting it.

"This is it!" said Emily. "This is what I saw, look, you can see this used to be a station. We need to get through this wall, it'll be on the other side."

"What if there's no door?" asked one of the girls.

"What if a train comes?" asked one of the boys.

Emily shared a look with the man whose hand she still held, both having the same thought. If a Tube train came down these tracks while they were standing there...

"Faster!" he boomed, dragging Emily after him. They all half-ran half-staggered along the tunnel, trying not to get close to the live rail in the middle. Now their voices and gasps and moans and screams echoed hugely, captured by the larger space. Emily's eyes went from the brick wall beside her to the tunnel mouth ahead, wondering if they would see the headlights of an approaching train roaring right at them, if the driver would even notice before it mowed them down...

They all saw it at the same time: a high concrete step in front of a rectangular opening in the wall. It was covered by a wide metal gate. Instantly the Polish man jumped on the step, gripped the bars of the gate and pulled. He pulled again, gritted his teeth, pulled and pulled.

"*Push*, you twat!" Emily yelled.

He pushed – and with a groan of hinges, a door-sized section swung inwards. Obviously! It wasn't going to swing out into the path of a train, was it? But she saved her breath for jumping up onto the step and through the gate. The others piled up after her, desperate to be out of the tunnel. Somebody heaved it shut behind them with a loud clang, as if a pack of wild animals were slavering at their heels.

They were in a grimy passage, every surface a dark grey. But at least there were working lights mounted on the walls. Cables were strung here and there, including a few from the tunnel that plugged into some kind of junction box. This had the word ON lit up red – looked like the tracks were live after all. The passage stretched ahead into shadows, but the Polish man was already heading through a narrow doorway near the gate. She followed, gesturing for the others to come along.

They all rattled down a few concrete steps and into a wide open space. It was clear they were now behind the brick barrier that lined the tunnel, in what was definitely an old Tube station. The curved platform wall was covered with cream tiles decorated with lines of brown and dark green, many crumbling away and all dulled by dirt. There were no roundels with the station name printed on them, but fired into the tiles in large letters were the words *BROMPTON ROAD*.

Also imprinted on the tiles was an old-fashioned *No Exit* sign, surrounded by a ticket office motif. But Emily couldn't see the opening it referred to. Instead of one long open space, the platform area had brick partitions built across it with narrow rectangular doorways in them, like the one they'd just come through. Dividing walls, she realised, turning the platform into several smaller rooms.

She turned to face the passengers who had come with them. As well as the four teenagers and the Arab man – still with earphones in – were the goth girl, a thin greying man in his fifties wearing battered

26

denim, and a woman in a leopard-print coat whose copious make-up had mostly melted. They were all talking over each other, babbling, crying.

"All right, take it easy!" said Emily. The booming echo of her voice startled her, but also made the others go quiet. "We're safe here, you can see this is an old station, we'll be able to use this to get out. Or there'll be a way of contacting London Underground, a telephone or something."

Why am I saying this? Not, she knew, because she was some kind of natural leader or had a clue what was going on. Only because nobody else was saying it. "So just sit down and wait for now, okay?"

The Polish man sat heavily on the ground as if she'd just snipped his strings. The others took this as a cue to lower themselves slowly to the concrete floor.

She stood there for a minute, breathing in stale, hot air. Maybe she'd believed her own words, because she felt calmer. Heart wasn't pumping, skin wasn't crawling. She didn't even jump when a callused hand slid into hers. She allowed the Polish man to pull her gently down to the floor beside him.

"You are called?" he asked.

"Emily. You?"

"Peter. Peter the twat."

She let out an abashed laugh. "Sorry."

"Emily, what happened? What did we run away from?"

"It was… I don't know. I thought…"

She drew her knees up, glancing at the brick wall between them and the tunnel. Trying to remember what happened ten minutes ago felt like struggling to recall a childhood memory. Only one thing was a cold fact. "I was so scared," she admitted.

Peter nodded. "Me too. Very scared. I don't know why." He shrugged inside his chequered overshirt. "Train breaks down, that should not scare me."

"It wasn't just a breakdown, though, it was like..." She ran a hand over her face, wondering how to phrase the ideas lurking in the back of her mind. "The doors were opened on purpose, weren't they? You said as much, it had to be deliberate. At first I thought it was to let us all get out, but maybe..."

*Obstructing the doors can    anger us.*

"Emily?"

She shook her head. "Sorry. I don't know what to think, to be honest."

"And skinny? What happened to him?"

She remembered the nurse crawling toward the driver's cabin, and his voice coming back at them, and then...

"I don't know," she repeated softly.

She looked at the people crouched on the floor nearby, all bedraggled and dirty. It was clear that shock was starting to settle in for some of them, and hysteria might not be far behind. She felt exactly what they felt: lost, scared, confused, under attack. Christ, she thought, we have to get out of here.

"I'm going to find the way out," she said firmly, getting to her feet.

Peter did the same. "I'll come with you."

"No, I'll be fine, this place is empty. You stay with

these guys, okay? They need someone to look after them."

His baby-face broke into a smile. "I need someone to look after me."

Her hand seemed to squeeze Peter's arm all by itself. "I won't be long."

Peter started to talk to the others as she turned and headed for the nearest brick partition. Ducking through the narrow doorway into the next section, Emily spotted a *Way Out* sign on the tiles, with the same ticket office design drawn around it and an arrow pointing left. Just like a normal station.

She supposed this was a normal station once, with normal people flowing through it. Not that she'd ever heard of Brompton Road. There was a West Brompton, on the District Line, but no Brompton Road. Weird to think it had been erased from that Piccadilly Line map she knew so well.

And shouldn't it be called – what was it – Shroud Lane? That might explain the glitch on the dot matrix display, if the train had detected the disused station when it passed. Maybe Brompton Road was its original name from decades ago. Like with Arsenal, which still said Gillespie Road on its wall tiles. That would make sense.

She badly needed *something* to make sense.

Through another dividing wall, she saw the exit she was looking for. It had a few concrete steps leading up to it, making her realise they had removed the entire platform and she stood on the same level as the train tracks. But it felt less like a Tube station in this section, with all the walls painted over in beige and green, obscuring the tiles. Right at the far end of the platform was a large off-white rectangle with the words *NO SMOKING PLEASE* in its green border.

It looked so absurd that Emily wondered if random signage was following her around wherever she went. Then she realised that this was a kind of miniature screen, for a film projector. Who the hell watched movies down here? Jeez, they'd never allow Secret Cinema into this place, health and safety would go mental.

Ah… maybe Brompton Road had been an air raid shelter during World War Two. Grandma Spencer used to talk about being taken down to Chalk Farm Station as a little girl, whenever the sirens wailed. Emily could easily imagine hundreds of people cowering on the platform, trying to entertain themselves to take their minds off the bombs raining above. Also, didn't she once read about old Tube stations being used as military bases? Perhaps that explained the partitions and the nasty paintwork. This could have been a wartime office for Churchill, for all she knew.

Emily walked up the little steps into the *Way Out* passage. There were more lights here, but it was dark at the far end. Halfway along on the right was a round opening – a stairwell leading up. She touched the handrail on the side and instantly regretted it, wiping off the gritty dust on her jeans.

Slowly, she walked up the steps. The emptiness of this place was draining. She was so accustomed to the look and feel of a normal Underground station that to see one in this derelict state felt unreal. Familiar and alien, all at once. She travelled below ground almost every day, in trains and subways and underpasses, yet this felt like being… deeper.

She was surprised to find a set of double doors at the top of the stairs, something she'd never seen in a station before. They were heavy but creaked open at her touch. On the other side the passage turned left, yellow lights strung along the roof.

Emily coughed, holding her hand across her mouth. The dust here was so thick it was basically grey sand. Little clouds of it erupted with every footstep, swirling under the lights like swarming insects. The atmosphere was thick with heat as well, making her face feel coated in oil.

This was obviously a passenger exit, so it should lead to the lifts. Not that they'd still be working, but there had to be an emergency staircase. She'd spotted signs for these at dozens of Tube stations, and once walked up the one at Covent Garden when she got bored waiting for an elevator. That was a mistake – her legs were killing her by the time she got to the top. But even if this one was just as long, she didn't care if it meant reaching the surface. Was there still a Brompton Road Station? An abandoned old building with those lovely dark red tiles and arched windows? If not then at least she should get signal for her phone.

All these thoughts collapsed when she saw that the passage ahead was bricked off, with a gated door in the middle. She grabbed and rattled it, but it was properly locked. "Oh, you son of a bitch!"

There were laminated notices stuck to the gate – signs, more bloody signs, wherever she went.

*AREA BEHIND THIS DOOR BELONGS TO TERRITORIAL AUXILIARY AND VOLUNTEER RESERVE ASSOCIATION FOR GREATER LONDON 306 BROMPTON ROAD.*

The Territorial Army? So this probably had been a military outpost once. She peered through the gate. No sign of life, no squaddies who could help, just more brick partitions and empty rooms. No getting to the emergency stairs this way.

She retraced her steps, pulling open the double doors, trod down the stairwell. She hurried back onto the westbound platform and through the narrow openings. The place where they'd got in from the tracks, the crossover passage, looked like it had a similar stairwell in it. She'd check in with the others then give that a try.

She came to a stop and looked around. Platform wall on her left, brick wall on the right, her in the middle.

They were gone.

She stared at the place where she'd left them. There were scuff marks in the dust. Had they wandered off?

"Hello?" Her voice was swallowed up by the arched ceiling. "Peter?" she called louder.

Silence. Had they gone to the other platform?

"Guys? Are you…"

It hit her quickly, a stomach cramp like she'd eaten something bad. Her mouth went dry. She felt her pulse speed up. Every hair on her body was prickling.

Moving her legs felt like dragging bags of sand, but she walked forward, up the steps to the nearest partition doorway. She stood in the original crossover passage through which they had entered. She stopped, because she had to. Her muscles seized up as another queasy wave rippled through her.

Nothing but silence.

Nothing but her own heartbeats and breathing and…

…and a sort of absence of noise, like a vacuum sucking at her ears.

Inch by inch, Emily twisted her body to the right. The gate built into the brick wall hung open. Behind it was darkness.

Had they gone back into the tunnel? But why? If a rescue train had arrived to pick them up, surely one of them, surely Peter, would have come to find her?

Something caught her eye. She looked down at herself, chest rising and falling, to find that her white blouse was now smeared with dirt, ripped in a couple of places, and… shining.

What? She blinked hard. Yes, the cotton blouse was giving off a sort of blueish-white glow, all by itself.

Her fingernails were glowing too.

She held out both hands. All ten nails were now luminous, in a way that seemed vaguely familiar.

As she stared at her outstretched hands, the darkness behind the open gate…

…*moved* from left to right…

…and the grey tunnel wall reappeared.

*Run*, said her entire body, *run now!*

Emily thought of Peter, of the four teenagers, of the Arab man with his tablet and the woman with the leopard-print coat and all the rest. She didn't run. She hauled leaden feet forward, scraping across concrete. Closer to the open gate.

Trembling hands gripped the metal bars and she leaned her head through, over the tracks. On her left, the direction from which trains entered, the tunnel mouth was empty – nothing was coming that would decapitate her. Her head creaked slowly to the right, toward the straight tunnel with the high brick wall along one side.

There was a symbol on the wall. A huge one, over a metre across, that she couldn't possibly have missed. It glowed on the brickwork. Shining blueish-white, like her t-shirt, like her fingernails.

Emily craned her head. It was hard to make out at this angle but it seemed to be a perfectly round ring with two straight lines crossing over it, like a flattened X, meeting in the circle's middle. It was fading before her eyes, eyes that dropped down to see…

…something moving away along the tracks.

Something black and metallic, lined with windows that were equally black.

Something train-shaped.

Looking at it hurt. An ache deep in the back of her eyes. She was making a noise, a baby's cry, and her whole body was shuddering, and it felt like she might have wet herself, and she wanted her daddy, make it go away daddy, oh God please make it stop and *run you stupid bitch just run!*

Her body locked into place, unable to even turn her head, only shiver from head to toe.

It made no noise. No electric-whine, no wheel-screech. The air itself felt drained of sound. All she could really hear was blood thudding inside her skull.

Slowly… slowly… the train-shape slid into the circular hole. It seemed to coil to the left, following the curving rails, and then vanished, indistinguishable from the blackness inside the tunnel.

Emily's sweating fingers slipped off the metal gate and she almost tumbled onto the tracks, scraping her knees on the high concrete lip. As she clambered back she saw that the symbol on the wall, the glowing circle and crossed bars, was gone. Nothing but filthy, bare bricks. And her fingernails, her blouse, no longer glowed.

Now that she was moving she didn't stop, scrambling back through the gate and down into the same space where Peter and the others had been, where she now collapsed. That strange hush had gone so she could hear her sobs echo off the walls, gasping for air and trying to cry at the same time. She knelt, quivering and paralysed, looking up around her at the ancient station, breathing in its filthy air, feeling the dust worm into the pores of her face, dampness spreading through her jeans, sweat blooming under her arms. More little-girl-terrified than she'd ever been in her life.

She wasn't sure how long she stayed that way, hunched over and rocking to and fro, keening like a grieving mother, like a wounded animal. That glassy, detached feeling soared back, making everything more unreal than ever.

What… *was* that?

Her mind couldn't think of it as a train. It was more like the absence of one. Logic told her it had to be some kind of engineering train, some weird test vehicle, but… no. No no no. It wasn't that, it wasn't anything remotely like that.

Emily wiped her face and looked up, realising that whatever it was, it would now be approaching the train they'd escaped from. The Night Tube that was still full of people, stranded in the tunnel with its doors wide open. She was straining to hear something. The crash of colliding trains? The screams?

Silence.

Only silence.

Oh God. I'm alone.

Terrified thoughts tumbled over each other. Totally alone, no phone signal, no food or water, no-one knew she was there, no-one would come looking. She would die down there, buried beneath the earth in a place nobody ever went.

What happened to the others? Peter, the teenagers, all of them, why have they vanished, why did they leave her?

She couldn't help but think: They've been taken.

That train-shaped thing *took* them.

Emily heaved herself to her feet and forced her numb legs to move in the direction of the *Way Out* sign. Her mind was visualising running back up those stairs, through the double doors, breaking down that locked gate with her bare hands, instantly discovering the emergency stairwell and rushing up toward… what? For all she knew, Brompton Road Station had been demolished years ago or flattened in the Blitz. Was anything left up there?

And was she really alone?

She staggered to a stop. She'd gone blundering about by herself through the dust-choked passages, assuming they were empty, but now it was easy to think that eyes had been watching her the whole time. That there were things hiding behind the crumbling brickwork. Faces in the shadows, turning her way as she went by. The station wasn't dead at all, there were things living down here, the way fungi and jellyfish grow and swell in the ocean depths, this was their home, and here she was, buried alive and alone and any moment now she'd hear them moving toward her, walking or crawling or slithering into view –

Strands of hair blew against her face. She knuckled her eyes dry. A low rumble was growing steadily louder, and the air was moving.

A stab of fear at the thought of that train-shape coming back, coming back for her… but no, she could properly hear this. She'd heard it a thousand times, whenever she'd been on a platform waiting for the next train.

Emily's legs finally started working, taking her back up the steps and into the crossover passage. There was a noise-burst as something once again moved past the open gate. Not black, but grey-blue-red.

A proper train, a fat ugly fantastic beautiful London Underground train!

She caught glimpses of people-shapes on the other side of its windows, smothered with light. Standing, sitting, sleeping, cocooned in their steel bubble. The sudden pangs of longing were so intense she felt like crying.

She realised it was slowing down. Its brakes echoed horribly around the empty platform. It can't be stopping here, can it?

As before, she held on tight to the metal gate and stuck her head into the tunnel. Yes, it had stopped, but not quite in the station. It stood in the straight part of the westbound tunnel. Its rear cabin was just inside the circular mouth, twin lights glowing red.

The sight of it was like cold water on Emily's face. There it sat, a piece of the normal world just within her view… just within her reach.

Not a train. A lifeboat.

Before she knew it, Emily had jumped down from the concrete step and was on the tunnel floor. She couldn't quite run with the rail between her feet so instead power-walked as hard as she could in the direction of the train, panting with exertion and fear. Fear that at any second it would start up again and pull away, leaving her alone in this pit.

The brick wall passed by on her right, dull grey flatness, no trace of the glowing symbol. The Tube train grew closer. Her nerves jangled, hurry, move faster!

It stayed still as she reached it. What should she do? Bang on the windows and let the passengers know she was there? Imagine their shock to see her face at the glass. She looked at the rear cabin of the train, painted bright red. There were sliding doors on either side and also a central door facing backward, similar to the interconnecting ones, with another oh-so-helpful sign, a blue *Piccadilly Line* sticker on its window.

A voice reached her, ghostly, muted – a woman's voice. Emily realised it was coming from inside this train. She strained to make out the words:

*"...for the delays to the service, ladies and gentlemen. This is due to an earlier signal failure on the Piccadilly Line. Repair work is underway and we should be on the move shortly. Sorry again and thanks for your patience."*

Her blood ran cold. That's what the driver said before. Before he abandoned his passengers to –

A loud hiss of compressed air made her jump. She'd heard that lots of times, always a few seconds before a train started moving. Do something! Now!

Emily placed one foot an inch away from the central rail – the rail filled with electric current – and lifted her other foot onto an iron tongue jutting out from the train's underside, the part that linked cars together. She shifted her weight and stepped up onto it, knowing that if the train moved right now then she'd go tumbling down on top of the live rail and probably die instantly... but it didn't move. Quickly she stepped onto a metal footplate above the tongue, in front of the central rear door.

The train juddered into motion. She lost her balance, falling backward. "Oh fuck *no – !*"

Both hands reached out, grabbing vertical poles on either side of the door. She heaved herself upright with a cry, face slamming against glass.

She stood on the footplate and gripped the hand-rails tight. The narrow door had a single window with a long windscreen wiper that pressed painfully against her breasts. She could see the cabin inside, although its lights were off. There was an upholstered seat and curved panels covered with chunky buttons and switches, all surprisingly primitive.

And the door had a handle. But to try that would mean letting go of one of the poles.

"Shi-*iiiit!*" She felt the train accelerate and bend sharply to the left. Its wheels shrieked, drilling into her ears, and the vibration of motors shuddered through her entire body.

Emily held on for dear life as she was hauled through the tunnel. The darkness was almost absolute except for the dull red glow from the rear lights. In the window, her ragged reflection howled silently back at her.

She knew it would have to stop soon. When it reached the first train. Surely that was still there?

But the speed increased, motors rising in pitch. More nerve-rending screeches as it veered to the right.

Emily's thoughts raced. Where was the train she'd left? Maybe the driver had returned, the doors closed, and it carried on as normal. Maybe the ones who'd got off with her had also been rescued. What the hell is she doing, risking her life by surfing the rails like a lunatic? If only she'd stayed put, maybe it would all have been…

She stared at her right hand, wrapped in a fist. Thumbnail glowing.

Emily's stomach lurched. She looked down, down at her torn and smeared blouse, her blouse that was shining blueish-white.

"No no no oh God oh God oh God…"

Here it came again, surging up from her guts and spreading across every inch of skin: that icy, nauseous shiver.

Sweaty palms slid down the handrails. An inch, then another. Her trembling legs started to buckle, aching from standing on the narrow footplate, aching and ready to collapse.

She felt the train turn once more to the left, but suddenly couldn't hear the wheels screech or the motors whine. Nothing but her own panicked breathing and…

…and a sort of absence of noise, like a vacuum sucking at her ears.

Emily knew. She knew it was there.

Sliding silently along the metal tracks. Coming up behind the train.

*Behind me.*

If she could turn her head, would she see it growing nearer and nearer? What if she glimpsed it in the glass? Did it have curved black windows at its front, fixed on her like the dead eyes of a shark? Was there a…

Was there a figure inside, driving it?

Her left hand let go of the pole and grabbed the door handle, yanking it madly over and over. Locked. No way into the cabin. Nowhere to go.

Her other hand started to slip. She was going to fall off, down onto the live rails, down in front of the un-train that must be only a couple of metres away, oh God she's gonna fall!

Eyes squeezed tight, Emily wished she knew how to pray, wished she could even scream, instead of just gasping for air in the hot dusty tunnel.

She felt the train slow… heard the pitch of its motors drop. She let out a cry as her right hand lost its grip and she slid halfway down, other hand wedged awkwardly around the pole, one leg coming off the footplate.

She spun round, expecting to see it right behind her: the thing in the shape of a train.

Her massive eyes drank in the empty tunnel.

Straining every muscle, she managed to haul herself upright again as the train came to a stop. Her blouse was no longer glowing. But there seemed to be more light from somewhere.

We're in a station, she realised, a normal station!

The rear cabin was just about inside the tunnel mouth, but the rest of the train was alongside a platform. She could hear the whoosh of opening doors, and the footsteps of people, and another announcement about changing for the District and Circle Lines. Oh yes, she could hear normally! And all those drab, routine noises chimed like melodies in her ears.

Checking below, she saw that the two live rails were now in the centre and on the right. She jumped to the left side of the tunnel floor, almost collapsing. She stayed there and caught her breath while the doors bleeped and closed. That hiss of pneumatic brakes, then the train started moving again. As soon as it did, she hauled herself over the concrete edge of the platform, with its painted white and yellow lines, its upside down *MIND THE GAP*. The gap she crawled up from.

There were only a few people on the platform, most walking to the exits, plus a middle-aged man in staff uniform. Nobody noticed her climbing up from the tracks, like a grotesque troll emerging from under a bridge to eat all the pretty humans. That's just how she felt: grotesque. But they didn't spot her. It was like she'd slipped under their radar.

Oh, South Kensington looked like heaven. Seeing the modern London Underground roundel in front of her felt like a hug from a long-lost friend. The whiteness of the wall tiles stretching ahead was almost dazzling. The bank of grey mesh seats nearby, the overhead lights, the colourful posters... all so beautifully ordinary.

"Thank God," she heard herself say, "oh thank God..."

Emily slumped onto the nearby bench, exhausted. Then she turned to look at the tunnel mouth, which was framed by a blue box-like structure. And her guts tightened again at the thought that...

... it was still in there.

That the darkness inside the tunnel might suddenly extrude into the light, shaped like a train.

She pulled her gaze away. The display board said that the next train to Heathrow was in nine minutes. Just a normal Night Tube service. Like nothing had ever happened.

A sudden rage fired through Emily, propelling her off the bench and toward the station guard, shouting "Where is it!"

He actually recoiled at the sight of her. "What?"

"The train before that one! Where is it? Where's the people?"

"Er…"

Emily made herself take a deep breath. "It was stuck in the tunnel. All the – "

"Oh, right," the guard nodded. "Yeah, we have had some delays tonight. The three-forty had to wait in the Kensington Bends for a bit. But they've fixed the signals now, we're getting the service back to normal."

She stared at him like he was speaking an ancient language. "But what happened to it! Where was the driver? Where were the people, for God's sake? Weren't some missing? Weren't the, the doors, weren't they all open?"

His eyebrows came together in a bewildered knot. "No, the train had a driver and passengers, like they all do," he said slowly.

"So where's…" She cast a desperate look around at the empty platform. *"Where's Peter?"* she wanted to demand. *"Where's the nurse, where's the ones that thing took!"*

The guard had turned his back and was wandering away, bringing a radio handset to his ear. She could barely hear his low voice, but the words 'transport' and 'police' were enough. Another instinct jerked her toward the exit, walking quickly.

That glassy, detached feeling washed back over Emily as she stumbled through bright corridors, past orange and yellow tiling and up stairways. She stood alone on the escalator. The people on the other side, being carried gently down to catch the next Night Tube, peered at her. Some frowned or wrinkled their noses, others staying rock-faced in case there was a drunken crazy demand for money or something. That London distance.

She glanced down at herself. Covered in dust, streaked with dirt, blouse clinging to her clammy skin, jeans stained with grime and urine, blonde hair tangled and lank. She wasn't the same Emily who had enjoyed a night on the town then jumped on a train to whizz safely home. That girl was long gone. She was different now. Changed.

Changed at Brompton Road.

Changed at Shroud Lane.

It was only when she stood at the top of the escalator, facing the ticket barriers, that Emily realised her coat and handbag were gone. What was she going to say to the guard who was even now giving her daggers? It took a while to remember that she always carried her Oyster card, along with an emergency £20 note, in a little plastic wallet in her back pocket. Who was that sensible, organised girl from a hundred years ago?

Once through the barriers, she shuffled into the South Kensington ticket hall. All the little shops at the front were closed, shutters down. The huge skylight overhead was dark. A few people were coming and going through a pedestrian subway that led to all the nearby museums. The thought of going into that enormous tunnel made her feel like being sick. Instead she walked up a flight of stairs and through a little shopping arcade, again all closed.

Out on the street. Tall, ornate, whitewashed houses typical of west London. Lots of shops for the tourists. Traffic and people passing by. The wind on her skin felt freezing after the cloying heat of the Underground. The sky was lightening and dawn was on the way, but all the cars' headlights were still on, streetlamps still lit up. Everything felt ordinary and mysterious at the same time. That sensation when you return from a long holiday abroad, and your own neighbourhood seems foreign.

Emily thought: What just happened to me?

It seemed impossible that her Night Tube had just rolled into South Ken as normal. Everyone on it had been so scared. So ridiculously scared. Surely there'd be ambulances and police, right here outside the station, and trembling passengers wrapped in shock blankets and all that. What about the group who'd got off the train with her, and tunnel-walked back to Brompton Road… God, did she really do that? It sounded insane.

One thing she did remember was all the doors on the train sliding open at the same time. The lights going off. The train sitting dead in the tunnel. And she remembered wondering if they had been deliberately opened, not to let people out but to let something in.

Like an offering. Like a sacrifice.

The guard could have been lying, she thought. Maybe they're all in on it. Maybe London Underground are keeping this all quiet. Maybe they're conducting some bizarre psychological experiment, or it's a freaky Tube-cult ceremony, or…

…maybe I'm still drunk. Maybe my drink really was spiked.

Emily shook her head, feeling that some connection was broken. Some of her memories looked so hazy in her mind's eye. Some of the things she'd done, the words she'd said, hardly felt like her at all.

Aimlessly, she wandered across a paved area decorated with large potted plants, past a row of closed shops and a bus stop. She needed to get home. Boston Manor was still a long way away, but the thought of travelling across London by herself made her want to cry like an abandoned child. She felt like calling Kay and Alicia, waking them up and begging them to come and get her.

There was even an impulse to call her mum. Not that she'd be much help. Zero chance of Mum ever coming back to London again, no matter how badly Emily needed her. Just the mention of London was enough to make her mother shiver and draw into herself, like people with phobias do. She'd been that way ever since… ever since their family broke in half.

She leaned against the bus stop shelter, near the intersection of roads in front of South Kensington Station. Even at this time of the morning, there was plenty of traffic rumbling along. Also a fair few people standing near the traffic lights, waiting to cross the busy roads. Just standing patiently…

Her eyes landed on four teenagers, lined up along the pavement's edge. An Asian girl, a blonde girl and two dark-haired boys.

Just standing there calmly. Eyes open, mouths shut. Waiting.

She stepped forward, wanting to call out to them, but hesitated. Why did she think that she might know a group of teenagers? It was like déjà vu, a nagging feeling that she'd seen them before.

There were more people farther along the intersection, also waiting to cross, and again a few seemed familiar. Her gaze fixed on an overweight Arab man with glasses. His shirt was filthy and torn, with red grazes beneath, like he'd been mauled by a tiger. Whatever he was listening to wasn't coming through his dangling earphones, which were plugged into nothing.

The lights changed to red, and the traffic came to a slow halt. On the pedestrian crossing, the glowing red figure changed to a walking green man. Red and green, stop and go. No need to think in London, it told you what you needed to know.

Everyone looked jolted out of half-sleep by the beeping sound. And Emily's skin prickled as she watched the strangers start to walk at precisely the same moment. All crossing the road in silent unison.

All receiving the same signal.

# Chapter 1

Friday 13th August 2010
12.23am

The train thundered through the tunnel, carrying Jake deeper into London.

He stood close to one of the doors, being gently swayed from side to side by the train's motion. His whole body was rigid as he held onto one of the yellow handrails as hard as he could.

None of the other passengers shared his tension. For them, this was just another quick trip on the Tube, and they took it in their stride. Ordinary, mundane, safe, nothing to worry about.

Jake stood apart from them all, holding on for dear life.

He glanced around the interior of the car, which was all very familiar. Rows of seats upholstered with geometric patterns, designed to hide the dirt of a million backsides. Rectangular adverts that nobody paid much attention to, below grilled air vents that never let in much air. London Underground stickers and symbols in primary colours: *Priority seat. Obstructing the doors can be dangerous. Emergency alarm.*

It was fairly busy, even for this time of night. Jake was surrounded by a few dozen people who sat or stood in groups. Late-night Londoners, heading home from the bars or out to the clubs. Some were even younger than him.

He coughed, keeping his mouth closed, and went back to watching the tunnel wall race by on the other side of the windows. At this speed it was just a blur, layered with grey cables that streamed past like never-ending snakes.

Jake's eyes refocused onto his own reflection, bent by the curved glass. It was the first time he'd looked at himself for a few months. All the mirrors were broken in the last couple of squats he'd stayed in. The derelict flat above the bricked-up corner shop, which he'd broken into a few weeks ago, didn't even have running water let alone mirrors.

His faded jeans were held together with black gaffer tape across the rips. Once-red trainers were nearly colourless now. The padded jacket was too heavy and thick for August, but he often had to sleep in it, on bare floorboards in a room where the wind whistled in through the cracks. Underneath that was a grey hooded top and three more layers, although two of the t-shirts weren't even his size. The rucksack on his back usually held the few clothes he owned, but tonight it bulged with the hard angles of more practical items.

A week ago, he had to cut his own thick blonde hair with a rusty pair of scissors when it started getting in his eyes, and now it looked so randomly spiky it might almost be fashionable. His blue eyes were the only colour on a smooth, paper-white face. Was it always that pale? Did he always have such visible cheekbones? He never shaved very often but could make out a wispy cloud of light fuzz across his jaw, matted down by dirt. His mouth was a thin line, lips dry and chapped.

He didn't look eighteen anymore. He carried too many years with him.

Jake broke into another cough, aiming it into the crook of his elbow to muffle the hacking sound. Lots of perfume and aftershave from the other passengers clogged the air. That must be it. That's all it was. He'd be fine when he got off.

His journey on the Tube tonight hadn't taken long, but had been difficult to deal with. Too many people, everywhere he looked. And too many lights stabbing down from above, making his eyes sting. He had moved fast: striding through passageways double-quick, jogging up and down escalators. He didn't need to follow the signs – he could have made the journey blindfolded.

From the squat, Jake had walked to Rotherhithe Station where he bought an old-fashioned ticket rather than an Oyster card. He took the Overground to Whitechapel, changing onto the westbound Hammersmith and City Line. That took him toward King's Cross, where he changed to the Northern Line train he was now on.

Change and change and change again. A laboratory rat running through a maze that it knew every twist and turn of. This was Jake's life now.

He felt the motion of the train begin to slow, slow... and then, with a drawn-out metallic squeal, come to a halt.

His hand gripped the rail, bone-white-tight. Through the window he saw the bare interior of the tunnel, lined with cables and coated in grime, no longer blurring past.

Jake looked around. Nobody was panicking. A few people tutted and moaned, clearly accustomed to Tube trains stopping between stations. Happened all the time. Any second now they'd hear the driver announce that they were being held at a red signal, or waiting for the train ahead to leave the platform, or that there were delays due to a signal failure. There's always bloody signal failures.

But no announcement came. The train remained still.

A few seconds later, its electric motors – a constant background hum that you only became aware of when they stopped – stopped.

The train went silent. Stuck dead in the middle of the tunnel.

It's happening, thought Jake.

His head whipped back and forth, mouth open, breathing fast. He gripped the rail with both hands, as if he were trapped on a plane falling from the sky. As if something bad were about to happen any second. Any second now.

It's coming for me.

I knew it would, *it's coming for me!*

He knew what was about to happen. All the lights would blink off, and the entire train would go black, and in the darkness there would be screams, proper screams, and he'd see –

A pneumatic hiss reached his ears, followed by a vibration and a hum of power. He felt movement. The tunnel wall continued passing by.

Jake caught his breath, frowning at all the normality, at the perfectly ordinary Tube train that dared to carry on travelling as if nothing were going to happen.

It *was* going to happen, he was sure. He was sure of it! He'd been expecting it for months now, every single time he got on a Tube. Why hadn't it taken this chance to –

*"The next station is Camden Town, High Barnet Branch."* He jumped as the automated PA system blared from a speaker near his head. *"Change here for Northern Line, Bank Branch. Please mind the gap between the train and the platform."*

The tunnel vanished, replaced by the brightness of a station platform. As the train slowed, passengers turned to face the doors, eager for their night to begin.

Jake prised bloodless fingers away from the handrail, pulled the hoodie over his head and took a deep breath. This was where his night began too.

With a beeping alert, the doors rumbled open. Jake allowed himself to be swept out by the surge of people. He kept his head down as he shuffled around iron railings – cattle barriers for humans – opposite the archway that led to the exit. He moved to the edge of the crowd, staying still while everyone else drained away like rainwater.

A uniformed member of staff wandered into view, keeping an eye on people. Keeping an eye on him, perhaps. Since the bombings five years ago, anyone carrying a rucksack on the Tube was viewed with suspicion.

Jake heaved his bag onto the floor, unzipped it and made a show of rummaging deep inside as if searching for his Oyster card, oh where is it, must be in here somewhere, silly me... This seemed to satisfy the staff member that the rucksack wasn't packed with explosives, and he turned away.

If he had peeked inside and seen the crowbar, hacksaw, bolt cutters, oxyacetylene blowtorch and the rest, it might have been a different story.

Jake glanced at the train. It was the final one of the night, so it would remain there with its doors open for longer than usual to catch the very last passengers. His eyes roamed over the platform. The wall was covered with brick-shaped yellow and blue tiles, rising to a curved ceiling from which dangled signage and lights. There were also two security cameras, but not aimed his way. Nobody was looking at him either.

Worth the risk, he decided. His hand fastened around one of the pieces of equipment in his rucksack.

The large Tube map on the wall beside him was printed on plastic, set into a metal frame. It showed the entire bewildering mesh of the London Underground. A map famous around the world, making sense out of the city's complexity by ordering it along neat, colour-coded lines. Dark blue for Piccadilly Line, green for District Line, red for Central Line, light blue for Victoria Line, yellow for Circle Line, brown for Bakerloo Line...

And...

Jake lifted the rectangular lamp. The glass tube within was jet black, not transparent, and gave off a faint purple haze when he turned it on. For a second he blinked, even though it wasn't bright. Then he turned toward the map, quickly running it up and down.

A dotted mess of smears and smudged fingerprints glowed under the ultraviolet light. But the white background of the map itself didn't, which meant it was printed on some phosphor-free material. Jake knew not to get too excited. He had done this on dozens of maps, at Tube stations all across London, but not once was there ever –

There.

Oh my God. *There it is!*

He leaned in close, aiming the UV lamp. He stared at the two black lines – branches of the Northern Line – running upward from Camden Town…

And the glowing blue-white line, angling off into an area with no stations.

It ended not with a T-shape like a terminus but with a circular symbol, like an interchange station. Except this circle had a slightly flattened X across it, radiating the same ultraviolet shine.

Jake's wide eyes traced the blazing stripe back to where it joined the Northern Line and ended at a point halfway between Camden Town and Kentish Town stations.

A nowhere place. Unless you knew what was there.

"It's true," he heard himself whisper. "They're real."

Jake swallowed down his hammering heart. With the lamp in one hand, he held up his mobile phone with the other, grateful to have charged it earlier at a coffee shop, albeit only to 87% before the staff threw him out for not buying anything. He struggled to stop his hand trembling as he opened the camera icon and took a picture of the Tube map.

The Tube map with the extra line.

A few people walked past. Native Londoners, fortunately, so they only spared him a microsecond glance, not giving a damn. Jake flicked off the lamp and phone, then dumped both inside his rucksack. He stood up too quickly, making his head spin, his vision blur.

He stared once more at the map. The fluorescent line was gone now, invisible to the naked eye... although he found that by blinking hard, he could just about see it again. An electric glow, outshining all the flat colours of the other lines.

He reached out and ran his fingers along the map, tracing the hidden path.

Hefting the rucksack over one shoulder, Jake ambled along the platform, doing his best to look like just another traveller catching the last train home. The words *MIND THE GAP* on the floor drew his gaze. The letters were scuffed by years of footsteps, as was the yellow line painted along the platform's edge.

Up ahead, a wall jutted out halfway across the width of the platform, with a brown door set into it. More signs: *Fire door. Keep shut. Danger. High voltage.* It then sloped ahead toward the headwall. Before the actual tunnel was a waist-high metal gate with yet more symbols emblazoned down it. *Danger. Moving trains. Passengers must not pass this point. Offenders will be prosecuted.*

He almost smiled. As if that would be enough to stop him.

The tunnel mouth looked ancient. It was smeared with soot and dust, and ringed by old cables stapled into place. No light reached inside.

It pulled at Jake's eyes. The emptiness of it.

That aching tingle came again. In his guts, his belly.

A cousin to hunger.

A pre-recorded female voice echoed down the platform. *"This is a Northern Line train to... High Barnet. The next station is... Kentish Town."*

"No it isn't."

That startled him. Why was he talking to himself? He never did that before. He doesn't do that when he's alone in the squat, does he?

Jake glanced round. He was in range of a security camera now. He made himself sit down on one of the metal seats nearby, retrieved his phone from the rucksack and hunched over it. It was an iPhone 3GS – last year's model – covered with a thick rubber case and plastic screenguard that made it waterproof, scratchproof and shockproof. It needed to be armoured in the places he took it.

He flipped randomly through a document on the device, pausing only when...

> *I'm screaming. I can hear it*
> *now, my own voice screaming*
> *as he drags me along, because*
> *up ahead there's... just a pitch-*

*black tunnel, there's nothing in*
*there, so why am I*

…only when something stood out…

*gap the mind the gap mindthe*
*gap thegap please god*
*mind thegap*

…from the text that he knew off by heart.

"Ladies and gentlemen!" blared a voice over the PA. "This is the last northbound service from this station. The train is about to leave. Please stand back behind the yellow line."

He pocketed his phone, picked up his rucksack and walked alongside the train to the sloping wall. Acting normally, oh so normal, la la la, nothing to see here.

He noticed the driver, scowling at him through the cabin window. Probably wondering if Jake might be a 'one-under'. That's what London Underground staff called those who tried to commit suicide by jumping on the tracks. Routine hazard for them, happened all the time.

A few more dry coughs came hacking out of him. Must be the train's motors, chucking out a load of dust.

The train's pneumatic doors all closed in unison. With a hiss and a rising hum, it started moving from right to left along the platform. Jake stood still, buffeted by wind as car after car whooshed past, offering glimpses of blurred faces through the windows. As the last car vanished, its rear wheels spat a sudden spark. He blinked, seeing the flare overlaid on his vision.

The train's rear lights disappeared, sucked up by the tunnel's blackness, and its rumbling faded away. All that was left was that wide-open circular mouth, ringed with cables and filth. Nothing inside at all.

Nothing the naked eye could see…

"You're in there, aren't you," someone whispered with his voice.

That same taut ache. A cousin to hunger.

Jake checked his wristwatch, the chunky one that could withstand the pressure of ocean depths, the one he got for his… sixteenth, seventeenth birthday, something like that. The station would close to the public in the next ten minutes or so. Staff would do a sweep, knowing there were always people dragging their feet on the last Tube home.

He'd be long gone by then.

He moved closer to the metal gate, to the very edge of the platform. His trainers stepped across the yellow line. Not minding the gap, like all the signs told him to. Bad passenger. Nobody likes a one-under.

He peered over, at the four metal tracks. Beneath them in the angular suicide pit scurried a couple of tiny mice, zipping back and forth. Just like the ones he heard at night, scratching in the corners of the empty room he slept in. You could spot them at most Tube stations, living their little lives in the gaps between trains, darting away when one arrived and emerging when it was gone.

"Mind the gap," he muttered. To the mice? To himself?

A quick glance over his shoulder. Yes, the sloping wall blocked the security camera, good. So all he had to do was take a step...

*"Would Inspector Sands please report to the operations room immediately."*

Jake went rigid as the strident female voice speared through the air, through his heart. It sounded like a routine PA announcement, but that was just to avoid alarming people. This pre-recorded message was a security alert. Sometimes because a fire alarm had been pulled or there was the possibility of a terrorist incident, but in this case he knew exactly what the threat was.

Him.

He twisted round, expecting to see station staff looking at him or British Transport Police storming his way, but the platform was empty. Somehow they must have picked him up on CCTV, and some bastard up in Camden Town's operations room was watching him on a screen and stabbing a big red button.

*"Would Inspector Sands please report to the operations room immediately."*

Jake hesitated, tempted to jump off anyway.

"Do it!" someone ordered – his own voice again.

...But no. He wouldn't get far, not now they knew he was there. And tonight was the one night that he couldn't risk getting caught.

Plan B it was, then. He'd have to meet the others after all.

He stepped away from the edge, stood back behind the yellow line like a good little passenger. Behave yourself or Inspector Sands will come to get you. Yes all right, I'm following the rules, look, I'm obeying your stupid signs...

Muttering under his breath, he strode back along the platform toward the cattle barrier – and skidded to a halt as a clutch of men appeared through the entrance all at once.

Shit! The police, here to arrest him?

No, Jake realised with relief, just engineers. They all wore hard hats and bright orange overalls lined with luminous strips, and carried heavy bags of equipment. It was clear they would be performing some work on the tracks once the power was shut off. Their voices bounced flatly off the wall tiles. The dull chatter of dull men doing a dull job.

He gritted his teeth. This could seriously screw with his plans. For now, though, he just had to get out.

He held his breath as he continued walking to the exit... but the maintenance team barely gave him a second glance and automatically stood aside as he went through. A teenage Moses parting an orange sea.

Jake joined the last few people leaving Camden Town Station without really seeing them. Instead, his mind's eye saw its entire layout: the northbound and southbound tunnels built on top of each other, the passenger corridors, the internal gates, the staff-only offices, the emergency exits, the twisting staircases.

He knew this place, knew its history. He even knew about the deep-level air raid shelter that had

61

been constructed underneath it during World War Two but never actually used. Few of the millions of people who passed through Camden Town ever suspected there was a rusting wartime relic below their feet.

Jake knew all of London's forgotten subterranean chambers. He knew how to get to them.

And he knew what else was down there, even deeper.

# Chapter 2

Friday 13th August 2010
12.41am

Jake found himself short of breath when he reached the station's ticket hall. This was despite standing on the escalator rather than walking up. It was more as if he were unused to the altitude.

On his left, the entrance-only side of Camden Town Station had huge iron gates pulled across it, leaving only a narrow gap. A uniformed TfL staff member stood there turning people away, explaining they had missed the last Tube. Their dismayed howls bounced off his craggy face like a mountain breeze.

On the right, by contrast, the exit side had something of a carnival atmosphere. Jake fed his off-peak single into the ticket barrier and walked through, into the noise and music and traffic of Camden High Street.

Crowds were spilling out of late-night bars, clustering around bus stops and queuing outside mini-cab offices. Squawking packs of girls. Braying gangs of boys. Old punks in their fifties. Kids younger than Jake. Energetic tourists consulting their maps. Lethargic locals hauling their shopping bags. Drug dealers roaming in circles, muttering offers under their breath. Club promoters trying to push flyers into people's hands.

Surface life. Clinging to the skin of the city.

Jake realised he was shivering, deep inside his jacket. It was a warm summer night, but the breeze felt icy on his face. That must be why he'd started coughing again, that or the exhaust fumes. There were so many lights – shopfronts, cars, streetlamps – that it hardly felt like night-time at all. It made him wince, dull stabbing pains behind his eyes.

He couldn't bring himself to raise his head. The night yawed above him, a too-empty cavern of air. Looking at the sky gave him vertigo, like he might fall upward.

He walked round to the other side of the Tube station, The stumpy building was clad in glazed dark red tiles, with its name on a blue sign and the familiar UNDERGROUND roundel jutting out above the street. It sat on the corner of a five-road intersection, the core of a star that radiated traffic and people in all directions. Camden was one of London's always-beating hearts.

With so much laughing, singing, arguing, kissing and throwing up going on, nobody paid attention to the three young men watching the station like hawks.

Just over the road, The World's End pub had closed but the Underworld club in the cellars beneath was still thumping away. It was in the alley alongside the empty pub that they lurked. All three wore dark tops with the hoods up, making them look shapeless, anonymous, dangerous.

Jake crossed Kentish Town Road and joined his people.

They immediately began hurling questions at him – why didn't he meet them outside the entrance, why weren't they already down in the station, why wasn't he following the plan – but he cut them off in a calm voice.

"Maintenance workers. They're already on the northbound platform. No way past them without being seen." He hauled off his rucksack and placed it against the wall beside a similar one.

"Bollocks!" exploded the biggest guy in the group. He yanked his hood down. "What bloody bad timing! I suppose that means we're not getting in there tonight, are we?"

Jake glanced up at him. He was in his early twenties and impressively built, well over six feet tall, broad and stocky. Not quite as pale as Jake but with freckles, short ginger hair, a strong jaw and a ruddy face. It was only the posh voice that stopped him from looking threatening. What with his size and the clipped vowels, it was easy to imagine he had a stellar history in grammar school rugby teams.

As with all of them, Jake didn't know the man's real name. On the online forums, he always signed off his posts with a mocking *'Try this at home, kids!'* Hence the nickname 'Disclaimer'. It was clear that a hunger for excitement was the main reason why he had joined the scene.

There were many names for it. Urban exploration. Place hacking. Environment access. A network of people addicted to finding ways into places they were not meant to go: sewer drains, old hospitals, neglected gasworks, dead power stations, derelict military bunkers... and of course, disused Tube stations. Anywhere they could feel like true explorers.

Almost always dangerous. Almost always illegal. Both were part of the appeal. To avoid prosecution for trespassing, the forum members used pseudonyms instead of their real names. As far as his companions were concerned, 'Jake' was just as artificial as 'Disclaimer'.

It was while scouring those forums that Jake found him. Although Disclaimer's face had been deliberately blurred to hide his identity, he was a familiar sight in the photo galleries. Images of him on the roof of Battersea Power Station, angling his body so it looked like one of the four gigantic chimneys was protruding between his legs: *'If you've ever met my girlfriend, this is why she smiles like the Mona Lisa.'* Or standing on a narrow ledge outside King's Reach Tower, silhouetted against the lights of London below: *'With about 300ft of empty air under my Caterpillar boots, I had finally found a place where my tungsten balls could swing freely.'*

Educated, bored, experience junkies like Disclaimer were ten-a-penny on the scene. But it was the pictures of him and his crew infiltrating Down Street Station that caught Jake's eye.

'Ghost stations' were a popular target for urban explorers. There were over forty of them dotted around the Underground, many of which were shut down decades ago and left to fall into decay. Down Street was typical of these, a forgotten station that was closed in the 1930s. It was unseen by passengers, the trains passing through but never stopping there. Like all disused stations, it was closed off to the public and impossible to gain access to.

And yet there was Disclaimer, inside it. Posing like

a superhero on a grimy spiral stairwell, and standing on an abandoned platform holding out a thumb as if hitch-hiking. That's when Jake knew he'd found someone he could use.

Someone he could recruit.

"I knew this was a bad idea," Disclaimer grumbled. "There's too many people around anyway, we're too exposed here, guys."

"Nah, that works to our advantage."

This was from the man Jake knew only as 'Subverse'. Here was someone you would cross the road to avoid. Shaved head, narrow face, dark eyes, spiky piercings, whole body corded with tight muscle, arms and neck covered with tattoos and scars. He stood next to Disclaimer, taking quick drags on a cigarette.

"Nobody's paying us any attention, we're blending in much more than if this was an abandoned site. It's the perfect camouflage, we're nondescript amongst the herd of conformity." He ground out his cigarette against the wall and spat on the pavement. "Still a frigging nightmare, though."

Maybe Jake shouldn't have been surprised, when he first met Subverse, that he talked exactly the same way as he wrote on the forum. But his pictures spoke more eloquently than his words. Subverse's art was in photographing cities from new angles. His photo galleries featured hundreds of shots of what he called the 'subterranea' beneath London.

Only a select few got Jake's heart pounding. Places like Mark Lane Station, abandoned since 1967. Aldwych, a one-stop spur jutting off the Piccadilly

Line that was closed in 1994. Platforms five and six at Holborn, walled off to the public. They were all there on the urbex forum, captured by Subverse's lenses.

Here was the second person he had to recruit.

"We have to abort," said Subverse. "If there's an engineering crew working in the tunnels, our odds of slipping down there are zero."

"We're not aborting," Jake told them.

Disclaimer and Subverse shared a mutinous look.

"I agree," the fourth member of the group said softly. "I think it might be too soon to give up. Let's just wait for a while. Yes?"

Disclaimer and Subverse nodded in agreement.

"You've all got into tougher places, I know," the man added. "I'm impressed with what I've seen of your work."

*"We* impressed *you?"* Disclaimer shook his head. "Our stuff's nothing compared to what you've done! Those shots you took in Brussels on top of the, what was it, the Palace of Justice? They were, like, legendary!"

"And the Augarten Flak Tower in Vienna," added Subverse, "and the Maillot Loop... inspirational stuff, mate, seriously."

The fourth man waved away their praise with a smile. At twenty-eight he was the oldest, and his goatee and glasses added maturity. His Canadian accent sounded quasi-American to British ears. Otherwise he was fairly plain. Short, thin, brown-haired... the sort of guy nobody looked twice at. But on the urban exploration forums, where he was known as

'Spatial Deconstruction', it was a different story. Over the past ten years, he'd done it all.

Unlike Subverse, he only posted pictures, always in black and white. From the highest towers to the deepest underground spaces, monochromatic views that no-one in the world had ever seen. And accompanying his pictures were those taken by other members of his crew, documenting the master at work: climbing sheer walls using only his fingertips, bending his small body under barbed wire fences, jumping across the sickening drop between buildings. Spatial Deconstruction in progress.

Those in his crews called him 'Deak' for short. The urbex forums simply referred to him as SD, with phrases like *'If SD couldn't get in here, neither can you, noob!'* and *'Back in 2003, long before getting rinsed by other groups, the Paris Catacombs were well and truly SD'd.'*

Everyone knew this man. Everyone respected him. Every cell of explorers in the international community would be honoured to meet him. And here he was, lurking in a grotty Camden back-street at one in the morning with this lot.

Jake knew why. The only way to interest an explorer of Deak's stature was to offer routes into places nobody else had been to. The perfect bait.

His final recruit.

It crossed Jake's mind that not so long ago, he would have been in absolute awe of these guys. They often risked their lives getting into places the public were either forbidden to reach or never had a clue existed. Nobody paid them to do it, and they took

69

nothing except photographs, seeking only the experience of being in a space where they should not be. Go back a year or so and he would have seen urban explorers as the coolest of the cool.

Now, they were nothing but human versions of the tools in his rucksack. There for a purpose, there to be used. There was no room for awe in Jake's thoughts anymore.

Deak asked "The York Road hack was one of yours, wasn't it? How did that feel?"

"Deeply satisfying on a fundamental level," replied Subverse immediately. "When I was at North London Uni, I used to go to Holloway Road all the time, and I always knew there was a reason why it took so long to get from King's Cross to Cally Road, you know? And when I became aware of this zone of blackness halfway between stations, where the tunnel walls just vanish and there's this absence of reality, I've always felt that one day I'd have to physically place myself into that void – "

"Bloody amazing!" grinned Disclaimer. "That's how it felt!"

A gentle smile from Deak. "And how did you manage to get down there?"

Subverse's features fell, while Disclaimer's remained buoyant. "Jake found us a way in, the kid's an absolute genius!"

"Yeah, genius," Subverse muttered.

Jake said nothing. He didn't even appear to be listening, sitting on top of his rucksack with his back against the wall. But he remembered showing the two of them how to achieve one of their goals.

York Road Station's upper levels still remained, a familiar red-tiled building now fitted with offices and presumably CCTV, which had put off many other crews. But Jake knew of the concealed doorway in Bingfield Street that led into its basement, where they found a grime-coated staircase that led all the way down to track level. He'd explained that it was an intervention point, a way of evacuating passengers directly from the platforms in emergencies, probably never used even when the station was open prior to 1932.

The only problem was the iron chain keeping the door closed, but Jake's oxyacetylene blowtorch got them past that. Disclaimer called it a clever little shortcut. Subverse called it cheating.

While Disclaimer ran around the mouldering platforms whooping so loud it echoed off the walls, and Subverse lit up the entire area with flashes from his digital camera, Jake had got to work.

"We were down there for ages." Disclaimer gave a satisfied nod. "It was a great night."

"Some of us didn't want to leave," Subverse remarked.

Jake didn't look up, knowing Subverse was giving him one of his knuckle-hard glares. He'd made them both wait for ages while he poked into every nook and cranny of York Road, methodically shining his UV lamp at every piece of floor, wall and ceiling.

What the hell was he looking for, they asked? What did he expect to find down here? He'd kept silent as he aimed the black light back and forth, examining anything that glowed in the dark. All he found were a few faint streaks on the ground that shone a luminous yellow. He knew these were nothing but traces of rodent urine. Irritation scratched along his nerves. Had he come all this way just to look at mouse piss?

Disclaimer and Subverse had called out in alarm when he went inside the tunnel mouths, knowing the tracks might still be live. He found a small, one-man signalling cabin and used his crowbar to rip open the rusted door. He swept the lamp across its bare interior, eventually kicking the door shut in disgust with a ringing clang that echoed horribly in the dark.

Jake had wiped both grubby hands down his face, smearing it from white to black. Only then did he agree they could return to the surface. There was nothing down there for him after all. Another failure.

Deak looked back and forth, as if sensing a memory not being shared. "And how about – "

A group of girls suddenly walked past, stopping right by the corner. Five of them, all tall with hair streaking down their backs, short skirts, tight tops, handbags, heels. The very air around them smelled sweet. For a minute, they talked animatedly to each other while checking their phones. Then they were off, long bare legs scissoring through the night, heading up toward the Koko nightclub at Mornington Crescent.

Three pairs of eyes watched them go. One pair continued staring into space.

It wasn't as if Jake didn't see the girls. He just... it was like he'd forgotten how to react to them.

"And how about the Museum?" Deak asked, as if nothing had happened. "How did you manage that?"

"Ohhhh man, *British Museum Station!*" Disclaimer beamed like the most enormous little boy in the world. "That was an epic hack, Deak, you'd have loved it! You won't believe the way we got down there, God knows how Jake knew about – "

"So what we gonna do now, then?" snapped Subverse. "Are we screwed or what?"

Disclaimer peered around the corner at the closed iron gates. "Well, the fluffers haven't turned up yet, so maybe we've still got a chance, yeah? Jake, we can still get to that emergency stairwell, right?"

He nodded.

"Well in that case, if the maintenance boys finish early, I reckon it's still worth a shot. Otherwise we'll have to leave it for another night."

"We're going down *tonight*," Jake said.

Everyone looked his way. After a tense moment, Disclaimer tried a cheery laugh. "Absolutely! Got to stay confident, yeah?"

"Why?" demanded Subverse. His whole face was clenched tight like a fist. "What's so special about tonight?"

Slowly, Jake lifted his head.

"Tonight's when things happen."

For a long moment there were just the sounds of traffic and people, before Subverse turned away from Jake, hawked up phlegm and spat loudly into the gutter. "I'm gonna get some shots." He fished inside the battered leather satchel over his shoulder, pulling out a digital camera. "Be good to capture the normality of the topside around the portal into the subterranea, get some juxtaposition with the unseen reality behind the façade."

And then he was gone.

Disclaimer shifted his weight from foot to foot. "Listen, if we're hanging around here for a while, I might grab something to eat. Either of you guys want anything? Bag of chips, something like that...?"

Deak shook his head. Jake remained motionless.

"Jake, you sure I can't get you some food? Looks like your mum's not feeding you enough, man!"

The breath that Jake drew was so deep it sparked off another attack of coughing. There was probably still some perfume from those girls lingering nearby. He glimpsed a concerned look on Disclaimer's face, and waved in a way that meant *I'm fine* and *thank you* and *leave me alone* all at once.

"Okay, cool. Back in a bit." Offering them a double thumbs-up, Disclaimer turned and strode down the high street.

Deak lowered himself on top of his own rucksack, next to Jake. They sat there in the alley, ignoring people passing by as they looked toward the station's closed gates.

"You have a secret, I think," said Deak quietly.

For a very long time it seemed like Jake hadn't heard him, but eventually Deak's renowned patience paid off. "What do you mean?"

"When you contacted me, you offered me access to places that you know even I'd never cracked before. You thought that would be the perfect bait."

Jake twitched involuntarily.

"You thought... the only way to convince Spatial Deconstruction to come to the UK and join my crew is to convince him I can get into disused stations on the London Underground nobody else has. Places that would make him even more famous. He won't be able to resist. He has a giant ego and he won't be able to stop himself. Yes?"

The corner of Jake's mouth turned up slightly, the ghost of a smile.

Deak produced a pack of Canadian cigarettes and lit up one of them, as if rewarding himself. "But I didn't come here to see those places. I came to see you."

Jake turned to face Deak properly, who tapped ash onto the pavement as he went on. "I've spent years working out how to break into secure locations. It can be complicated, takes a lot of time to scope out routes, dig up plans, watch people till you know their routines, all of that. But you... you just *know* how to get in. You amaze your friends not because you're good but because, somehow, you already know exactly where all the ways into the Underground are."

Deak dragged on his cigarette, breathed smoke away from Jake, then turned back to meet his eyes.

"Wherever this knowledge comes from... it's a gift. So that's the real reason I'm here, Jake. I want to hear your story." He smiled. "To learn from the master!"

Jake felt his own expression change, eyebrows rising, mouth opening.

"A gift?"

Deak nodded. "So many people would waste it, but you've – "

"You think... knowing this shit... is a *gift?*"

Jake talked so slowly that it didn't seem like he was angry. His blue eyes were just as wide as normal, his voice just as level. But Deak could tell that he'd walked into trouble. He held up a placatory hand. "Listen, I don't expect – "

"It's not *my* story."

Jake suddenly stood up. He pulled out the iPhone from his coat pocket, tapped in a passcode and turned the security off. Then he tossed it toward Deak, who caught it with one hand.

"A gift," said Jake, making it sound like anything but.

Deak looked at the phone, fingers wrapped around the ridged rubber case protecting it. The screen displayed a text document with no title. Jake knew what words his eyes would fall upon, on the page he'd recently skimmed past.

> *Crosses on the doors of*
> *No that can't be right.*
> *Coincidence. Just because they used to paint*
> *No no no no no*
> *Please oh God*
> *I'm dead*
> *I'm dead*

"Holy Christ," muttered Deak. "What's...?"

Jake turned away to lean against the corner of the building. He folded his arms and stared at the Tube station.

Behind him, Deak used his thumb to turn the digital pages and started reading the document from the beginning. In his other hand, a forgotten cigarette sagged between his fingers, ashes falling to the ground.

# Chapter 3

Sunday 23rd July 2000

I've been sitting here for hours, wondering how to start writing this. It doesn't really matter, I've decided, so I'm just going to start. Treat this like a first draft then come back and sort out a proper structure later, give it a catchy headline, killer opening paragraph, the usual. Right now I just need to feel my fingers typing, get the wheels moving.

It's been two weeks since Chalk Farm. I'm not ready to write about that properly just yet. Other than to say it scared the hell out of me... me and everyone else on that train.

Julia was terrified, of course. I've never seen her that scared before, but she clearly thought she was going to die. I can still see it on her face even now. It's sort of lingering underneath her smiles to the kids.

I haven't told Julia I'm writing this. She would stop me. And I would stop, if she asked, because part of me wants to stop right this second.

Ever since Chalk Farm, I've been debating with myself about whether or not to do this, to finally get down in print all the things I've seen, and what I know about my dad and everything. Or, or... just forget it all, let it lie. That would be easy. I've been doing that for much of my life.

But I can't stop thinking about the past. And I can't shift that feeling that everything's connected, if only I could lay it all out properly and see it from the right angle.

So I've decided to approach this in a professional way, by doing what I do and writing a proper piece on it all. I've no idea who might read it yet, but right now that doesn't matter so much. The only audience I need to worry about at this stage is me.

It's not like there's a shortage of material. There's bags of stuff up in the attic that I never planned to look at again. Letters, photographs, blueprints, newspaper clippings... the research of a lifetime. Really, several lifetimes – my family's lifetimes.

It needs something central to build around, some text, so that's what this will be. I'll need to properly explain who I am when I redraft it. Add some credentials. Something like – Mike Thames, writer and researcher, used to work as a journalist for some of the biggish newspapers, now freelance for magazines and colour supplements and even Websites more and more (which are probably going to make dinosaurs out of the papers at this rate). Maybe list some credentials, whatever makes me look like some kind of authority.

Oh and stick in something self-aware about my name. Somebody with the surname 'Thames' writing about London will be a good selling point for whoever publishes this. Although God knows where this article will end up. It will be an article, I think, of some kind anyway. Very different from all the exposés and hack-jobs I used to fill column inches with. I'll need to clarify my aims in the first few paragraphs.

This is a story about the London Underground.

No. This is about what's *under* the Underground. Not the behind-the-scenes stuff, the machinery of it, but… what's underneath even that.

It is a kind of exposé in a way. I suppose it's also an exposé on my own family, a side of them nobody knew was there. How about 'Beneath the Thames' as a title? No, that sounds like it's meant to be funny. Julia always says I've never been much cop at funny.

There. I've started. That's always the hardest part. I didn't write as much today as I hoped… this has taken hours. I'll have to keep coming back to this whenever I get some time.

But I've convinced myself now that it all needs to be written down. Even if it's only going to be read by me.

Saturday 5th August 2000

It's been difficult finding time to get back to this. Not just because of all the daily crap, looking after two young kids, looking for new clients, meeting dead-lines for old clients, painting the upstairs banisters, etc. Excuses to the mirror is all they are, I realised today. The truth is I've been scared to write any more. I think it's the idea of seeing things that have only been in my head put down on the page in black and white. They'll be harder to ignore then.

But I'm glad I forced myself to begin this article two weeks ago, as picking up something is a lot easier than starting from scratch. So let's keep typing, carry on.

Need to get introductory stuff in early, some facts and context about me. Get the readers trusting the author, like we were taught to.

So: Michael David Thames, forty years old, born on 17th May 1960 to Robert and Angela Thames, an only child. I take after my dad a lot. Same eyes, same nose (I say 'Roman', Julia says 'big') and the same tight black curly hair. Lots of other ways too, it turned out.

I was brought up in Brookwood, which is a village in Surrey. We had a little two-floor house in Connaught Crescent. My mum's still there actually. Supposedly she's looking after Aunt Claire (my dad's sister) who's in her seventies now, but actually I think it's the other way round. Aunt Claire is the toughest old bird you've ever seen, and my mum... isn't, anymore.

Brookwood is a small place, even now. It's one of those places where you know a lot of people's names, even if you've never spoken to them. There weren't so many buildings when I was young, but plenty of open spaces that I remember haring across. On one side of the village was a river and on the other was a train line, neither of which kids were allowed to go anywhere near – so of course we did, if we thought we'd get away with it.

There were always trains running through the village. We grew up with the sound of them chuffing and click-clacking and whistling in the distance, wherever we were, whatever game we were playing. It was our birdsong, our wind in the trees.

Beyond the train tracks was the huge cemetery. This didn't seem like anything special when I was young, it was just local landscape. Every kid had seen the big mausoleums ringed with pillars, the rows of white crosses, the moss-coated headstones. We all knew... funny now, to think that this was so ordinary... we all knew there were dead people on the other side of the tracks.

It's because of trains that my family were there in the first place. My grandfather, Albert Thames, moved from London to Brookwood because he used to work on a railway route that went between them, and according to my dad, "He wanted to live at the nicer end of the line."

Mum often remarked that Grandpa Albert had been a smart one because anything was better than living in London, even living next to a cemetery. At least it was peaceful there, she often said, London never stopped moving, it made her head spin. A big day out for my mum was a trip to nearby Woking or Guildford, which were also hotspots for gigs and clubs later when I was a teenager.

"Your grandpa died in London," she'd remind me, as if the same fate would befall me should I ever dare to 'go down the Smoke'. Seeing as the cause of Albert's death was the Blitz in 1941, I didn't think that was likely. My parents used to talk about the war all the time... planes, doodlebugs, air raid shelters, evacuations to the country. I suppose it dominated their own youth.

Even when I was very young I knew that train driving was the Thames family profession, for men anyway. Apparently even my great-grandfather used to work on the railways. I was the one who broke that mould, which I felt guilty about for a long time, although I can remember for years wanting nothing more than to drive a train and carry on the tradition. (1975 put an end to that.)

Grandpa Albert wasn't any normal train driver, though, as my dad proudly told me many times. He worked on the Necropolis Railway.

The very idea seems bizarre now, but it was a practical solution to the horrific number of deaths in 19th Century London from cholera and other diseases. The old cemeteries and graveyards were literally overflowing, so Brookwood was set up as an enormous new burial ground where citizens of the metropolis could be laid to rest. This was to be the London Necropolis, a city of the dead placed far away from the city of the living. Being the golden age of steam engines, its hearses ran on metal tracks, with locomotives for horses. The world's first dedicated funeral train.

The route was straightforward: from Necropolis Station near London Waterloo, trains ran southwest directly into two stations situated inside Brookwood Cemetery. (The mainline Brookwood Station didn't appear until ten years later.) South Station served the larger and sunnier Anglican part of the cemetery. The North was for 'nonconformists' – all those other lesser religions and atheist heathens.

This wasn't just about ferrying the deceased but also providing a funerary service for their family and friends. The passengers – both alive and dead –

travelled first, second or third class, and the quality of service varied accordingly. They actually had 'coffin tickets' for the corpses, which were of course one way, since they wouldn't be making the trip back to London.

Class and death were both a big deal to the Victorians. They turned mourning into an art form. Compared to some of the other common practices at the time, like including recently deceased family members in their photographs, the Necropolis Railway wasn't that bizarre at all.

Everyone in my neighbourhood knew about this. It was our history. The burial grounds came first and the village was built around them.

My Aunt Claire used to say that back when she was a girl, she would watch the 'stiff express' bringing funeral parties to Brookwood. Every three or four days, a steam locomotive would come thumping and hissing through the cemetery gates at a slow, respectful pace. Drawn behind it would be a mixture of passenger carriages full of mourners and hearse vans full of coffins, stacked four-deep on shelves inside sealed compartments.

I remember her telling me that you could almost set your watch by it, always arriving at about quarter to one in the afternoon and heading back to London an hour later. Although she swore that a few times she heard the train in the early hours of the morning, when everyone was asleep and the stations were empty. She said her father, my Grandpa Albert, told her that she must have dreamt it.

Even when Aunt Claire was young, the funeral

trains only came a couple of times a week. By then, the London Necropolis had been superseded by several new cemeteries in the suburbs that were easier to get to. It closed down during the war and became just another weird piece of Victorian history. By the time of my own youth, the only people who cared were trainspotters and historians. Both would turn up in the village fairly often to ask about the Railway, and get fleeced by locals taking them on expensive guided tours of empty fields.

But like I say, this was just part of the landscape to me. I was a turned-on and tuned-in child of the Sixties, I had my own record player and everything, so to me it was 'old stuff'. Necropolis trains had stopped running twenty years before I was born.

I do remember Dad taking us for lunches and snacks at South Bar (which had once been South Station) a few times when I was six or seven. There was a joke sign above the bar saying 'Spirits served here' that nobody ever laughed at. It was hard to eat there because of a dank smell they tried to hide with too much air freshener. You had a funny taste at the back of your throat for a couple of days afterwards. Aunt Claire refused to come with us, saying she remembered watching train porters carry coffins from the hearse vans down into the cellar. From the smell, it was easy to imagine they were still there.

North Station had already rotted away. The old chapels remained but otherwise there was little trace of the Railway. All the tracks had been pulled up long ago, leaving parallel strips of yellowing scrubland running across the grass. Only the old platforms survived, concrete islands rising up from a green sea.

Nobody was surprised when South Bar closed. It always felt like a decaying relic, no matter how many coats of paint they gave it. This was followed by years of strange rumours about something being kept locked in the old building, and voices coming from it at night, and one kid was taken into it by a man and never seen again, and someone's dog got trapped inside and came out rabid with all its fur stripped off… village stories. These ended when a gang of boys set fire to South Bar in '72, which was one of the most dramatic things ever to happen in Brookwood. The remains were knocked down afterwards.

I knew those boys – they went to my school. Nobody grassed them up. We all thought they were heroes but could never have told an adult why.

That's enough of Brookwood. I need to talk about Dad. Next time.

Saturday 12th August 2000

Robert Thames, my dad, followed Grandpa Albert's footsteps and worked in the transport industry. It was pretty normal back then for sons to take the same career path as their fathers, although it's rarer nowadays.

Instead of the mainline trains, Dad was pretty much a lifetime employee of London Underground. Like his own dad, he lived in Brookwood with his family while working in London, travelling back and forth. Mum made it clear she wasn't keen on him being in that filthy overcrowded rats' nest, but put up with it. I realise now that was because of the good steady wage he earned, far more than any local job would bring in.

Dad was a Tube driver, or 'Motorman' as they used to be called. It was shift work so it made sense for him to stay there and only come home on his days off. His residence was in a big house in Paddington, which he told us was used as temporary lodgings for Motormen and other Underground staff. He never invited us to visit him there, and Mum would have kicked that idea to the kerb straight away if he had.

So throughout the early Seventies, while I was at secondary school, my dad was often away for up to a fortnight. Phone calls were expensive back then, so we would stay in touch by writing letters once or twice a week. (This is probably where my interest in writing stems from, and I suspect my dad knew this and was using the letters to encourage me. He probably hoped I'd be a great novelist or something, and not just a part-timer for the tabloids. I have the same hopes for my own two. You want better things for your kids, don't you?)

Yesterday I went up into the attic looking for Dad's letters. They're all written by hand on letterheaded paper with the old London Transport logo at the top. The ink has faded a bit but not much, and the colour occasionally changes when his pen ran out. His handwriting is surprisingly neat, but then everyone's was in those pre-word processor days. Something else he got me into the habit of doing was dating everything I wrote, which my teachers patted me on the head for, but I was just copying my dad.

I'm going to transcribe his letters as best I can so they are more readable in print and not full of spelling mistakes, ink blotches etc. Otherwise I'd be writing [sic] after every other sentence – journalist's habit.

I can't find the very earliest ones he sent, but here's a fairly typical example.

> *20th of February 1971*
> *Dear Mike,*
>
> *I hope you are well. Some good news, I managed to find that album you wanted by Trex or whatever he's called. I found it at a big record shop called The HMV Store in Oxford St. that I will take you to when you next come down, you will love it it has millions of records. Bit pricey though, 37 and 6 for a record, hope it all gets cheaper in new money!*
>
> *This week I am off the trains because they have sent me back to school! Yes I'm at school too and I even have homework. (Booo!) I have to do a course on some new procedures at a place called the Railway Training Centre. This is where I did my training as a Motorman years ago. They have a train simulator here which broke down more often than it worked (so proper realistic then!!) and mock-ups of train cabs too.*
>
> *What's really neat is their scale model of a whole Tube line which they use to teach all sorts of things. It's like the railway set you got for Christmas but ten times bigger and all remote controlled. It even has a few fake Tube stations called things like Oak and*

*Ash, <u>you won't see those on any map!</u>*

*The training is in a place called White City, although the only white thing I've seen around here is dog poo. (Don't tell mum I said that!!) It's over the road from BBC TV centre, the big round building where they make all the programmes. I've seen a few stars come and go, so you never know I might spot the Goodies (your favourites) there one day.*

*Let me know if you managed to see the Dad's Army film at the cinema and if not we will go when I am home next week. Don't panic don't panic!*

*Lots of love,*

*Dad*

*P.S. <u>Mind the Gap</u>!!!*


I'm crying.

Stupid I know, but so many things I'd forgotten about just came rushing back when I read this. I'd forgotten my dad used to be light-hearted and fun.

He was so normal then.

I'm a mess. Need to pick this up another day.



Sunday 20th August 2000


I had to wait until Julia and the kids were out of the house before I could get back to writing this. I think she's starting to suspect I'm keeping something to myself. Maybe my poker face isn't as good as I thought it was.

So, partly thanks to Dad's letters, I had a proper fascination with the Tube when I was a kid. My mum kept telling me how dirty and dangerous it was, which obviously to a young boy made it irresistible. On the rare occasions when I managed to badger her into visiting Dad in London – never at his lodgings, he always met us at Waterloo – the experience of actually travelling on the Underground only made it more exciting.

I can remember thinking there was something slightly magical about going below ground in one part of London and coming up in another, finding yourself in a totally different place. It was like being teleported rather than actually travelling, since you never saw the areas between A and B.

And that famous map of all the Underground lines, I loved that too. The genius of erasing distance from a map! You never wonder how far apart the stations are, all that matters is the number of stops between them. Who cares about geography, the map says, who cares what the world above is like? It's all about you, and where you're going.

Most fascinating of all were the names of all the Tube stations. Why were some of them so strange? What did they actually mean?

My dad had all the answers. I listened to his stories of the medieval knights on horseback at Knightsbridge, of the guns and bombs at Arsenal and Cannon Street, of the Seven Sisters who nobody could tell apart, and of the little houses with cuckoo clocks at Swiss Cottage.

Oh, and so many more, it's all coming back to me

now. He pointed out the holy men – St Paul (who owned a cathedral), St James (who owned a park), St John (who owned some woods) and St Pancras (who owned a lot of trains). These, he said, were all searching for the Angel, helped by the friars who wore black. Plus, of course, there was London's King who was always *very* cross.

I can remember asking one day if there really was an earl at Earl's Court, and if Dad had ever seen him. "Seen him? I pick his lordship up on my train every day," he replied, "and I pick up the barons from Barons Court and all the poor people at Paupers Court and all the ravens at Ravenscourt Park, although birds go half-price!"

And yes, of *course* there were circuses at Oxford and Piccadilly. Hadn't I heard about the elephant who escaped from one of those circuses and got stuck in a castle? Or the road full of gold hawks? How about the road where black horses grazed?

That was my dad – he couldn't just tell you some-thing, he had to turn it into a tale or give it a punchline of some kind. He made all those ordinary Tube stations sound like fantastical domains. Again, looking back, I can see his influence on me. Maybe that's why I got into journalism… that art of mixing up facts and rumours, knowledge and legends, histories and yarns.

As I became a teenager and a little less gullible, Dad's letters still fed my imagination. He'd tell me plenty of stuff about his everyday work on the Underground, and seeing the sights of the big city, but spiced up his letters with what he knew I wanted to hear: ghost stories!

To begin with, he would simply relate some of the legends that had sprung up over the decades. London was – is – full of urban myths. They flow through it, like all the lost rivers that have been concreted over, occasionally bubbling to the surface here and there. It's to be expected that some of them rise up through the Underground.

A few of these have stuck in my mind. The murdered actor walking through Covent Garden. The woman in black lurking outside Bank. The 'Screaming Spectre' heard at Farringdon. There were lots like that, combining historical tragedy with unexplained sights and sounds to make a good solid ghost story. (If ghost stories can ever be called 'solid'.)

I would bug Dad for details when he was home. He never seemed to get tired of me asking about them. I remember being thrilled when he said there'd been so many strange goings-on at Aldgate Station that they actually kept a 'ghost logbook' there, in which the staff noted down the details of each reported sighting. "They showed it to me the other week, and I spent so long reading through it that I was late for my shift," he told me. "You wouldn't believe what people have seen down there over the years!"

Much more creepy was the letter – I can't seem to find it right now, but I remember it well – where Dad said a workmate of his, a station master, had asked for a transfer from Bethnal Green because of all the voices. Every night for a week, when he was locking up, he could hear the sound of children and women crying in agony from somewhere in the station, echoing along the empty hallways. Dad wrote that his mate was normally a rough-tough bloke, but this had reduced him to tears. In a later letter he mentioned that he'd discovered the cause: in 1943, nearly two hundred people were crushed to death on the station steps during a panicked rush caused by air raid sirens.

About a year after he wrote this, I came across the exact same tale in a book about World War Two. At the time this confirmed to me that his story was 100% genuinely true... and now makes me wonder if my dad had read the same book.

(It's surprising how often WW2 crops up in Dad's letters – but then as I said, my parents talked about it a lot. Tube tunnels were one of the few ways that Londoners could hide from the frequent bombings. The government even built proper air raid shelters underneath existing stations like Goodge Street, Camden Town, a few in Clapham. I don't think they ever got used but they're all still there. And Down Street, a disused station in Mayfair, was turned into a secret operations bunker for Churchill. Lots to say about disused stations later. Maybe rewrite this to connect to it.)

Here's another cute story, part of a letter from October 1972:

> *Yesterday a mate of mine, who does track maintenance, told me about something strange. He was part of the crew building Vauxhall, one of the new Victoria Line stations which opened last year. Quite a few of them kept seeing a really tall bloke,*

*over 7ft, wearing overalls and a cloth cap who never spoke and just walked past them. My mate's gaffer told him this was a builder who died in an accident when they first started construction years ago. He'd been the superstitious type and asked not to work on Friday 13th, but was told he had to, and that was the day he fell down a shaft and broke his neck.*

*After that they kept seeing him walk through the site but only in the early hours of the 13th of each month.*

*The reason my mate told me was because last week, some passengers reported seeing an extremely tall man walking along a platform at Vauxhall after the last train had gone, just after midnight on the thirteenth. Unlucky for them!*

Looking back, I wonder how many of these tales were totally made up, or if some were built around real events such as a builder dying in a tragic accident. At the time I didn't care, finding them all fun in a shivery-goosebumpy way.

The first one to keep me awake all night with the lights on wasn't technically one of Dad's stories, because it actually happened to him.

Tuesday 22nd August 2000

I had to go digging in the attic again, but I've found the letter. His handwriting isn't quite as neat in this one. Looks like the nib of his pen went through the paper a couple of times too.

*9th of November 1973*

*Dear Mike,*

*I hope you are well. I need to tell you about what happened to me yesterday.*

*I've been working on the Northern Line for the last few months. Last night I was on a return trip back up to Edgware. That means at Kennington we take the southbound train into a tunnel which circles back round onto the northbound platform, so we end up pointing the other way and ready to do the return journey. They call it the Kennington Loop.*

*I did the usual 'All change!' at Kennington and waited for the passengers to leave, then got the whistle to continue. (I didn't have a Guard on with me, they don't always have them that time of night – this was about 11.30.) They shifted the points and I drove into the Loop.*

*It always sounds weird going round because it's a pretty tight turn and the wheel flanges make a right racket on the tracks. The screeching comes in through the cabin windows and gives you a proper headache. About three quarters of the way round I see the signal to stop and shut down the motors. I have to wait till the train ahead has left the northbound platform.*

*So I'm sitting there in my cabin in the dark. The motors are off so it's totally quiet. I'm there about two minutes when I hear this thumping-clanging noise. No idea what it is or where it's come from but it sounds quite far away.*

*Then the same noise happens twice, a few seconds*

*apart, but they're both a bit louder. That's when I realise what I'm hearing. It's the sound of the interconnecting doors between cars. One being pulled shut, then the other.*

*But there's nobody on my train.*

*I know there's not, the station master at Kennington always checks before blowing the whistle. There's just me up in the front cabin.*

*Now I'm listening out for it and my heart's going too. Sure enough there's the clunking sound of a door being pulled shut and then the same sound again, even louder this time. Like someone's just walked from one car to the next.*

*I thought about calling control, but that would mean clipping my handset to the tunnel telephone wires and I'd be stuck there. (Remember I told you the wires kick off circuit breakers that cut power when they're used or rubbed together.)*

*I want to open the J-door behind me and take a look down the train and see what's happening. But I can't move, I'm just sort of frozen there. My heart's doing twenty to the dozen and I'm as cold as ice. All I'm doing is staring at the tunnel ahead and telling myself there's nobody else in the Loop but me, <u>there's meant to be nothing there but empty tunnel</u>, no platforms or doors or anything. So how come it sounds like someone is moving inside my train?*

*I almost jumped out of my seat when the sound came again – dead loud. And sure enough a second clanging soon after but this time I felt the door slam vibrate through my chair. Whatever was coming up through my train was now in the same car as me.*

*That was when the signal changed to a green light. I
slammed down the deadman and drove the train at
full speed and it shot into Kennington like a bullet,
way too fast and I had to cram the brakes on to stop
overshooting the platform. I got out of the cabin
sharpish with the station master coming up hollering
and wanting to know what I was playing at.*

*I went back to look through the windows of the first
car, sure I would see somebody in there. But it was
empty. Its back door was hanging wide open with the
handle down.*

*I told the station master what I'd heard and we both
realised that the interconnecting door hadn't been
shut properly, and going round the Loop must have
jogged it loose. The noise I'd heard was the same door
being blown back and forth by the wind that's always
running through the tunnels.*

*We had a good laugh about it and then I told him I
was calling it a night and he'd have to get someone
else to take the train northbound. He weren't happy
but I didn't care much, told him to get stuffed.*

*So there you go Mike, my very own ghost story! Let's
hope my hair doesn't turn white overnight (there's
enough grey as it is!). I'll write to you again at the
weekend.*

*Lots of love,*

*Dad*

*P.S. Mind the Gap!*

When I first read this, I knew that my dad was
trying to be comforting at the end. He'd realised after

writing about his experience… which, I see now, must have been a kind of therapy for him… that he needed to make it seem like just another silly, spooky story to his little boy.

I saw it another way: ghosts aren't real, but *something* in the tunnels is.

Something that can open train doors from the outside.

I didn't press Dad for more details on this one.

It was about this time that his letters started arriving less frequently. He wasn't coming home as often, either. And the letters he did send were telling a different sort of story.

# Chapter 4

Jake had to remind himself to blink from time to time, as he continued staring across the street at Camden Town Station. He'd hardly budged from leaning against the corner, even though his legs were stiff. It didn't bother him. He was familiar with numbness.

There were fewer people in the area now, although still plenty staggering out of the bars and clubs, piling onto night buses and queuing for mini-cabs… faces weary, shoulders slumped, feet shuffling. The wind had grown colder, blowing scraps of garbage across the streets. The ever-ticking clockwork of Camden was slowly winding down.

The iron gate across the station entrance remained unopened no matter how much Jake glared at it. He could tell that the others were losing their eagerness. Adrenalin turning sour, bottled up with nowhere to go.

Not that he felt the same way. Not that he felt much at all. Nor did he say a word, only the occasional bout of coughing as the night air bit into his throat.

Behind him, Deak continued reading the document on Jake's phone. Occasionally he stood up, wandered around a bit then sat back down again, but his eyes hardly left the screen. There was a moment when he drew a breath, perhaps to ask Jake a question, before thinking better of it.

Leaning against the alley wall, Disclaimer finished his second bag of chips and let out a huge sigh. "What on earth do you think they're doing down there? Digging a new tunnel? I can't believe they've been... oh hey, Sub, get some good shots?"

Subverse was swearing under his breath as he stomped up to them, camera swinging from a lanyard around his tattooed neck. "Nah, there's not enough spatial contrast between bodies and architecture, can't achieve one end of the isolation spectrum or the other, it's coming out shite."

"Bad news," tutted Disclaimer as if he heard this kind of thing a lot.

"Those bastards still down there?"

"Yep. Doesn't look like we're getting in tonight, does it?"

Subverse's hard features twisted into something close to sorrow. "Um, Deak, look, I'm really sorry about tonight. We really wanted to, you know, give you a proper London exploration experience but sometimes, and I know you know this already, it just doesn't – "

"What about the air raid shelter?" said Deak, lifting his head from the phone.

Disclaimer frowned. "The what?"

"The one underneath Camden. Is it still there?"

"Yes!" Subverse's eyes went wide. "Of course it is! The deep-level shelters from the war," he told Disclaimer, "there's eight of them, and one of them's right under this station, haven't you seen them on the forum, I think the Infiltrator Crew cracked them a couple of years back, we could try that instead."

"Bloody marvellous!" Disclaimer grinned. "Jake, do you know a way in?"

Without looking round, Jake replied "The south entrance is on Underhill Street. Round the back of Marks and Spencer, down the road." He jerked a thumb over his shoulder.

Subverse had the expression of a dog watching another pet play with his favourite toy. He rolled his shoulders, baring his teeth. "I tell you what else, a lot of these shelters had passages leading to the Tube station above them, so people could get in and out if the main entrance was blocked by rubble or whatever, so I reckon if we get into this one, we could sneak onto the Camden platforms right under their noses and then – "

"It's sealed."

Once again, Jake managed to ignore three pairs of eyes as he added "In the shelter cross-tunnel there's a stairwell going up to a metal grille, which was an emergency exit onto the Northern Line, like you said. But it's been bricked over."

Deak stroked his chin. "You've been there."

Jake nodded. "About two weeks ago."

Subverse looked like he wanted to howl or bite Jake's throat out or something. Instead he just prowled up and down the alley like a caged animal.

"Well," said Disclaimer after a while, "I haven't seen this shelter thing, so if you guys don't mind…

oh, hang on. Looks like the fluffers have turned up."

All four of them peered round the corner. A large white van with a Tube Lines logo printed on its side had parked outside the station. Half a dozen men and women in orange overalls were clambering out. They all had white face-masks slung around their necks, and carried torches and small equipment bags. Teams of cleaners such as these worked during the hours when current to the tracks was turned off. Their job was to manually remove all the garbage, left behind by passengers, that had been blown into the tunnels.

The craggy-faced station supervisor appeared behind the iron gates, unlocking them so the team could walk inside the ticket hall. Seeing this brought a single hand-clap from Disclaimer. "Guess that's that, boys. No way we're getting in there now."

"There's another way down," said Jake.

Disclaimer spun round. "What? Really? Are you serious?"

Subverse waved his arms. "Are you taking the piss now or what! Why didn't you mention this before?"

Deak raised an eyebrow. "Where?"

"It's a short walk from here." Jake picked up his rucksack and heaved it onto his back. "We should get moving."

Subverse stomped in front of him. "Hang on a second, 'boss'! You know we never deviate from the script when we're on a hack, and we certainly don't play follow-the-leader just 'cos you reckon you can get into any – "

"It's dangerous," Jake told him, meeting his stare.

"That's why I never mentioned it. Going through the tunnels from Camden would have been easier. This other way has more chance of being caught, and I didn't want to put anyone at risk."

Behind him, Disclaimer let out a laugh and rubbed his hands together. "Well, if it's more dangerous then I'm definitely in! Bring it on!"

Subverse continued glaring. "This isn't how we do things. You know that. You should have discussed all potential routes with us."

"It's a backup plan," shrugged Jake, "that's all. If you don't fancy it then don't come."

For a moment it looked like Subverse might swing for him, until Deak appeared by his side, voice low and soft. "It's worth checking out Jake's alternative, don't you think? He's led you guys to some pretty interesting places before now. Yes?"

Disclaimer nodded. "He's got a point there, mate. We'd never have known about the Cumberland route. Worth a punt, and if it's no good we call it a night, eh?"

Jake could see a memory rippling across Subverse's features, of the night the three of them broke into British Museum Station.

Here was a station that was obviously intended to bring tourists to one of London's great attractions, but had been disused since 1933. With the surface building long since demolished, the only way to reach it was via the Central Line tunnels. Plenty of urban explorers had tried this from nearby Holborn, and plenty were spotted or arrested. Jake had assured them that taking the long way, approaching from the other direction, would work. They were astonished when he explained how they would get into the tunnels: via a four-star hotel.

One by one, they had walked through the gleaming lobby of the Cumberland Hotel in Mayfair at around midnight. They were pulling wheeled suitcases and wearing jackets and ties, so as to blend in with the wealthy guests. None of the staff did more than nod and smile politely at them, as they got into an elevator and pressed the lowest button.

The enormous hotel actually had six basement levels, the deepest only accessible by stairs, and it was down there that they rendezvoused. That level was laced with pipes and air ducts, filled with massive boilers and rusting ovens. It was abandoned, staff never venturing down there because their radio handsets had no signal. It would be easy to get lost in that labyrinth, but Jake had led them directly to their target: a large manhole cover set into the floor of an old storeroom.

Disclaimer's strength came in handy as he heaved the iron disc from its resting place – and almost dropped it as a blast of air surged up. He and Subverse had gaped down at the sight of a Tube train speeding directly underneath their feet. Jake's expression hadn't changed.

Sweating from the heat, they stripped off their hired suits and changed into black clothing and balaclavas. They unpacked their equipment from the suitcases and waited until one in the morning, when the trains stopped running. Subverse set up a tripod mount over the manhole from which a climbing rope could be winched down. He slowly lowered himself into the darkness, swaying back and forth in the tunnel wind, and eventually planted his feet beside the tracks. Jake went next, Subverse pulling him to a safe position. Disclaimer let go of the rope halfway down, landing with one foot either side of the live rail. That guy lived for near-death experiences.

Jake had watched Subverse remotely retract the rope back up through the manhole and felt satisfied with his recruitment choices. These two would help him get into places he'd never reach on his own.

He'd led them along the eastbound Central Line. It was nerve-wracking enough walking through the tunnel, with every sound they made echoing back at them, expecting to bump into maintenance workers or fluffers at any minute. But they also had to pass through the eerily silent platforms of Bond Street, Oxford Circus and Tottenham Court Road. They remained on the tunnel floor, awkwardly hunched over to avoid being picked up by CCTV.

After scurrying through three brightly lit stations, they finally emerged into one so dark that it swallowed up their torch beams. Disclaimer had bellowed victoriously, his voice echoing off once-white wall tiles that were now filthy grey. Subverse had taken a thousand pictures of the cavernous desolation. And Jake had once again inspected every wall and doorway, shining his UV lamp across any surface within reach.

It revealed nothing. Nothing glowing back at him. Nothing but another waste of time.

For him, anyway. For Disclaimer and Subverse it

was one of their greatest adventures. Their reports had set the urbex forum alight, gaining them massive kudos. They didn't give away the Cumberland Hotel route, and only mentioned Jake's name in passing. Not that he cared.

But he could see now, on Subverse's face, how much another triumph like that would mean to him.

"How come you know all this, anyway?" Subverse asked, taking a step back.

"Research," Jake said.

Was Deak going to make a comment about that? No, the Canadian remained quiet. By now, he knew whose research was leading the four of them, and it wasn't Jake's.

Another harsh cough kicked in as he stepped from the alley onto the high street. The Underworld club was still pounding with music, disgorging drunken people up into the night air. Youngsters like him, enjoying themselves, partying, having fun.

No, not like him, with his grime-streaked face and gaffer-taped jeans and soot-stained jacket. He wasn't the same as them anymore. Their Underworld wasn't his.

Deak grabbed his own rucksack, then stood beside Jake. He angled the rubber-encased phone toward him and asked "Kid sister?"

Jake barely gave the phone a glance. He didn't need to look at its wallpaper image: himself with longer, thicker hair and a more rounded face, beside a twelve year old girl with similar blonde hair. Big smiles in bright sunshine, the greenery of a park behind them.

He said nothing. He felt nothing. Easier to pretend he hadn't seen it.

Disclaimer and Subverse followed Jake as he walked away from Camden Town Station. Trailing behind, Deak continued reading the document.

# Chapter 5

Sunday 27th August 2000

I've been doing more digging, reading more old letters, whenever I can. Julia doesn't seem to be out of the house as much as normal… maybe she's sniffing around? No, I'm just being paranoid. She'd have said something if she thought I was keeping secrets. Which I suppose I am. Anyway, she's finally taken the kids to the park this afternoon so I can get some writing done.

As I became a teenager, Dad's letters from London dropped the ghost stories and were more about the realities of working on the Underground – the more interesting aspects, at least. I welcomed this, as it made me feel like I was growing up and that my dad was making an effort to educate me, even when he was so far away.

He also used to send me envelopes packed with little souvenirs: used season tickets, timetables, metal badges, pens and pencils, old posters from platform walls. I loved getting this stuff. Back then I refused to drink tea from anything other than the canteen mug from the Ealing Common Depot that Dad nicked for me, which had a strange griffin logo on it rather than the normal roundel. I wonder if I've still got that mug somewhere?

But what really put a smile on my face was when my dad told me 'Secrets'. That's how he referred to them: *'Got another great Secret for you, Mike!'* These were things that only someone who worked in the tunnels would know – hidden corners that ordinary travellers never saw.

From ghost stories to ghost stations. Over the space of a few years, my dad gave me a handwritten tour of the unused stops on the London Underground. There were dozens of them, he said, all shut down for various reasons and closed to the public, in some cases without any surface building left at all. Some had been sealed for decades, abandoned and left to rot beneath the earth. Most people who took the Tube never had a clue they were there – proper Secrets.

Every time he was transferred to work on a different line, he would write about the dead stations that his new route passed straight through without stopping. He'd describe the empty platforms looming in his train's headlights as he drove alongside them, their passageways black with shadow, their walls coated with dust. These were invisible to passengers on the train, who only ever saw darkness through the windows. He once wrote that sometimes he felt like stopping the train at a ghost station and opening all the doors, just to – as he phrased it – *'put the willies up the punters!'*

Flicking through his letters now has reminded me of some ghost station names. York Road, Down Street, Brompton Road, Mark Lane, City Road... and I'm going to admit that even writing those down (especially York Road for reasons I'm not ready to write about yet) has given me a sort of tingle. Places that officially no longer exist.

Back then, I had studied the Tube map so often that I could almost close my eyes and see it. So the unfamiliarity of these 'lost' names was exciting. I carefully drew them onto my fold-out copy of the Tube map using a red biro – little X symbols in the gaps where Dad told me the stations were. I suspect I chose red crosses because there was a similar cross over Strand, which my map informed me was closed for rebuilding. Also, it made them look like the sites of buried treasure. X marks the spot!

As well as souvenirs, he would often send me official London Transport documents, grainy black and white photographs, and even old blueprints – proof that these Secrets were real, not stories. There's a whole bunch of this stuff still up in the attic. (Go through this in detail to find suitable illustrations for the finished article.) A couple of them have got things like *'Shhhh!'* and *'Hush-hush!'* scrawled on them. I suppose he'd have got in trouble if he was caught posting them to me.

I felt so lucky. The Motormen were an exclusive club who got to see things nobody else did, and one of their number was giving away all their Secrets, smuggling information out of London like a spy in the enemy's base.

Of course, Dad being Dad, he couldn't stop himself from spinning the odd yarn about these ghost stations. The difference was that since I was older, he didn't try to sell them to me as real. Like the rumour about there being some kind of train station under-neath Buckingham Palace. He told me – one time when he was home, maybe Christmas '73 – that he'd actually met a bloke who claimed to have seen it, and who swore blind that the Queen had her very own personal Tube train. That made Dad laugh his head off. "Imagine that! The Elizabeth Line!"

I asked where it went, and he said it varied depending on who you spoke to: maybe Windsor Castle, or the Houses of Parliament, or even all the way up to Scotland. "Load of old codswallop," he reckoned, which coming from the Codswallop King himself was saying something.

I wasn't so sure, though. There was a lot of worry over nuclear war back then... surely a secret Tube line would be just the thing to whoosh the royal family to safety during the four-minute warning?

Here's another that I've just come across. Proper urban myth stuff, and you'll see WW2 gets mentioned yet again.

> *Have I ever told you about the BBC's <u>secret station</u>? The Bakerloo Line runs right under Broadcasting House pretty much, and there's meant to be a way down into the tunnels to a platform where they could board a Tube train in an emergency. Great story which I know is made up because I've been down there looking for it! Last week I went track-walking with a repair team along there and there's not a dicky bird.*
>
> *Mind you, Vic's son in law is an engineer at the BBC and told him that there's a massive concrete bunker in the basement of Broadcasting House called the Stronghold, which they built to keep all the studios running during the Blitz in case the building got*

*bombed. He told Vic there's a weird staircase in there
that doesn't go anywhere! It goes down two flights
and then the steps just come to a dead end with a
brick wall. So maybe that was meant to be an escape
route onto the Bakerloo, but Auntie Beeb never got
round to finishing it?*


Saturday 2nd September 2000


I've brought down another batch of letters from the
attic. They were all wrapped together by a thinning
elastic band that snapped when I picked them up.
From the postmarks on the envelopes, these are all
from 1974. I must have started trying to keep them in
some kind of order.

Last week, Julia and the kids came back just as I
was hitting my stride. Annoying! But I still need to
keep this to myself for now. I've started hiding all the
letters and things down in the garage, behind the old
paint tins – not much chance of Julia nosing around
back there. This way I can get more time to read them
even when everyone's at home.

I was going to follow up on my dad's little tale
about the BBC by making the observation that this
love of storytelling obviously runs in our family. My
grandfather, Albert, seemed to have done the same
thing to my dad back when he was a kid.

*The other day I remembered a story your Grandpa
Albert told me when I was young, about something*

*that happened to him when HE was young, and that's going back a bit! He talked about being taken on a trip when he was four or five years old by his own dad – this is your great-grandfather. This would have been around 1905, I think.*

*"He took me out of the house in the middle of the night. There was frost on the cobbles and a bitter fog," your grandpa said. He wondered if he was sick because he was taken to a hospital somewhere – "but it was a strange kind of hospital with a train going through it."*

*He remembers his own dad trying to drag him onto the train, even though he was scared and crying that he didn't want to go wherever they were going. "I ran away and got lost in some tunnels, but then some nurses found me." Someone took him on a coach (horse-drawn, I guess) back home.*

*Not much of a story, I know. He looked sort of surprised when he told me this, saying he'd forgotten all about it for years and it just came flooding back to him.*

*That was the last time he saw his own dad. Jacob, his name was. He showed me a death certificate from London Hospital, this ragged yellow scrap of paper. It said Jacob Thames died of cholera in December 1906. Cheery old bugger your grandpa, wasn't he!*

My dad mentioned Albert Thames quite a few times in these later letters. Here's another extract from one dated 16th January 1974:

*I've been thinking about your Grandpa Albert a lot lately. I sort of wish he was still around for me to ask him questions. I've ended up following in his footsteps, what with working on the trains in London and only coming back home every so often, just like him. Some other ways too. At least I don't stink of coal and smoke when I walk in the door like he did! (Don't tell me I stink of other things, cheeky sod!)*

*I know your Aunt Claire says our dad was a mardy old so-and-so, but that's not how I remember him most of the time. Considering what he did for a living, he was pretty cheerful, always making me laugh and telling stories. All the funerals never seemed to rub off on him at all, except towards the end maybe. We rarely saw him in the last few months and when we did he hardly spoke. Or rather he didn't speak to us. He was always mumbling away under his breath. Sort of there but not there, gone someplace else in his mind. So perhaps all the death and sorrow he saw did get to him eventually.*

*As you know, he passed away when I was seven, so I never got to know him as well as I'd have liked. Your Aunt Claire never cried once. I'd forgotten that, but it's just come back to me. I bawled my head off for weeks, course I did, but she didn't. She took over a lot of housekeeping and helped your Nana Martha out, but wouldn't talk about what happened. It was like she never missed our dad at all. I did though and I still do.*

I felt uncomfortable hearing such things... at thirteen, you don't really want your parents opening up to you about their feelings. (I'd never do that with my two, not in a million years.) But I can see now that he was writing to himself as much as to me. He was trying to remember his father – the same way I am, I suppose, with this article. God, are we doomed to become carbon copies of our parents?

That notion must have been on Dad's mind too. Not only did he have a similar job driving trains, and a similar lifestyle all round, he was even staying at the same lodgings near Paddington.

I already knew how Grandpa Albert passed away. In fact so did half the population of Brookwood, since the entire Necropolis Railway died along with him.

The air raid on 16th April 1941 was the worst night of the London Blitz, killing over one thousand people and badly injuring twice as many. Imagine: the blasts, the noise, the flames, the dust, the bodies in the streets. All those ordinary lives gone in a matter of hours. It seemed impossible to me in 1974 – even more impossible now, in the year 2000 – that an attack on that scale could ever happen. At least not to a modern city here in the Western world.

Necropolis Station took a direct hit. A single bomb utterly demolished over half of it. Once the war was over, rather than spend money rebuilding what was already an unprofitable line, they simply closed it down. Coffins still came to the cemetery by rail for a few more years. Aunt Claire told me they were hidden away in the brake cars of ordinary services to Brookwood, which would have horrified passengers if they'd known. But the days of the world's first funeral train were over.

I remember standing with an energetic Dad and a bored Mum outside what was left of Necropolis Station. It was on Westminster Bridge Road, very close to Waterloo where he always met us as our train came in. This would have been in '72 or '73, on one of our rare trips to see him in London. (Talking of bombs, I can also remember how worried my mum was of 'getting bombed by the Irish'. The IRA ran a brutal terror campaign during the Seventies, leaving incendiary devices in litter bins, especially around the West End. Naturally this made London even more dangerous in her eyes.)

Dad pointed out the magnificent dull-red building with its columns, arched brickwork and wide gateway. Horse-drawn hearses used to be taken right into the station itself with its mortuaries and waiting rooms, leading out to boarding platforms alongside the steam engines. All long gone, of course, save for the front building that was now rented offices.

I tried to imagine it in its prime, blending the quiet reverence of a funeral parlour with the bustle and noise of a railway station. I could see from Dad's eyes that he had no trouble visualising that, even as we stood there. When he started telling me how they used to stack up coffins in the arches underneath the viaduct during busy times, Mum snapped at him in disgust that we had to get moving before the lunch-time crowds.

I've also seen (but can't recall where or when) a black and white photo of the station after the bombing. It shows a train with broken windows nose-dived into a pit, surrounded by shattered buildings, bent rail tracks and rubble. And I remember looking at that photo and thinking *Grandpa's in there*. That's what my parents told me, and what was common knowledge in Brookwood. Albert Thames, one of the very last drivers on the Necropolis Railway, perished in the explosion that destroyed the station.

And it's only now, while writing this, do I stop to wonder: *Why?*

Why was he there all by himself at 10.30pm on 16th April 1941? What was he doing in the middle of an air raid? None of the funeral trains ever ran that late at night, so he couldn't have been working. Why wasn't he in his lodgings at Paddington, or hiding in a shelter? Was he sleeping there overnight? Had he been saving money by bedding down inside the luxurious padded carriages without anyone knowing?

Writing about the Blitz has made me remember something I once read. You'd think that as soon as war was declared, all the Underground stations would be converted into shelters, but the government initially forbade it. The same thing happened during the German air raids of World War One – people were actually prevented from hiding on the platforms, even when the bombs were falling. The authorities had a serious concern that Londoners would develop a 'bunker mentality' and never want to come back up again. They might feel so safe and secure down in the tunnels that they'd never return to the surface. Wartime governments were actually more worried about this than their citizens being blown to pieces!

As crazy as that sounds... when I think about Albert hiding away in the Necropolis Station as if it were his second home, and when I think about what happened to Dad... maybe they had a point.

Tuesday 5th September 2000

Last night I spent some time in the garage reading through the 1974 letters, and came across something as disturbing now as it was then: my dad's sudden obsession with plague pits.

Nowadays it's common knowledge that during medieval times, the number of people dying from the Black Death was so huge that individual burials were replaced by mass graves. London's very success meant that it suffered more than most. The riverside docks bringing trade and wealth also brought the rats and fleas that carried bubonic plague into the streets. In both the 14th Century and the 17th, the city was turned into a festering, sickening nightmare. The Great Plague of 1665 alone took a *hundred thousand* lives! How did the city survive that? The Blitz feels mild by comparison.

Like most people, I learned about this at school. I didn't expect to be learning about it from my dad as well.

*20th of March 1974*
*Dear Mike,*
*I hope you are well. I had a weird sort of flashback going through the Kensington Bends last night. Have I told you about the Brompton Rd ghost station*

118

*on the Piccadilly Line? Add it to your map if I
haven't. It's between Knightsbridge and South
Kensington. It's one even I can't see because it's
walled up. It used to be an army base during the war.
There's a proper Secret for you!*

*But the Bends are just after that, where the tracks
swerve sharply and the noise of the wheels made me
think of Kennington Loop, all that screeching. I
remembered being stuck in there by myself and
hearing those noises in the empty cars behind me.*

*God knows what I'd have heard if I'd been stuck at a
red light in the Bends, seeing as I was an arm's reach
away from the biggest load of skeletons you can
imagine. The tunnel bends because it's going around
one of the plague pits from olden times. All the clay
under London is chocker with bones, but the burial
pits are the worst because they just used to heave in
corpses in their hundreds, no time to bury them
properly, had to get rid of the plague carriers quick.*

*All the Motormen know where these are and where
the Tube turns to avoid them. See, they couldn't
tunnel through the one at Kensington. They tried,
but the bones are packed together too tight. The
official story is the tunnel swerves because it's
following Brompton Road, and that Tube lines were
dug under public roads to avoid foundations and
suchlike. But that's just what they tell the punters,
Mike. <u>It's us who knows where the bodies are buried</u>.*

*Similar thing happened when they were digging the
Victoria Line some years ago. More than a few lads
told me about how a boring machine went straight
through a plague pit at Green Park, covering them in*

*bits of skull and bone. They normally know where
these are but there's so many under London that
sometimes they only find out when they plough right
into one. Imagine the tunnel drills hitting all those
bones. Bet it sounded just like the same metal
screeching sound on the Bends and the Loop. Drills
right into your head it does.*

*Can't think what else to write today so will send you
more Secrets soon.*

*Love,*

*Dad*

*P.S. Mind the Gap*

Maybe I should have found this fascinating, but
actually I can remember feeling vaguely disgusted to
read this. It made London seem diseased and rotten
rather than a cool, mysterious place.

It also gave me a crazy paranoia that the Tubes
might still be full of plague, which my dad might
have been exposed to – and therefore had infected me.
Every time I started coughing, or the glands under my
arms started aching, I wondered if it wasn't just
another bug but the beginning of the end. Funny to
look back on… 'I was a teenage hypochondriac'! Even
nowadays, a persistent cough always reminds me of
that fear.

Plague pits crop up again in his subsequent letters,
sometimes connected to whatever Secret he was
telling me, but often more randomly. He mentions
that Aldgate, the station where they kept a logbook of
ghost sightings, was actually built right on top of a
pit. There's another remark about Farringdon Station

being near the biggest mass grave of all, containing the corpses of thousands of medieval Londoners.

And then there's this, from 8th November 1974:

> *Went looking at the London Road Depot last night, after the power was shut off. Down the south end are two tunnels – one goes to the Bakerloo Line at Elephant & Castle, the other is called an overrun tunnel and just ends with a wall. But it's <u>a false wall and the tunnel carries on behind it</u> for a way before being properly bricked up. Guess why? They had to stop because of what they found behind it. The bones. Plague bones.*
>
> *None of the depot staff wanted to take me down there. Not at night, a couple of them said, we never go at night. Had to steal a torch and go through the false wall myself. There's tracks that go into barriers and a sand drag, but otherwise it's just black in there. The air is thick and hot and the walls are running damp. I was down there for hours before they found the balls to come get me. Station master weren't happy but screw him.*

You can see how the tone of Dad's writing has changed. He's becoming almost confrontational, like a man on a mission. He never explained why the depot staff wouldn't accompany him at night, even though I recall asking him when I wrote a reply.

And he says he 'went looking'… for what? I asked him that too, but he never gave me an answer. Like Grandpa Albert toward the end, it wasn't his son who he was really talking to.

Sunday 10th September 2000

Julia knows something's up. God knows how, I've been so careful. But yesterday she waited till the kids were in bed and then asked me outright what I was doing. Obviously I acted confused and innocent, but she wasn't having any of it... said she knew I was up to something behind her back and that she had a right to know what it was.

I lied to her face.

I don't like doing it, I really don't, but it's too important that I keep this going, especially now that I've got to this stage. I need to write about Moorgate.

Even before 1975 began, things were strange. For the first time, Dad didn't come home for Christmas. There were some presents under the tree that were supposedly from him, but they were so 'not-me' that it was obvious Mum had bought them... Dad would have known exactly what I wanted. She told me he was just really busy in London, but I knew something had changed. I was sending three letters to every one of his, and his replies were becoming shorter, scratchier, odder.

The last letter I ever received from him is still inside a transparent plastic bag, more carefully protected from the attic's dust than the others. Kind of ironic considering it's also the shortest. It arrived a couple of weeks after Moorgate – which surely needs no introduction? But maybe that's because I still feel its impact... like a bomb crater, distorting everything around it. So perhaps I'd best get some facts down for the article.

The Highbury Branch of the Northern Line always looked kind of cute on my Tube map: a mini-line with only five stops, running from Drayton Park to Moorgate. It didn't even deserve its own proper colour, just white outlined in black. Nowadays it's called the Northern City Line and has been extended to link up with Overground rail services, but back then it just went across Islington and the City, shuttling to and fro, to and fro.

On the morning of Friday 28th February 1975, a Tube train on this branch crashed at Moorgate, killing forty-two people and hospitalising seventy-four of its 300 or so passengers.

I woke up that day to find my mum on the phone trying to call Dad, then calling London Transport, then the Metropolitan Police, then members of our family, then trying Dad's number again... shuttling to and fro, to and fro.

I barely got to speak to her at all. There was no talk of going to school, so I didn't. There was no sign of food, so I ate toast and cereal all day. There was no word from my dad, so I re-read his recent letters for some mention of the Highbury Branch. But it was one of the few lines he never worked on, or at least he hadn't mentioned it if he did.

The news on the TV was dominated by it, with cameras showing all the fire engines, ambulances and police cars outside Moorgate Station. God, it was horrible. Uniformed men emerged with their faces coal-miner black. Figures were brought out on stretchers covered with blankets – the survivors and the dead. But no pictures of what was happening beneath. No clue whether or not my dad was down there.

The evening news programmes revealed more facts, including the reassuring one – to me, anyway – that the driver was named as Leslie Newson, not Robert Thames. But we still hadn't heard from him.

Hunched on the sofa and still in my pyjamas, I watched the haunted, dirty and bandaged faces of those who either saw what happened or had been on the train itself. They explained how it hadn't slowed down as it entered Moorgate. In fact it seemed to accelerate, whooshing alongside Platform 9. This was the Highbury Branch terminus, a dead-end tunnel like the one at London Road Depot, lined with a sand drag and buffers to slow down any train before it reached the concrete wall. Unless that train went roaring into it at thirty-five miles per hour.

I can't remember anything about that weekend. But I do recall, the week after, feeling shocked at how people at school or around the village talked about the Moorgate crash in an unsurprised manner. "Typical London," was the sort of thing they said. As if life were cheap there, and disasters happened every day. It's London, they shrugged, what do you expect?

For days, I watched every programme about Moorgate, listened to every radio report and read every newspaper. It wasn't the tragedy that was addictive so much as the mystery. London Transport stated that the train itself hadn't malfunctioned, its brakes were all working perfectly. So maybe the Motorman deliberately killed himself? But Newson was known to be a cautious, safe and experienced Tube driver, with no suicidal tendencies, and had cash in his pocket with which he planned to buy his daughter a car that day after work. How could he simply forget that there was no more track after Moorgate, that Platform 9 was the end of the line?

Time went by with no word from Dad. My mum started becoming visibly stressed, so I calmed her down by saying that he was probably busy helping, somehow. Driving replacement trains, or assisting the investigation. After all, if there were anything wrong, London Transport would have contacted us, of course they would. "He's just busy, Mum, that's all." I must have said that a hundred times, repeating the same words she'd been reassuring me with for months.

I started believing it myself. I so badly wanted everything to go back to normal. I was studying for my mock O levels, hanging out with friends, buying music from the record shop, doing all the things fifteen year olds do... I wasn't prepared for anything to change.

Nearly two weeks later, lying on our welcome mat when I woke up one morning, was an envelope with my name on it. No address, no stamp or postmark, literally just the word 'MIKE'.

*9th of March 1975*
*Mike*
*I hope you*
*Mike I have a lot to tell you soon as I can don't listen to them you have to read between the lines like I*

125

*I know why he did it I know where he was trying to get to*

*None of them are talking about it but some of us saw it happen at Shroud Lane and down the Cross we KNOW what happens to us*

*it happens, he wasn't the same anymore he'd <u>gone under</u>*

*deadman should have stopped it that's how it works the gap is*

*I love you but <u>mind the gap</u> and*

Reading this again now, for the first time in many years, I'm as short of breath as I was after I'd ripped open the envelope and yanked it out. The handwriting is scrawled, unlike his usual copperplate script, with his underlining slanted rather than ruler-straight. The paper is crumpled as if scrunched up then smoothed out later. And the words...

That's my dad, but it's not.

Even now, it turns my guts to water.

I never showed the letter to Mum. Perhaps I was scared she would take it away from me. Perhaps I was scared that this single scrap of paper was the very last contact I'd ever have from him.

I was right.

Days became weeks. I wrote a reply, a second, a third, a fourth, but there were no more letters from him. The phone number we had for his lodgings at Paddington went out of service.

The letter hadn't been sent via post, so did Dad stick it through the letterbox, meaning he was actually in Brookwood? I quickly realised he could have asked someone else to drive up and put it through our door, or paid for a courier. He obviously wasn't trusting Royal Mail anymore.

Mum clammed up tight. Sealed herself away from everything, doing all the mundane housework and meals and shopping as if on autopilot. It was to be expected under such stress, and yet... thinking back on it, I realise what was missing from her behaviour: sadness. She wasn't actually upset as such, it was more like a defensive reaction, a retreat into a shell. Had she expected this, somehow?

There was a night when Aunt Claire, my dad's sister, came to visit. They sent me to my room while they talked in the kitchen for hours. Aunt Claire left without saying goodbye – which was weird in itself, since she was always very fond of me. Mum then called me down to sit at the kitchen table and told me, with no preamble, that my dad had changed.

"Changed?" I asked.

"Like your grandad. I mean, you know, before he died. He's gone down London for good now. London's took him."

I was chilled to the bone, too stunned to move or ask anything more – maybe scared of hearing more – as my mum calmly told me that we wouldn't be seeing Dad again so the two of us would just carry on, that Aunt Claire was going to help with the money and sort out a few things for us, and so everything would be fine, nothing to worry about, and would I like spaghetti hoops for my tea?

It seems insane now, writing it down like this, to

think she could accept that my dad – her husband – would never walk through our front door again. It seems even more incredible that I was meant to just nod and eat my tinned spaghetti. Which, as far as Mum was concerned, is exactly what I did.

But that was the moment when my secret mission to find my own father began.

After a visit to our local library, I found telephone numbers for London Transport's head office at 55 Broadway. I called every one of them from the battered red phone box up near the cemetery, crammed inside with my notepad and pen, writing down whatever number or extension they gave me to try. I spoke to secretaries and admin assistants and staffing managers, all with the same question. Where is Robert Thames?

Of course there was no master record of all the members of staff working on the London Underground – even I didn't expect that. But it was a bigger bureaucratic tangle than I thought. It seemed as if every line or depot had its own payroll department, as if they were still independently owned companies competing against each other for passengers. Since my dad had worked all over the network, I assumed he'd be on *all* of their lists. But I was repeatedly told that they had no record of that name.

Until an office dealing with the Northern Line told me that yes, they'd found a listing for a Mr Robert George Thames. Excited, I started asking a babble of questions when the line went dead. I pumped more coins into the phone box and punched in the same number only to get the engaged tone, and again on the next six attempts. When I called back the next day, a different voice told me they had no-one with that name on their books.

I'm embarrassed to recall that, in my rage, I vandalised the phone box. Yanked the handset loose, kicked in panes of glass, shredded the directory's pages.

I'd hit a dead end. They'd erased my dad! His name had been struck from the records of every single Underground line.

But what did his last letter say? I had to read _between the lines_.

On a wet and overcast Monday in May, I avoided my school and walked up to Brookwood Station, where I bought a return ticket and got on the train to London. I was familiar with the fifty-minute journey from when we used to visit Dad, although we hadn't done that for nearly two years.

The old British Rail train squeal-clunk-rattled its way into Waterloo, while I stared out of the rain-streaked window at the swollen clouds. Somewhere under that grimy grey sky, somewhere in that grimy grey clench of metal and concrete, he was there. He had to be.

I was prepared to spend the entire day knocking on office doors, asking around at depots, throwing stones at 55 Broadway's windows and basically being a pain in the arse to London Transport until they told me something useful. But there was one logical place to see first. I went down into the Tube, bought a ticket and got a Bakerloo Line train to Paddington.

Remembering my dad's advice from when he

showed me round the city, I made sure to travel in the rear car where a blue-uniformed Guard kept an eye on youngsters travelling by themselves. I watched him at work: pressing buttons on a panel to open the train doors, leaning out to bellow "Mind the gap!" or "Stand clear!", and ringing the starter bell after the doors closed to tell the Motorman he could proceed. He also offered cheerful hellos to passengers, and told off rowdy kids for being too noisy. I glared at the Guard for the entire journey, as if he were the evil monster responsible for my father's absence, for Moorgate, for everything that was wrong and shit in the world.

With only the fur-lined hood of my parka protecting me from the belting rain, I followed the crowds out of the gaping maw of Paddington's main entrance. The streets were choked with traffic and people, making Brookwood feel like a ghost town. I walked for a while, squinting up at street signs and down at the paperback London A-Z in my hands with a route drawn in pen.

Before long I was standing outside my dad's lodgings, his home away from home. I'd never been there before. I expected something as squat and grimy as a Tube station or an army barracks, so was surprised at its tall poshness – a five-storey Victorian house painted pure white. It looked exactly like all the other buildings in the street albeit with no house number, which I had to work out by looking at the numbers on either side. But this was definitely the right place.

I remember how nervous I was. Did I expect him to

be inside? Not really, but perhaps one of the other Motormen living there might know where he'd gone. Or maybe he'd left a clue for me, maybe another letter. There'd be something, I knew, something...

The enormous black door was more than twice my height and bordered by white columns, with no doorbell or sign. I knocked loudly and waited in the rain. Knocked again. Called "Hello?" a few times. I would have peered in through the windows but there weren't any on the ground floor so instead I looked up, hoping to spot a sign of life. The upper windows were decorated with ornate balconies and arches, but their panes were black. Not just curtained. Flat black. Almost like they'd been painted over.

Puzzled, I walked down a narrow side-street to the back of the building, hoping to find a rear entrance. Instead there was just a wide brick wall with no door. I waited until nobody was looking then jumped to grab the top and haul myself up, where I saw –

Nothing.

An enormous space where a whole house should be. Only a few steel girders crossed the empty air, buttressing the buildings on either side of the...

(Oh God, it's just hit me. There's only one word for it.)

Either side of the *gap*.

I almost fell off the wall when a train suddenly appeared. Down below street level, in a pit where the house's foundations should have been, were parallel sets of tracks leading into two tunnel openings. The grey Underground train burst from one of these, racing below me before vanishing again.

Dad's home no longer existed. It had been swallowed up. Like Mum said, London had taken him.

But I quickly realised it was much worse than that. This hadn't happened recently.

Dad's home *never* existed.

I suspect none of this will come as a surprise to most of my article's readers. Loads of people know about it nowadays. The two buildings that had to be demolished to allow the locomotives of the Metropolitan Railway to come above ground and vent excess steam before descending again. The false frontage facing the road that is only a few feet thick, a façade to make sure the street remained attractive to its wealthy residents.

But in the Seventies, this wasn't anywhere near as well known. Especially not to a fifteen year old boy for whom 23 Leinster Gardens wasn't an amusing architectural oddity for tourists to visit. It was the address where his father was staying.

The address I'd been sending letters to for years, for *bloody years!*

I never did go on to make a nuisance of myself at the London Transport offices. I never made any more phone calls or enquiries. I spent most of that day slumped against a huge black door that never opened. Staring out from under my parka hood, watching people with umbrellas hurry past as the rain spattered against the pavement, up through which came the regular vibration of trains passing below.

I stayed there until long after the sun went down, hunched up against the empty shell of a home, feeling even emptier.

# Chapter 6

Jake was starting to feel the cold now. The wind had picked up, blowing all the empty bottles and garbage across the streets of Camden. His whole body quivered under all the old clothes, hands balled inside jacket pockets, hoodie covering his head.

But still he kept walking. And still the other three followed.

He'd avoided going straight up Kentish Town Road, knowing there would be fewer people if he took a roundabout route. Even at three in the morning, there were still some die-hard clubbers roaming around or waiting for night buses. Jake couldn't bear any more people. They had been surrounding him all night, everywhere he went. The constant friction of crowds, grating against his skin even through all the layers, making it feel as if his nerve endings were exposed and all the faces and voices and bodies were grinding against them like sandpaper…

Deep breath. And another.

He'd be back down there soon.

Not long now.

The four of them walked unhurriedly along Royal College Street, crossing Regent's Canal. Occasionally,

Jake glanced at Deak as he continued reading the document on his phone. His calm expression had become a frown, outlining twin grooves in his forehead, but otherwise there was little reaction so far.

Another cough ripped through Jake's chest. He tried to swallow it down but couldn't. It's because of this cold wind, he knew. Soon as they were out of it, he'd be fine.

"You all right, mate?" asked Disclaimer.

Jake nodded, muffling his coughing with a gloved hand.

"Sounding a bit rough there. If you're getting sick or something, we can always call it a night?"

"I'm fine," he said.

Disclaimer continued walking beside him, tall and plummy-voiced. "So, like, what's going on with you then?"

Jake looked up sharply. "What?"

"I mean, you know, what's new? Are you living at home, or studying at college, dating a girl?" He shrugged. "Or a boy even, that's cool, whatever…"

He shook his head. None of the above.

"Oh, okay. So what are you doing with your life?"

Jake held out both hands, taking in himself, the four of them, and the night-time streets. "This."

He was grateful when Disclaimer took the hint and started chatting to Subverse instead. His throat hurt too much. And there was nothing he wanted to talk about anyway.

Jake rubbed his eyes. Had all the streetlamps along this road been turned up to maximum? Bright little daggers trying to stab into the meat of his brain, that's what they felt like. He wished he'd stolen some sunglasses from that corner shop near his squat.

Laughter rang out as Disclaimer and Subverse discussed some of their previous escapades. They were talking about Tube stations they had explored, which for some reason was making both men giggle like schoolkids.

"And there was that one time," Subverse said with a smirk, "when I hacked West Ashfield Station…"

Disclaimer let out a public-school guffaw. "Oh, good one!"

Jake's head twisted round. What was this?

"Yup, in fact I managed to get a good look at all the stations on that line. Let's see, there was Hammersmith Bridge, Kensington Palace, Strand-on-the-Green, Hobbs End…"

"Hobbs End!" hooted Disclaimer. "Must have had the *devil* of a time getting down there!"

Jake felt his pulse start to thump. What were these names? Were they… did these two know? *How could they know?*

"And then there's Walford East… that's a pretty depressing old place."

"That's nothing mate, I hacked Sun Hill once, nearly got caught by the Old Bill…"

"Oh yeah? You reckon that's dangerous, try getting into Vauxhall Cross, you have to be some kind of secret agent to get down there."

"Bet you were shaken not stirred after that one!"

Jake relaxed as he realised what they were talking

about. But Deak looked up with an even deeper frown. "I don't think I've heard of any of those. Are they disused stations?"

Disclaimer shook his head, beaming. "No, we're just messing about, Deak. They're not real places."

"West Ashfield's *sort* of real," Subverse added. "I went on a tour once to Ashfield House, where they train all the staff, and they've got this mock-up of an entire Tube station on the third floor. It's in the west wing of their offices so that's why it's called West Ashfield. It's totally accurate, has tracks and sound effects and display boards, the lot! And there's this big model railway to demonstrate signalling, with all these fake station names... Hammersmith Bridge, etcetera."

"Ah." Deak nodded. "You won't see those on any map."

Jake knew he was quoting the document on his phone – from one of Robert Thames's old letters – but Subverse just blinked. "Um, no, you won't."

"The others are all from old TV shows or films," explained Disclaimer. "Doubt you get them in Canada. Well, you've probably seen the Bond movies..."

"Right. Just stories," said Deak. "Like the station under Buckingham Palace. Yes?"

"That's no story!" yapped Subverse, eyes huge. "I know a guy who's been on the Queen's train, it's real!"

"Jeez, Sub," laughed Disclaimer, "not this again."

"Straight up! I've seen pictures! There's a train with

137

the royal wossname on it, the royal crest, it's 1938 stock, all in gold and red. It's locked away in some sidings under St James's Park but it's definitely there, the track hooks up with the Q-Whitehall tunnels, it goes right under Downing Street too. I'm telling you guys, that's no story, it's absolutely true."

Disclaimer was shaking his head. "Load of old rot and you know it. Everyone's always making up stuff about weird things underground. Ghosts and monsters and giant alligators…"

"That's the New York sewers," Subverse muttered, stopping short of claiming he'd seen pictures of those too.

"What do you reckon, Deak? Ever come across anything spooky?"

The Canadian gave a semi-smile. "I've been inside catacombs, asylums, basements in old hospitals, Soviet nuclear bunkers… not once have I ever seen anything remotely supernatural or weird."

Disclaimer swung a light punch at Subverse's shoulder. "There you go. Total bollocks!"

As the four of them walked over a zebra crossing, Deak asked "What about Shroud Lane? Is that from a movie too?"

Jake's head jerked round again, but he managed to stop himself before the others noticed. A fresh shudder rocked him. Must be getting colder.

Disclaimer scratched his jaw. "Shroud Lane? Not heard of that one, I don't think…"

"Me neither." Subverse's face tightened with concentration. "That's not a ghost station, or an old name.

Where's that meant to be, then? You sure that's in London?"

Deak looked his way. "Jake?"

He thought of what he might say. He thought of the glowing ultraviolet lines on the map back on the platform at Camden Town. He thought of all the names he knew, names that ate through the jelly of his eyes like acid and seared into his skull, names Deak would also soon know.

"We're here," Jake said, coming to a stop.

The others looked up at the two-storey building they now stood outside, which was dark and closed up like all the other nearby shops. There were plenty of signs and adverts in its windows announcing it as a branch of Cash Converters, offering financial services such as loans and cashing cheques. But the oxblood-red brickwork and the arched windows instantly announced what the building had once been.

Deak looked at Jake. "This is it. Yes?"

He nodded. This was their target for tonight: South Kentish Town.

In a city full of abandoned Underground stations, this one was truly lost to history. It hadn't been popular even when it was open, with trains frequently skipping it and moving on to the next stop. Closed in 1927, the only activity since then was being used as an air raid shelter during the Second World War. After that it became a place where nobody got on or off, a place where nobody ever went.

In other words, urbex catnip.

Now, the old station entrance was just another

high street shop. Smaller signs advertised that the level above the Cash Converters was a massage parlour. Disclaimer let out a tut of disappointment, as if offended that this historical building was now being used for the most seedy of transactions: money and sex.

Subverse spun to face Jake. "What the fuck are we doing here?"

"I was wondering the same thing, to be honest," said Disclaimer. "They'll have closed up the station entrances years ago, won't they?"

"Course they did," Subverse snapped, "you can *see* they did. There's a frigging shop here now! You think I haven't cased this place already? There's stairs in the back of the shop going down to a landing where the lifts used to be, but it's all sealed up. There's no way down into the tunnels from up here, absolutely no way. And if you were thinking of trying the emergency exit staircase, then you can forget it because I can tell you for a fact that it's been capped with concrete, so what's the point of – "

"Only one of them," said Jake.

Subverse's jaw continued moving silently for a few seconds, like a badly dubbed actor in a foreign movie. *"What?"*

"The second stairwell isn't sealed. Technically it's one of the emergency egress routes from the Northern Line, although it hasn't actually been used for decades."

Disclaimer gawped at him. "But… I mean, if you knew there was a way down from here – "

"Then what were we doing wasting our time at

Camden!" Subverse demanded.

"I told you, it would have been easier to tunnel-walk up from Camden Town if we could get in. That was the safer route. Now we have no choice."

Subverse was again glaring and knotted with tension, but Disclaimer bounded up like an eager puppy. "Hey, if it means we can get in there tonight then I'm not complaining! Down here?" He pointed to the narrow alley alongside the red-tiled building.

"No, it's round the back. This way."

Jake set off again. He didn't have to look back to know the others were following him. The little rabbits were starving and the carrot he'd dangled was particularly juicy.

Subverse started muttering again after a while, complaining that South Kentish Town was a stupid name for the station considering Kentish Town was literally just up the road, they should have stuck to calling it Castle Road like it was meant to be, for some reason they changed it just before it opened in 1907, that was a much better name, would have given it its own identity… and so on. There was no response from Deak, who was still reading the document. Disclaimer was busy singing The Jam's 'Going Underground' to himself, something Jake knew he did every time he was about to place-hack the Tube.

They turned right off the main road and into a much quieter area. The others stopped talking as they trod softly along a silent road, past residential blocks and parking bays full of cars. There was nobody around, no apartment windows lit up, no sign of life. Ordinary people slept on in their ordinary homes, oblivious to the four figures passing by.

The road curved into a large housing estate that a green sign identified as Castle Court. Jake stood in the middle of an open parking space, getting his bearings.

"Okay. That's number five, there." He pointed to the rear garden of a flat filled with overflowing trees. "We need to get over that wall right at the back."

Disclaimer grinned. "Brilliant. Sub, give me a leg-up and I'll – "

"Listen!" hissed Deak.

They all froze. Rising above the distant hum of traffic came the wail of a police siren.

Jake looked back the way they had come and saw coloured lights playing across the buildings. The siren grew louder.

"Shit!"

"Oh God!"

"Get down!" Deak gripped Jake's arm, yanked him behind one of the parked cars then dragged him to the ground.

Disclaimer and Subverse immediately did the same thing, diving behind a transit van. The four of them lowered their heads, squatting on the tarmac and staying perfectly still.

They heard rather than saw the police vehicle as it roared up the road, siren howling.

Jake squeezed his eyes shut and called himself every name under the sun. Should have anticipated this. Should have been more careful. What must they look like – a gang of young men in hoodies, creeping through a housing estate at four in the morning? Of course someone spotted them and called 999. And now everything was dead in the water because…

He held his breath as the vehicle drove by, then screeched to a stop. Its siren cut off. He heard the sounds of sliding doors, boots on tarmac, crackling radio handsets. And then an abrupt crash – breaking glass – that made all of them jump.

Jake inched his head up, looking through the windows of the car he was crouching behind. He saw the police van, parked at an angle across the road about ten metres ahead. Its flaring lightbars sent red and blue flashes across a hundred nearby windows, making the whole estate sparkle. Uniformed men and women spewed from its side and tromped into one of the buildings. He noticed a shattered pane of glass on the second floor, with figures moving within and the distant sound of bellowed voices. Something was definitely kicking off up there.

Lungs aching, he finally exhaled. The police hadn't come for them. This was a domestic squabble or a drug deal gone bad or a drunken argument, something like that. Not 'four suspicious blokes', which was all that mattered.

But if they were spotted…

Jake looked across at Disclaimer and Subverse who were hunkered down behind the transit van, their eyes aimed at him: *What's happening?*

He gave them the thumbs-up sign: *It's okay.*

Disclaimer nodded and gestured downward with the flat of his hand: *Stay put.*

Jake realised that their wide-eyed expressions weren't fear, but excitement. They were loving this!

To be so close to their goal, to be on the verge of getting caught… this was the 'edgework' that urban explorers talked about on the forums. For some of them, place hacking was a way to chase an adrenalin high. The risk of the long arm of the law feeling your collar gave meaning to the whole thing, made it an adventure, and increased the personal triumph if you got away with it.

The only thing Jake felt was frustration, gnawing at his empty stomach. He looked at his watch. Time was running out!

Deep breath. And another.

He'd be back down there soon.

Not long now.

He turned to Deak, expecting to see the same excited expression as the others. But his features were as calm as ever. Of course – he'd done this a hundred times. Hiding from the cops in the small hours was just another day at the office for Spatial Decon-struction. He wasn't there for the edgework. He was there for information.

As Jake watched, Deak noiselessly turned round to sit with his back against the car's wheel. He pulled out the rubber-clad phone, adjusted his glasses and continued reading.

# Chapter 7

Sunday 17th September 2000

I was shattered after writing that last part, so much so I had to take a day off work. I hadn't realised how exhausting it would be to dredge up Moorgate, or to write about my dad leaving. I've hardly ever spoken about it out loud, let alone put it down on paper, and it just drained me. For a while I thought about giving up this whole article, now that was all out of my system.

But here I am. Writing again, hiding away from my family again, lying to Julia again. One day I'll have to explain to her why I barely hear her voice these days, and spend so many hours staring into space or locked away in the garage. I feel bad – she doesn't deserve this.

I can't help it. I've got that familiar 'mission' feeling tingling through me, which I haven't felt for years. There's a lot more I want to get down.

When I left school in 1977, I managed to get an office job with the Woking News and Mail. For quite a while, I'd had an ambition to become a journalist. At the time it felt like the perfect combination of things I was keen on... writing, investigating and storytelling. I had that romantic view that journalism was about digging up the facts and presenting them as an exciting but truthful tale. I was 100% confident of that. I was sixteen, after all, so I knew everything.

I wasn't totally naïve, aware that it would take time to build my skills before I had a shot at what I really wanted. A job at a family-owned local newspaper, despite its limited print run and small office in nearby Chobham, seemed like the ideal place to start.

So I worked. I stuffed a lot of papers inside big metal filing cabinets, I hauled a lot of ring-binders up from dusty basements, I bought a lot of biros and typewriter ribbons from the local Woolworths, and I made a *phenomenal* amount of tea.

I also applied for every training opportunity the paper offered. I was the only boy on the touch-typing course, where smirking tutors told me I'd look great in a mini-skirt when I became a secretary.

Three years later, I had enough experience to apply for a junior researcher position with one of the national tabloids. (Not sure if I am going to name them in this article… partly out of shame, also they might sue.) And that meant leaving home and moving closer to their head offices. On Fleet Street.

After everything that happened, I should have wanted nothing more to do with London, but the pull of the big city hadn't decreased as the months and years went by. That weird magnetism wasn't repelled by anything in my mundane life: working, going to the cinema, riding my Chopper bike, battling Space Invaders machines, fancying girls from afar or learning how to drink cider. It had stayed with me, grown with me.

More important than all of those things was that 'mission' feeling… the same one I'm getting now. My dad might have been done with us, but I wasn't done

146

with him. I needed to know why he'd hidden his real life from us – from me. And I needed to know what really happened at Moorgate to affect him so badly.

I expected a blazing row with my mum when I told her about the new job. She always hated London even before dad vanished, but now her only child was asking for permission to live and work there... so I expected squabbles, reassurances of my safety and promises to visit often. In fact she just nodded.

This makes my chest ache now, thinking back.

At the time I saw it as a victory, that I'd won the argument. My hindsight sees deeper, though. That wasn't resignation or acceptance in my mother's eyes, it was defeat... despair. She'd known, hadn't she? Somehow, Mum knew all along that she would lose her only child to the city, the same way she lost her husband.

Why didn't I see that, back then? Why didn't I stop and think about what I was doing to her? Only now, with two young kids of my own, do I realise how easily they can reach right inside you and crush your heart.

It all happened so quickly. Getting the job was followed by getting a place to live, thanks to a colleague's friends in Finchley needing a fourth person to share a house. A couple of train journeys to move in all my stuff, a leaving party at the Woking News and Mail, a drunken night out at The Nag's Head to say goodbye to my mates, and that was it. In the autumn of 1980, I left Brookwood and became a Londoner.

And it was shit, to be honest.

To begin with, anyway. My visits when I was younger hadn't prepared me for the reality of daily life in the capital. I never realised just how difficult things could be... how difficult *people* could be. It wasn't that everyone in Brookwood was the soul of courtesy but most hadn't been stubborn, unhelpful, get-out-of-my-way bastards, which seemed to be the norm.

What really depressed me was the Underground, because it turned out to be very different from my dad's fantastic, imaginative stories. It almost felt like a betrayal. He might as well have been telling me about the metro system in Narnia.

The grim reality of the Tube assaulted my senses afresh each day. The rickety wooden escalators that vibrated unsteadily as they carried me down, their grooves filled with trodden-in cigarette butts and chewing gum. Old advertising posters peeling away from yellowing wall tiles with mouldy edges. Puddles of piss on the platforms, overflowing rubbish bins, plastic bags and crisp packets blown onto the tracks. Trains arriving with a tremendous noise, rumbling, rattling, squealing, shrieking, with their grey shells covered by the messy scrawl of graffiti. The smell inside them of damp wood, fag smoke, stale booze and rank sweat, like being trapped inside a pub on wheels.

And the people. Christ, the people. Buskers and beggars lurking in dim corridors, cawing for attention despite being ignored (and nobody can ignore you like a Londoner can ignore you). Punks with multi-coloured Mohicans and safety pin faces, skinheads with braces and bovver boots, New Romantics with eyeliner and headscarves. Women in trouser suits, men with blow-dried hair. Skin tones from countries I only knew about from watching Whicker's World.

Just travelling to work was exhausting, let alone what happened when I got there. Being the youngest member of staff at a national newspaper was a kind of modern slavery. Every single person seemed to think I was their personal dogsbody, asking me to fetch their lunch or wash their car or pick up their dry cleaning, all piled on top of my usual tasks. It got to the point that I was too shattered at the end of the day to really notice how alien London was...

...which is how the city gets you. Within a matter of weeks I was just another commuter, as blank-eyed and silent as the rest as I was shunted along corridors, escalators and streets. I followed the signs, followed the crowds, stopped when the lights were red and started when they were green. I found it easier to ignore my surroundings because it took less energy.

Nobody can ignore you like a Londoner can ignore you. And before long, I was that Londoner.

Time seemed to move differently there too. At first, each day had about thirty-eight hours in it. Weekdays crawled, weekends sprinted. Then 1981 came out of nowhere, and one day I blinked and realised I'd been there for a whole year. In London, time was both whippet-fast and dog-slow all at once.

Eventually, the newspaper started using me to do proper research for articles. I even had my own desk and telephone, and a business card with my name on it. That seemed like another London rite of passage. In a village they all knew you, but in the city you were nobody unless you had something official with your name on it.

Armed with these, I once again started making enquiries to London Transport, but now in an official capacity. These were about very ordinary things, like fact-checking for the latest Tube strike or getting the biography of some new senior board member. But it meant making proper contacts at their head office in 55 Broadway, which I even visited a few times. They started recognising me as a bona fide media contact and handing over information whenever I asked.

Among the many interesting things to fall into my hands was a bound copy of the Department of the Environment's 'Report on the Accident that occurred on 28th February 1975 at Moorgate Station'.

By this time, I knew a lot more about the Moorgate crash. I'd found pictures in the newspaper's archive, taken on the soot-blackened Platform 9 by the rescue services. Seeing the back half of a carriage emerging downwards from the tunnel mouth at an angle, wheels above the tracks, just felt unnatural. That was the third car – the first two had been crushed to half their original length, concertinaed by the impact. I knew there had been four days of hacksawing through the wreckage, freeing trapped passengers and extricating dead bodies, before they could winch those cars out of the tunnel.

I spent a long time reading the official report, which was written in a detached scientific manner. This made the eyewitness accounts from those who saw the crash all the more disturbing. It was easy to imagine being there, watching the Tube train race into the platform at a much faster speed than normal, as if simply passing through toward the next station... but there was no next station.

What fascinated me the most was that a few people on the platform glimpsed the driver as it sped past. Motorman Newson wasn't panicking, or unconscious, or ill, or gripped with suicidal anguish. He was sitting upright and facing forward with his hands on the controls, eyes wide open, staring straight ahead.

In my dad's last letter, there was this line:

*deadman should have stopped it that's how it works*

The report made clear that at the time of impact, Newson's hand was still on the 'dead-man's handle' part of the master controller. If his hand had slipped off, through him falling asleep or losing concentration, then it would have sprung up, cutting out the train's power and kicking in the emergency brakes. That's all he had to do to stop the train – let go. But he was still gripping it when the train rushed headlong into a closed tunnel. This must have been what Dad was talking about...

Or was he talking about a person? The report briefly mentioned Newson's training instructor on the Highbury Branch, another Motorman called Mr R.C. Deadman. Such a weird name – like a comic book villain – but he must have been real enough to have been interviewed for the report.

Should Motorman Deadman have done something to stop Newson? He couldn't possibly have known this would happen, but it was hard to see what other 'deadman' might have prevented this tragedy.

> *it happens, he wasn't the same anymore he'd <u>gone under</u>*

This was another line from the letter that made my blood run cold. There was something about it that made me think I almost might know what Dad meant, even though I didn't have a clue.

> *I know why he did it I know where he was trying to get to*

And this was the most unsettling idea of all. Had it been deliberate? Where did Newson think he was going when he drove his train straight into a dead end?

No, it wasn't the most unsettling thing. What was worse was the idea that this might all be nonsense. The ramblings of my insane father. Latching onto a genuine, horrific tragedy and spinning another stupid story around it, another serving of bullshit to his believe-any-old-crap son.

That was far worse.

Wednesday 20th September 2000

I'm not meant to be here writing this. I was meant to be taking my kids out tonight to the cinema. I'm not sure Julia believed me when I told her I wasn't feeling well and she'd have to take them herself. I'm trying not to think about the disappointed looks on all their faces, but can't let myself get distracted right now.

Too much I need to get down, my head's bursting with memories. I'll make it up to them all later.

So, for me the early Eighties went by very quickly. Living in London and working on a tabloid newspaper meant my life was filled with a million things. Some of the work started getting genuinely interesting, and some of the people I met became good friends. I discovered, as we all do, that looking after yourself takes up a lot more time than being looked after by your parents. Plus, being a young man in a big city rather than a small village meant I could go out every weekend and never see the same girls twice, a novelty that brought its own distractions.

That's not to say I lost interest in finding out more about whatever my dad was involved with. However, I became sidetracked by London itself. The city was so enormous it was as if I'd emigrated to another country, and each borough was a different town or state, with its own local rules and customs. I visited Greenwich, Westminster and Hyde Park (mainly for tourists, who I learned to sneer at like a proper Londoner). I went out in Camden, Islington and the West End (fun but expensive on my salary). And I heard all about Hackney, Brixton, Whitechapel and the Isle of Dogs (avoid like the plague).

I was also surprised to find that two thousand years after the Roman Empire established Londinium on the banks of the Thames, their influence could still be felt. A defensive wall built around the town had stone gateways that lasted for centuries, and their medieval names – Aldgate, Cripplegate, Ludgate, Newgate, Bishopsgate, Aldersgate plus, of course, Moorgate – all lived on as modern streets and wards. Even parts of the London Wall itself survived, and traces of Roman homes and temples were continually being unearthed. It amazed me to think that London's founding fathers were still with us in these small ways, millennia later.

Something that I remember being especially fascinated by happened shortly after I arrived in 1980. A journalist, who naturally became an inspirational hero to me, broke into some top secret government tunnels and published photographs of them. They were supposedly called Q-Whitehall, since they ran beneath the Whitehall area (and we all know from the James Bond films that 'Q' keeps the secret service's secrets).

These passageways joined up the basements of Downing Street, MI5, government buildings, army barracks, fallout shelters and places like that. They even included hidden military 'citadels', designed to keep things functioning during wartime. And it was possible to get down into the passages if you knew the right manhole cover to lift.

The rumours were that Q-Whitehall was merely the southern part of an enormous subterranean network that stretched north up to Holborn and King's Cross, east to Bethnal Green and Bishopsgate, and west all the way to Paddington. Now that's a proper labyrinth! Assuming it wasn't just urban myth, of course. But the journalist's photos were enticingly real.

Naturally I went looking for a way into Q-Whitehall myself, fantasising about being the one to make an even more amazing discovery, despite the risk of getting arrested or even shot as an intruder. Sadly, whether they tightened up security or I was just not very observant, my days and nights prowling around Westminster trying to find an unsealed manhole cover led nowhere.

Although, there was one burst of excitement when I thought I'd spotted a street beneath a street. This was while walking toward Soho (somewhere many journos went for after-work drinks, and whatever else they fancied). On a traffic island in the middle of Charing Cross Road, my shoes clanged on a large metal grille. I glanced down through this and saw, on a mouldy brick wall below ground level, an old-fashioned sign for *Little Compton Street*. But there was no such place. Had I stumbled across some buried Dickensian fragment of Ye Olde London Town?

Later, I found out this was merely part of the Cambridge Circus utility tunnels that ran below the West End, carrying pipes and cables. An old street sign had simply been moved down into the tunnel. Not as exciting as Q-Whitehall but it still impressed me how many of these passages, sewers, conduits and so on there were, all to keep the city functioning.

It was 1984 before I found a way to make serious headway in my 'mission' to find out more about my dad. By that time I had enough journalistic qualifications to perform actual interviews. Not with celebrities or big names, obviously, but ordinary people. So I came up with an idea.

My contacts at 55 Broadway were more than pleased with my proposal to interview a wide range of their staff, as a multi-part feature on how hard-working and wonderful London Transport were. They were so pleased that they never checked with the newspaper to confirm it was genuine, which it absolutely wasn't. If my boss found out... well, he'd probably just nick all my work and slap his name on it, like the arrogant turd always did.

Over many months, I visited a lot of Tube stations and depots, interviewing anyone who agreed to be interviewed. By this time, I'd learned the hard way that asking direct questions to London Transport got nowhere. This way, I could ask the ground troops rather than the generals. Surely, I thought, there had to be scores of people who remembered my dad. At least one of them would know what happened to Robert Thames.

My frustration mounted during the year. I met veterans with soot in their pores, and fresh-faced newbies just out of the training centre at White City. I met the men who repaired broken lengths of steel track, and the women who trudged through the tunnels cleaning those tracks. I met the Motormen who sat at the front of the trains and the Guards who stood at the back. They all had their stories – I could fill a book with them, based on the notes I still have.

A few of the tales they told me were ones I'd already heard from Dad, including some ghost stories – the tall man who only appears on the 13th of each month, the screaming at Bethnal Green, and so on. And I spoke to two Motormen who told me about the time when their train was sitting in the Kennington Loop and they heard something moving through the empty cars toward them. Which meant either my dad lied about it happening to him, or his colleagues had stolen it for themselves.

But none of the staff gave me the story I wanted. Every time I mentioned the name Robert Thames, I only got blank looks.

How could this be? There weren't many people with the surname Thames, so surely someone would have remembered him. He worked on the Underground for twenty-five years! How could Dad have been airbrushed out of all those people's lives, as well as the official records? What the hell was going on!

Then in November 1984, I met Otieno.

Thursday 21st September 2000

I had planned on waiting till the weekend before writing more, but it's three in the morning and Julia and the kids are asleep, and I can't stop thinking about those days. Now that I've made myself remember them, it feels like I've uncapped a volcano. It all needs to come to the surface before it burns me up.

The man I met was called Otieno Kibore. I'd seen him before on a previous visit to the Acton Depot: a tall black man with short greying hair and large thyroid eyes. He was in his forties, but his dark skin was dry and cracked as if much older, or he hadn't seen sunlight for a long time. He wore the usual dark blue uniform of a train driver (as they were now officially called, but many still referred to themselves as Motormen) complete with flat cap, which he twisted in his large hands as if wringing a flannel.

Last time I was at Acton, he'd vanished while I was talking to someone else. This time, a day in late November, he sat still in the depot canteen – where a lot of my interviews took place, over a mug of tea – and watched me approach, notepad and Dictaphone in hand.

I explained what I was doing there. He said hello and told me his name. He spoke with the flat vowels of a Londoner but plumped up a little by an African accent. And then he asked "Are you Robert's boy?"

No, I've got that wrong. He said it like a statement. "You're Robert's boy."

It took me a moment to remember why I was really there. Suddenly excited, I confirmed that Robert Thames was my father and asked if he knew him.

Otieno looked at me like I'd said something sad and then nodded. "Years away. Years back."

I remember looking over my shoulder, like the crappiest secret agent in the world, as I started asking questions in a hushed tone. Gradually I pieced together that not only had Otieno worked with my dad, presumably in the Seventies, but it sounded like he had been trained by him.

"When I started… he took me with him… on some of his runs." He spoke as if having to dig deep for the words. It didn't seem like his English was poor, more as if he were trying to remember how to hold a conversation. A lot of Tube drivers were the quiet type, I'd discovered.

I couldn't help but ask outright where my dad was – what happened to him – what did Otieno know – anything – anything at all?

He twitched under my barrage of questions, but didn't blink. Those slightly bulging eyes rarely blinked. All he said was "I know he's gone. Don't know where."

Somehow I resisted the urge to grab and shake Otieno and maybe punch him in the face until he told me more. Him being twice my size wasn't the reason why I didn't. He would have sat there and let me do it, and it would have been pointless. There was a feeling of immobility about him, like he was chained to the floor.

I had other questions. "When did you last see my dad? Was it in 1975?"

Otieno's head angled, like a dog puzzled by something new. I got the impression that time might not mean the same to him as the rest of us.

"Before Moorgate?" I clarified. "Or after?"

Now he nodded. "Before. He came with us. Down the…"

"Down the Cross?" My heart jumped at this mention from my dad's last letter. "Which one is that, King's Cross? Charing Cross?"

"Tyburn…"

"What?"

"Tyburn Cross."

My breath caught in my throat. I knew every single Tube station on the map. I knew all the original names of those that had changed. I knew about all the empty ghost stations. And I knew for a stone-cold fact that there was not, nor had there ever been, a station called Tyburn Cross anywhere on the network.

When I asked him where this was, Otieno's head lowered again. He seemed to be closing up in front of me both verbally and physically, drawing his huge frame into himself. But I wasn't about to let him stop now.

"Have you ever been to a station called Shroud Lane?"

Otieno's whole body jolted for a second. His head lifted and those large eyes met mine.

I can remember the thrill that ran through me. This was something that had grown over the years from a vague niggle at the back of my mind into a full-blown obsession: the weird station names that my dad occasionally spoke or wrote about. The non-existent ones.

When I was a kid, and he mentioned Paupers Court in the same breath as Earl's Court and Barons Court, I'd just accepted it as one of *millions* of stations in the *ginormous* mega-city that London was to my young eyes. All of the station names sounded historical and mysterious, so that was no different. Years later, poring over old Tube maps Dad had sent me, I realised that names could change – Barbican, for example, was labelled as Aldersgate until 1968. I assumed the same thing had happened to Paupers

Court, whatever it was now called.

It wasn't until I was much older, doing my research, that I tried to look it up... and found no trace of any name resembling Paupers Court. Not on any map.

By this point, there were a few others my dad mentioned that I had confirmed were not genuine names, even though they felt as if they could be. I can still recall a couple of them now... like Wakebridge, which sounded like a station out on the rural north-west Metropolitan Line. There was also Still Street, a name so mundane I missed it for ages. That one felt like it should be somewhere central and urban, in the middle of the map.

And then in Dad's final letter:

> *None of them are talking about it but some of us saw it happen at Shroud Lane and down the Cross we KNOW what happens to us*

For a long time, I'd assumed that my dad had been suffering some kind of mental breakdown at this point. Certainly his letters became stranger toward the end, and the last one still made no sense. Inventing imaginary place-names might just be part of that. As for Paupers Court and the others that Dad came out with when I was younger... well, the Codswallop King's flights of fantasy were one of the reasons I'd loved him so much.

Now everything changed. Otieno had changed it with just one look, confirming that *these non-existent stations were real after all!*

Weren't they?

Making Otieno say any more was difficult, no matter how much I tried to get him to confirm what he was suggesting. I even offered to pay for his time, which I'd done with a few other Underground staff and they always took my hand off. But money didn't seem to matter to him and my offers received no reaction.

"Can you take me there?" I asked. "To Tyburn Cross? Or any of the others?"

At last, his head lifted and he met my eyes again. "Take you? Yes."

"When?"

"When the next one comes around."

I sensed that I'd got as much out of him as I was going to. So I wrote my home telephone number on one of my business cards and handed it over, urging him to call me whenever he was ready. It occurred to me that he might be breaking all sorts of regulations by even having this conversation, so I assured him this would all be kept between us, not published or shared with any of my colleagues.

Otieno nodded as if he had been about to say the same thing. "Secret."

For days, I waited in a state of tension. I glared at the silent telephone on my office desk, and got annoyed when any of my housemates spent ages chatting on our single shared phone. I went back and forth between feeling ridiculous, that I was chasing pure nonsense, to the excitement of being on the cusp of a terrific story.

Meanwhile, I tried to find out if there ever was an actual place called Tyburn Cross. It felt like there should have been… the name had a definite sense of 'London-ness' about it.

As with the Roman gates, this Saxon name had survived in various forms through the capital's history. There was of course the River Tyburn, one of many London rivers (like the Fleet and the Effra) that had been culverted or turned into sewers, long since hidden from sight. The Tyburn was once famous for its pure clear waters, which allegedly never froze even during the coldest winters. There was also a village called Tyburn that had a long history stretching back to the Dark Ages. That used to be in the area now occupied by the west side of Oxford Street, which was called Tyburn Road in the 1700s.

More disturbing was the fact that public executions took place there for centuries. Near where Marble Arch now stands was a famous gallows called the Tyburn Tree, at which many thousands met their end. History books told me that 'taking a ride to Tyburn' and 'dancing the Tyburn jig' were all common references to being hanged there. And those were the lucky ones… others were burned at the stake or drawn and quartered. All in front of a roaring crowd of spectators, the football matches of their day.

So as London names went, this one had an especially murky undercurrent to it. And wherever Tyburn Cross was, both Otieno and my dad had been there.

A week went by and my phone refused to ring. I even returned to the depot and asked around, but nobody I spoke to had ever heard of Otieno Kibore. Many snorted and said they'd remember a name like that, but even those staff members who weren't old-fashioned white men didn't recall him.

I was alarmed, then a little frightened. Had Otieno been 'disappeared' for talking to me? Maybe London Transport had deleted him the way they did with my dad!

I went over and over my conversation with him, wondering what I'd missed. What had he said at the end? *"When the next one comes around."* Was he still talking about these oddly named stations? He made it sound like they weren't proper places, but surely they couldn't actually move.

I wondered if they were somehow temporary… like events, rather than physical spaces. Perhaps artificial names like Tyburn Cross and Still Street were applied to normal stations only when something special was going on there?

I started wondering if I'd fantasised the whole encounter, when one day I answered my home phone and heard:

"Tonight. One o'clock. Outside King's Cross."


Saturday 23rd September 2000


I'm writing this on one of the PCs in my local library, working off a floppy disk. It's too risky to write in the house any more. Julia is being frosty with me and the kids seem to be even more demanding than usual.

Had to get away. Especially for this part. It feels like I should be out of the house before I write about what happened… like typing the words under my own roof means bringing some weird infection home.

Christ knows why I feel like this. Just get on with it.

That night in November 1984, I caught one of the last trains into King's Cross St Pancras. I stood on the pavement outside, watching while they drew gates across the entrances. All the people wandered away and left only me, standing in the wind and wishing I'd brought a warmer coat.

Every time I think about King's Cross I get uneasy, but I've always assumed that feeling was caused by the King's Cross fire. I think all Londoners were sick with dread when that tragedy happened. I remember shuddering as I watched the TV news, seeing all the fire engines and ambulances surrounding the station, with thick grey fumes pouring up from passenger stairwells. Then later, pictures of those blackened, blistered wooden escalators that had been ignited by a single discarded match… the charred wreckage of the ticket hall, where an abrupt fireball known as a 'flashover' scorched the life out of thirty-one people.

As with Moorgate, the disaster gave the station's name an abhorrent new meaning. Even nowadays, people still say they remember 'when King's Cross happened'.

But the fire took place in 1987. So maybe it isn't that which gives me the shivers whenever I think about King's Cross. Maybe it's what happened to me three years earlier.

I remember casting my eyes up and down the nearby Euston Road, feeling nervous. The area was scary, very different from the way it is nowadays. The enormous railway station was surrounded by dilapidated buildings, some of them little more than shells. Porn cinemas, cocktail bars and run-down amusement arcades glowed in the dark. Knots of drunken blokes drifted past with jeering laughter and the crash of thrown bottles. You could just about spot shadowy figures standing or sleeping in doorways. It was a different city here with a different population, made up of prostitutes, squatters, addicts, dealers, gangs and desperate men. Back then, everyone knew to avoid walking through King's Cross at night. For a village boy like me, it looked like the end of the world.

I paced up and down for nearly an hour, fondling my house key inside my coat pocket, pretending it was a switchblade or a gun or something, avoiding the eyes of anyone passing by, wishing I'd taken up smoking which might have made me look older and tougher, less like someone you could mug or beat up or knife to death, and wondering what the hell I was doing there at that time of night – when suddenly Otieno was in front of me.

Without a word he walked around the corner, heading up a street called York Way. I followed.

He led me past the railway tracks that emerged out of the rear of King's Cross, on which sat enormous engines, steaming and hissing in the dark. Giant circular gasometers and empty warehouses loomed above us as we walked along the pavement. I somehow knew Otieno wouldn't answer me if I asked

166

where we were going, but it didn't matter because I had guessed our destination.

It was slap-bang in the middle of a modern housing estate: a fence of corrugated iron around a squat building that looked like a bomb had hit it. The arched windows on its upper floor were all shattered, its oxblood-red bricks were grey with dirt, and old signs for Victor Printing Co Ltd covered up its true name. But there was no mistaking a London Underground building, even when it was barricaded away and wreathed in shadows.

I knew all about York Road – a Piccadilly Line station between Caledonian Road and King's Cross, abandoned fifty years ago. It was one of the many little Xs that I'd carefully drawn onto my old copy of the Tube map as a kid, adding ghost stations in their rightful places on each line. Just by being there, I was probably remembering all those old stories Dad told me, and feeling like I was about to discover something amazing…

Note that I'm saying 'probably'. Because to be honest, I don't really know what I'm writing about.

I'm not sure what words I'm about to type.

The fact is, I don't remember anything from this point on.

Not properly. Not like I can remember all the little details of arriving at King's Cross and everything else. That's still perfectly clear, even after all these years. But from arriving at York Road onwards, when I try to think back…

I get images. Flashes.

Otieno heaving a sheet of corrugated iron aside, me

following him through the gap.

A set of keys, jangling in his big hands as he opens a padlock, and there's a dark red door.

Standing inside a very dirty room, the floor is covered with wooden boards, broken glass and debris.

I'm following a solitary bobbing light as it descends down a stairwell.

On a platform… no, there's no platform there. Our feet are on the same level as the tracks. The walls are covered with patterned tiles, and the amount of dust floating in the torchlight is like a swarm of grey bees.

We're walking beside the rails. To the headwall. The tunnel mouth is pure blackness inside which the tracks disappear, we're getting closer, Otieno is leading us right to it, and…

Then he's pulling me in.

Bloody hell. He really is. I can see it when I close my eyes. He grabs me, his big hand hurts my upper arm, and he's just dragging me along with him as he walks straight into the train tunnel, we're inside the actual tunnel.

I can see myself trying to pull away, even hitting him to make him let go, and bellowing something, probably panicking that the rails are still live, that we'll be electrocuted or

Oh

It was in there

Inside


I don't want to write any

I've come back to this after two hours of walking around the block, and throwing up in the library toilet, and standing outside and crying, actually crying. Because I'm so scared.

What I can see – these flashes – have made me feel like something bad is about to happen any second, something unbelievably bad. I can't explain it, I don't know why I'm so frightened all of a sudden, all I know is I want to stop. I want to stop all this and go home and forget this whole thing.

I don't want to carry on but I'm going to. I've got to.

I can see it. When I close my eyes.

Otieno pulling me along after him through the darkness, my feet tripping over the slats beneath the rails but he's not letting me fall over, we're just going deeper into the tunnel, and I'm

I'm screaming. I can hear it now, my own voice screaming as he drags me along, because up ahead there's… just a pitch-black tunnel, there's nothing in there, so why am I

I'm trying to pry his thick fingers off my arm, his fingernails are shining, and so are mine, all our fingernails are glowing as I try to pull his hand off me.

I think I'm begging him to let me go, but he's just looking ahead and his teeth – he's either smiling or grimacing and his teeth are sort of shining as well, and his eyes are even bigger than normal.

The dark tunnel is even darker ahead, the torchlight is hitting something, an object, huge and wide, squatting on the tracks in front of us…

Something black.

Something train-shaped.

I'm too busy thrashing my head from side to side to make out much as he pulls me nearer to a pair of gigantic empty eyes – flat black, like the windows at 23 Leinster Gardens. Yes, they're the windows of a cabin, I see that now. It has five circles on its lower right instead of headlights either side, but there's no light coming from it whatsoever, no light and no sound…

I can't hear anything. It's not that I don't remember what I heard, more that there's a sort of absence of noise and I can't actually hear anything, not even my own screaming voice, or whatever noise Otieno makes when I swing my arm round and jam my door key into his face –

Jesus fucking Christ.

*I stab him!*

I can see myself doing it. I actually stabbed a man right in the eye!

He must have let go because I can see myself running… just running in the dark, stumbling and scrambling to my feet, then running up stairs…

Then running through the streets…

That's it.

Thank God, I did it, I wrote it down, I remembered. I've never remembered that much about it before. I feel ill again. Like I've sicked up something that's been festering in my guts for ages.

And afterwards – what?

I must have gone home, mustn't I? I don't know. I must have slept or eaten or done something ordinary because…

When I think back to that time, to November 1984 and afterwards, it all seems normal. In fact from that point on, my life became very normal.

I know I went to the newspaper's Christmas party and made a complete tit of myself trying to pull a woman ten years older than me. I know that I moved out of the Finchley house with one of the guys there and we rented a much nicer flat near Farringdon, making it easier to get to work. I remember how exciting it was seeing my name in print for the first time, as I started writing proper news pieces. I remember visiting Mum and Aunt Claire back in Brookwood, once or twice a year. And I have hazy memories of the rest of the Eighties: pubs, clubs, movies, gigs, relationships with girls, video nights with mates, learning to drive, changing jobs, going on holiday, all the things you'd expect a twenty-something Londoner to get up to.

I've always remembered all that – but not this. Not being dragged into the tunnels under York Road. Not driving a rusty Yale key right into a man's eye, my God, I might have actually killed someone that night and *I never remembered any of it!*

Not until this year. Until Chalk Farm.

And that's what I have to write about next.

Sunday 24th September 2000

Julia knows.

Shit.

She's found out about all of this – my article, Dad's letters, everything. *Shit!*

All she had to do was ask. That's the ridiculous thing about it. She put the kids to bed last night, came down and sat next to me on the sofa, and asked outright what I was doing that was such a big secret. Just that. And I caved, instantly.

Be honest. I did more than cave – I crumbled. Broke down in tears right in front of her. I must have been more upset about remembering York Road than I thought, because all my excuses just melted away and I blurted out the lot.

Well. I'm lying to myself here. I had the presence of mind not to tell her about that night in 1984, which now comes to me only in flashes. I didn't mention Otieno, or whatever it was in that tunnel, or actually gouging out a man's eyeball with a door key. Of course I didn't! Christ. It's bad enough seeing the way Julia looks at me now.

What rips at my heart is how relieved Julia was when she found out why I'd been so secretive all these weeks. She was properly relieved. Compared to having an affair, a drug habit or a gambling addiction – which were the top three on her list (Julia loves making lists) – obsessing over my family history barely entered her 'bad things' chart.

She said she understood how what happened at

Chalk Farm might bring back some memories... including some I never knew I had, although I kept that to myself... and that writing about them was a good, healthy way of processing my thoughts.

So now I'm doing what she told me to do, and finishing it properly. Explain what happened, write it all down, then put it in the past.

"Get it out of your system, Mike, and then come back to us." Those were her words. She also added "You big-nosed pillock."

I bloody love her.

And of course she's right – she knows me too well. Lord knows what my life would have been like over the last ten years, if I hadn't met Julia.

It probably speaks volumes that I met her, of all places, outside 23 Leinster Gardens. That gives me my answer right there, doesn't it? What would my life be like? I'd still be standing outside that white lie of a building, as I did every couple of weeks since the day I moved to London.

I can imagine what I must have looked like: standing in front of an enormous door that wasn't a door, looking at flat black windows that weren't windows. She came right up and asked if I'd lost my keys. I told her I'd lost a lot more than that.

Julia hadn't believed me when I explained that the entire building's front was fake. It made me laugh to see the way she banged on the not-door and threw a stone up at the not-windows... this short, sparky girl with bright blonde hair and really tight jeans.

I had to lead her round to the street behind Leinster Gardens and lift her up so she could see over the wall, at the massive gap where the building once stood and the train tracks down below. I was surprised at how light she was. Funny that I just physically picked her up without thinking and without permission, as if I'd known her for years. And she let me.

It's amazing how quickly things moved after that day. I got to know Julia Spencer very well, very fast. She was still living with her parents in Islington, and worked as a cashier at the Barclays Bank on Highbury Corner. I used to tease her for being a 'spoilt little rich girl' and that she was slumming it every time she spent the night at my shared third-floor flat in Farringdon.

If she wasn't visiting me then I was visiting her. I lost count of the number of times I made the trip to her family's lovely huge house overlooking Highbury Fields...

And the Underground would call for me.

The first time it happened was a shock. I got off at Highbury & Islington Station, crossed the road, walked past her bank and turned onto the street alongside the park... when a sudden blast of stale, dusty air swept over my face. Tunnel air – I knew it, tasted it, instantly. With it came a wail of wind that stopped me in my tracks.

There to my left were the arched windows and engravings of a station building. I hadn't recognised it at first because its once-red brickwork was nearly colourless with decay. A filthy opening was covered with a rusting iron gate, which rattled with gusts of air from the blackness inside.

I once prided myself on knowing where all of the abandoned stations were, so this caught me by surprise. Later I discovered it was the original entrance for Highbury & Islington, closed down and replaced in the 1970s by a new one on the other side of Holloway Road. At the time it felt like stumbling across a crack in the surface of the earth, through which the world beneath was howling like an abandoned pet.

By then, the autumn of 1990, it was six years since I had put any effort into what I'd once seen as my 'mission'. Life had got in the way. But for months, every time I went to visit Julia at her family home, I would pause outside that forgotten gateway, listen to its cry and feel its dry breath brush across the skin of my face. Then I would shake myself, walk away and continue thinking about the girl in my life.

Things went at a hectic rate for Julia and me. Before the end of the year, my flatmate had moved out and she'd moved in. I barely noticed how much I missed making that journey to Highbury, thrilled by being able to spend every day in her company. That was when London seemed at its best to me. Once I had someone to explore it with, who suggested visiting places I would never go to by myself, then the city seemed to reveal its joyful side. Now it felt like home.

And then in 1992, it was home to three of us when we were joined by Jacob Gareth Thames. Unplanned, if I'm honest, but certainly not unwelcome – we both exploded with excitement when we found out she was pregnant. For some reason I'd never expected be a father, but with Julia it looked like anything was

175

possible.

I suppose this is the place to confess that his first name was my idea. I've never told Julia that our little boy is named after my great-grandfather. She actually suggested naming him Robert – knowing a little of what happened to my dad – but that felt too close for comfort. Calling him Jacob made me think I was doing something to honour the Thames legacy, while not having to be reminded of it every time I looked at my son's gorgeous little face.

It wasn't until 1994 that Julia and I finally tied the knot. It was the cheapest registry office wedding you've ever seen, much to her parents' dismay, because all of our money (and a fair bit of theirs!) went toward buying our own three-bedroom house in Hampstead. Writing about the financial gymnastics we had to perform to achieve that would be an article in itself, but it's our home to this day.

And a couple of years later our baby daughter came along, the spitting image of her mother. I didn't think I could get any happier by that point, but that perfect, adorable little girl proved me wrong.

All right.

All right. I'm not putting this off any more. In a way I've been holding off on writing about this for two and a half months now.

Let's finish it.

It happened on Friday 7th July… although it was gone midnight, so technically it was the Saturday. Julia and I were on our way back from a night out in Soho (nowhere near as seedy as it had been twenty years ago), where we'd had dinner with a few friends.

It's a pretty rare thing nowadays for us to properly go out, but we'd been trying to get our social lives back and her mum and dad were happy to babysit. We lost track of time, but still managed to catch one of the last Northern Line trains from Leicester Square that would take us straight to Golders Green.

Both of us had been happy, and a little drunk too. We barely noticed our train stopping at Chalk Farm, passengers leaving and entering as normal before the doors closed and it carried on.

We did notice when the train slowed, gradually coming to a stop in the middle of a tunnel. It had done that a couple of times since we boarded, and the driver had spoken over the PA with the usual excuse: *"Our apologies for the slow running of the service tonight. This is due to an earlier signal failure..."* We'd joined the chorus of tuts and sighs from other jaded Londoners. All very typical. There's always signal failures, especially on the 'Misery Line'.

This time there was no announcement and it just sat there in the tunnel for a minute or so. We were talking away when I noticed the feeling of motion. I looked through the window at the grey wall outside, and my stomach lurched as I realised it was moving forward.

Which meant the train was going backward.

The chatter from the other passengers dipped as everyone realised that something was wrong. Julia wondered if it was reversing because there was some problem ahead. My mouth was too dry to tell her that I couldn't hear the train's motors, only the faint squeal of wheels on the rails.

It wasn't under power. It was sliding back along the track by itself.

Light flooded through the windows as Chalk Farm Station reappeared. We saw rows of astonished faces – people waiting on the platform for the next train, only to see the previous train reappear and come gliding past them. Their wide-eyed stares were met with our own.

Some passengers started hitting the glass and pulling the emergency alarms, calling for the driver to stop the train, stop the train, *stop the bloody train!*

It didn't stop. It sailed past the platform into tunnel-darkness, rolling backward, rolling downhill... faster and faster.

That's when the screaming started.

Not only in our car but echoing along the whole length of the train. A hundred trapped and terrified people, and I was one of them. I knew this wasn't the last northbound train, which meant there was one behind it, heading in the opposite direction – with us falling down to meet it.

Julia's fingers were digging into my arm and she was screaming too, screaming my name, telling me to do something, *"For God's sake do something Mike!"*

But I was paralysed with vertigo, like we were dropping down a sheer cliff face. All I could think was: crash, we're going to crash. The trains collide and kill all these people, just like at Moorgate, we're all going to – wait – is the same thing happening now?

Yes, it had to be. There had to be someone deliberately holding down the dead-man's handle to stop the brakes kicking in.

I could stop this. *I could stop another Moorgate.*

It was pure luck that we were sitting in the first carriage, what's known as the saloon car, with the train's cabin at the front. I shook off Julia and strode forward, grabbing handrails to haul myself along, like an ape swinging through the trees.

Obviously the cab door was still sealed. I kicked against the square of glass over its handle until it shattered. Then I twisted the lever inside, straining to push the stiff door wide enough for me to squeeze through.

The cabin was a narrow space and mostly in darkness. Various lights and alarms were going off on the front consoles. And there on the left sat the driver, upright on a small seat. He didn't react to me at all, just stared straight ahead through the window. His right forearm was resting on an armrest, fingers wrapped around the traction brake controller – a modern dead-man's handle.

I grabbed the driver's arm but found it didn't budge. He wasn't resisting as such, yet his arm was locked in place. I started panicking as the cabin echoed with screams from along the train. For a second I considered punching his head to knock him out like they do in the movies, but instead gripped his fingers and, with serious effort, prised them away from the red lever.

Instantly it sprang upright – and I was thrown back, my shoulder hitting the cabin door. The entire train jolted as the brakes engaged with a shriek, bringing it to a stop.

I picked myself up, gasping for air with my heart galloping inside my chest. I stared at the driver. He was a balding, stocky white man in his fifties. His eyes were round and wide, and his chubby features seemed as rigid as his whole body.

The report into the Moorgate disaster raced through my mind, recalling the eyewitness accounts from Platform 9. Motorman Newson hadn't been panicking, or unconscious, or ill, or gripped with suicidal anguish. He was sitting upright and facing forward with his hands on the controls, eyes wide open, staring straight ahead.

Exactly the same as now.

Exactly what I'd expected to see.

I jerked in fright when the driver suddenly moved, getting out of the chair. For a second I thought he might attack me, but his eyes remained unfocused, and he tilted his head to an odd angle. It was like I wasn't there. Actually it was like he was listening out for something.

He pulled down the white lever of the cabin's front hatch, known as the 'M' door, and swung it outward. This killed the train's headlights but special detrainment lights came on instead, illuminating the tunnel floor.

I watched as the driver jumped down from the cabin. He simply walked along the tracks with a steady pace, as if going for a stroll across a garden, caring nothing for the live rail inches from his feet.

The driver's silhouette faded into the darkness of the tunnel ahead.

Where had he gone? Where was there to go to?

What was out there…?

I think I yelped when two men came barging into the cabin, shouting and pulling me out. They both wore yellow overjackets and rumpled uniforms – Tube workers, catching a train home. I barely got a chance to look at them before they manhandled me back out into the saloon car and pushed the door shut. I heard the thump of the 'M' door being sealed as well, the crackle of voices over a radio, barked words and commands.

Julia came bolting up to me, her own voice melting into the surge of noise filling my head, from inside the cabin, from the terrified passengers.

There was another jolt, but this time the train moved forward. This triggered a ripple of relief from everyone. Slowly it continued in the right direction for a couple of minutes until Chalk Farm Station appeared once again through the windows, complete with even more dropped jaws and wide eyes. The doors all slid apart with a clunk and there was a mass exodus, people running onto the platform and away from the train as if it were about to explode.

Nursing my injured shoulder, I had to be pulled out by Julia. I couldn't take my eyes away from the cabin door. I was desperate to go barging in again and demand answers. But my quivering legs only allowed me to be led to the escalators, back to the surface and then into a taxi home.

There was no sleep for me that night. That week.

The TV and newspapers were soon full of the story of the runaway Tube train… but it wasn't the full story at all. I don't know why I was surprised, since as a freelance journalist I know how often the press tailor the facts to serve an agenda. This time, though, the lies came from the source. London Underground admitted they had no idea why the train rolled backward. They said it was possible the driver – never named – fell asleep with his hands on the controls. But they also claimed that the train travelled back through a red signal, triggering an automatic device on the track that stopped it.

There was no mention of a passenger breaking into the cabin. And certainly no mention of the driver abandoning it and walking into the tunnels, never to be seen again.

*'A very full investigation has been launched into what happened. We have never had anything like this before.'*

...Except for when exactly the same thing happened twenty-five years ago, at Moorgate. Motorman Newson sitting wide-eyed and motionless in his cabin, seeing something that wasn't there, taking the train somewhere it wasn't meant to go.

That was when another memory crossed my mind, one that I'd deliberately buried. That line from my dad's last letter:

> *it happens, he wasn't the same anymore he'd <u>gone under</u>*

I never knew what this meant, and I still don't. But that's what the driver had looked like: gone under, drowned. Fallen somewhere deep.

Julia was outraged when she read the papers, and

wanted to call them straight away to set them straight. "You're a bloody hero, Mike!" she said, waving a tabloid in the air. "They need to know what you did. You probably saved everyone's life!"

I told her to leave it. Just leave it. I eventually had to get angry with her, rip the newspaper to shreds, and order her to just leave it for Christ's sake! And then I held her tight and said I was sorry, and told her I didn't want publicity, think of how it might affect the kids, let's not make a fuss, all that matters is we're both safe.

It was easy to lie to her. Of course that wasn't the reason. Of course I'd told her that the train driver simply looked groggy, like he was on medication or something. Of course I hadn't said that he walked into the tunnel.

Whatever it was that really happened at Chalk Farm, it unlocked something. Something that I realised I'd been carrying around inside my own head since I was a child. So many memories came surging back, of the letters from my dad and his Secrets and all the stories of the Thames family...

That's when I decided to write it all down. My experiences, my history, the lot.

But...

Julia is right. As always.

I have to let this all go. I have to stop. Am I going to be niggling away at this forever? Seeing things in the shadows every time I hop on a Tube?

No. It's time to change. History can stay in the ground. Up here in the sunlight I've got two beautiful little pains in the arse who need their daddy, and a woman I can pick up with one arm but who is strong enough to support my entire life.

I'm sorry, Dad.

This article terminates here. All change please.

# Chapter 8

Friday 13th August 2010
4.04am

Jake held both gloved hands to his face as another cough ripped through him. He managed to muffle it but it still seemed to echo in the night air, bouncing off the housing estate walls.

And surely, surely reaching the ears of all those police officers, standing a stone's throw away…

He held his breath and listened. No bootsteps approached the parked car he was crouched behind. They hadn't heard him.

He looked sideways to where Disclaimer and Subverse were still hunkered down behind the transit van. Disclaimer lifted his huge frame and peeked over the bonnet, then gave Jake a smile and a thumbs-up sign. Behind him, Subverse's expression was far less cheery.

Jake shifted position again, legs aching from being folded under him all this time. He couldn't believe how long they'd been there, waiting for the police to leave. When a second van turned up, he'd been convinced that reinforcements were being brought in to collar the four painfully obvious lads making a pig's ear out of hiding from them. But instead the officers trooped into the same block of flats as the first group, drawn to all the shouting-banging-crashing up on the second floor.

As the minutes passed, Jake kept as much of an eye on Deak as he did on the police. The Canadian hadn't budged – still sat with his back against a tyre, reading the document on Jake's phone. He barely seemed aware of where he was, thumb-flicking digital pages on the screen. You'd think he was having a relaxing afternoon on his living room sofa instead of dodging cops in the middle of the night.

That was all part of Deak's reputation, according to the urbex forums. Many spoke of how he remained calm even in situations where his fellow explorers were, by their own admission, bricking it. One of the most popular videos was of Deak walking across a girder several hundred feet above the bright lights of a city, his face stretching with a big yawn.

Jake peered up through the windows of the car, and instantly ducked down again. The police were filing out of the building. It didn't seem like they'd arrested anybody, which was a surprise considering how rowdy the domestic, or whatever it was, had been.

Disclaimer and Subverse hurled themselves flat on the tarmac as if enemy soldiers were firing machine-guns over their heads. Jake listened to the murmur of officers' voices, the crackle of police radios, the whoosh-clang of sliding doors… and then the growl of engines. With a crunch of tyres, both vans swivelled around and drove up the road away from them.

He decided to stay put until Disclaimer and Subverse, who were more experienced at this kind of thing, judged it safe to get to their feet. It was a good couple of minutes before they slowly rose, scanning the silent estate. Jake's bones ached as he also stood, and his clenched chest finally allowed a proper bout of coughing to come tearing out.

"Man," whispered Disclaimer as he sauntered over, "that was intense. That was seriously intense!" He had an addict's grin, surfing the hit of adrenalin.

"Such a bloody waste of time," hissed Subverse. "Establishment stormtrooper tax-vampire bastards, had to come piss-balling around this part of town, didn't they? We need to get a move on, our schedule's way off, the trains start up again in a couple of hours. Deak, you good?"

Deak eased himself off the ground as if rising from the sofa to make a cup of tea. He pushed his glasses up his nose and turned to Jake.

How far has he read? How much does he know? Is he going to ask questions? Is he going to tell the others? Is he going to say that they're crazy and storm off?

Barely had these thoughts crossed Jake's mind before Deak pocketed the phone, said "I'm good," and jumped over a wall.

It really did happen that quickly. Without even a run-up, he turned to the brick wall and scaled it like a gecko up a taverna window. Then he dropped down on the far side with barely a sound. Seconds later, a length of rope sailed over the top.

Subverse allowed himself a rare smile as he grabbed the rope and pulled himself up. Disclaimer let out a whistle at the privilege of seeing Spatial Deconstruction in action.

Jake didn't react. This was what he'd recruited them for.

One by one, they climbed over the wall using the rope Deak held fast on the other side. He whipped it back and stowed it in his rucksack while Jake got his bearings. The four of them stood in an unlit alleyway between two buildings, mostly taken up by some kind of extension with a sloped roof.

It looked like a dead end until Subverse pulled out a small torch from inside his jacket, expertly keeping one hand over the beam. In its flesh-tinted glow, Jake pointed to a narrow gap alongside the extension. He led them down it in single file until they reached a steel-framed gate. The blue sign on it was written in the Underground's recognisable font: *Keep clear. Exit from emergency escape route.* A smaller yellow sign probably warned them how dangerous it was, but nobody read that one.

"This is it!" said Disclaimer, lightly punching Jake's arm. "You little superstar!"

"Yeah? You reckon?" Subverse stabbed his torch at the padlock keeping the door's iron bolt in place, as if to say *What about that then?*

Jake unshouldered his own rucksack and drew out a pair of industrial bolt cutters. He handed them to Disclaimer as if bestowing a ceremonial sword to an honoured diplomat. Bowing respectfully, Disclaimer took them with a gracious air and then set about busting the padlock.

"Not cool, this is not cool," muttered Subverse. "We shouldn't have to resort to breaking and entering, we're not criminals, that's not what

188

exploring's all about! We're meant to slip through the cracks, not make our own, you know? Exploit the blinkered thinking of society's systems, isn't that right?"

Jake realised that this was aimed at Deak. Subverse clearly expected the urbex guru to adhere to the same principles. But once Disclaimer had snapped the padlock in two, it was Deak who slid open the bolt. He clearly wasn't struggling with his conscience.

Jake ignored Subverse's curled lip as he followed the others through the open gate.

Disclaimer had already found the way in – a large door set into the very back of the station building. But it refused to budge when he yanked at the handle. "Bugger. Locked from the inside."

"No it isn't," said Jake. "It's just the difference in air pressure. Pull harder."

Disclaimer gripped the door with both hands and tried again, cords standing out in his thick neck. This time it flew open with a burst of air. "Bloody marvellous!"

Jake stowed the bolt cutters in his rucksack and took out his own small torch, as did Deak and Subverse. The four stood for a moment, staring at the blackness on the other side, before Disclaimer led them all in.

They found themselves walking down an angled stairwell to the side of an enclosed space. Circles of light from their torches swept across the brick walls and a wide double-gate below, decorated with a green *Emergency exit* sign. Everything was grey, with dirt particles floating in the beams. The cool night air was quickly replaced by a dry closeness.

Disclaimer pushed the gate open. On the other side was an ancient corroded boiler, boxes of switches on the walls and, incongruously, a long-dead fireplace. But all their torchlights converged on another staircase that led into darkness.

Four sets of footsteps rang out as they went down one by one. The metal stairwell coiled round inside a huge shaft. Its girders were coated with the browny-grey residue left by decades of dust and rust.

Jake was surprised to reach the bottom so quickly, knowing the station was more than twenty-five metres below ground. Then he realised that halfway down, the shaft had been floored over. They trod along a short walkway with a metal grille for a floor, through which came a steady updraught, and found a second spiral staircase.

At the bottom of this one was an enormous ventilation fan. Jake knew that one of the reasons disused stations weren't demolished was that they still served a purpose, in allowing air to escape to the surface. The Tube would soon become unbearable without its many vents, shafts and cracks, bleeding the heat away. And here they were, worming into one of its open wounds like specks of bacteria.

With the other two behind him, Jake followed Disclaimer across the shaft floor through an archway, hearing him mutter "Oh yes, baby, here we go!" As he went through, he understood why.

Up to this point everything looked generically industrial, but there was no doubt now that they were inside a genuine London Underground station. The corridor was lined with familiar cream wall tiles, decorated with dark red in both horizontal lines and concentric rings across the ceiling. But the tiles were muted by layers of grime, and the concrete floor covered with dust. There were plenty of official signs dotted around: some with arrows pointing back the way they came, some saying *No unauthorised persons beyond this point*, and others displaying mysterious serial numbers. The air was stale and thick, as if it weighed more down there. Beyond their torchlights, the corridor vanished into shadow at either end.

Jake found it easy to imagine how people had once passed back and forth along this corridor, the lights and noises and smells. Any Londoner would project their experience of living, breathing Tube stations onto this decaying corpse of one.

"We made it. We're in." Subverse's voice was hushed and excited, having forgotten his distaste for how they gained entry. "Welcome to South Kentish Town!"

Other people – normal people – might have stood there feeling reluctant to go on, scared at what might be lurking in the shadows. Disclaimer and Subverse, however, went into full-on hacker mode, just like Jake had seen them do on previous infiltrations. Roaming around in a kind of eager crouch, they aimed their torches in all directions and peered into every nook and cranny, like palaeontologists in a dinosaur graveyard.

They discovered broad openings that once led to passenger lifts but were now covered with rusting gates. Behind these were enormous vacant shafts, their elevators long gone. The only ungated archway led into another shaft that rose upwards to end abruptly with a concrete cap. Subverse deduced this had been the original emergency exit stairway. He tended to announce everything he saw, as if labelling his discoveries, whereas Disclaimer became more of an Exclaimer with comments like "Look at this!" and "God, that's so cool!"

Neither of them noticed how unimpressed Deak was. Jake glanced his way to find him once again reading on the mobile phone, as if killing time.

Jake himself was also aiming his torch in every direction, but not with urban explorer enthusiasm. He looked for footsteps in the dust, but found none. He looked for doors or hatches in the shadows, which were not there. He looked for some sign of recent use even though the station had been left to rot years ago, yet spotted no traces.

There would be. He knew. They just had to go deeper.

The end of the corridor turned into a long, straight stairwell heading down. Jake put his hand on the railing as he descended, feeling the gritty dust stick to his fingers. He could hear his own pounding heart, and was mildly shocked by the sensation. It had been so long since anything got his blood pumping. He took another deep breath of stale air, feeling it tickle his throat and fill his lungs with dust and dirt... but didn't cough.

At the bottom of the stairs, Jake turned left and found himself in a larger open space: one of the station's platforms.

Except the actual platform was gone, removed entirely. He stood on a short concrete block with a few steps down to the floor. There was all sorts of junk along the curved wall such as lengths of rail and old mechanical parts, some covered by thick tarpaulins. Either they were being stored here or, more likely, had long been forgotten. The circular ceiling rose high above, ringed with more coloured tiles. And running before him from left to right – from northbound to southbound – were the actual tracks of the Northern Line, raised off the ground on concrete posts.

He switched off his torch, no longer needing it. The whole area was bathed in light. Spaced along the length of the bare brick wall were several lamps, all with power cables dangling from them. Their glare did nothing to add any life or warmth, but they outlined every detail of the derelict chamber.

Even though Jake had known these lights would be switched on during the engineering hours, it still startled him. It gave the impression that this place had been prepared in advance… waiting for him to arrive.

He licked dry lips. It was so silent. So dead. Shockingly empty of all the things you expect on an Underground platform – the lights, the roundels, the adverts, the electronic display boards, the benches, the *MIND THE GAP* signs, the voice announcements, and of course the people. It felt as though he'd time-travelled into some post-apocalyptic future. Hard to believe that somewhere that had been abandoned for seventy-six years could still be connected to London's transit system. It was even harder to believe that ordinary Tube trains passed directly through here, but they did, a hundred times a day. And none of their passengers ever had a clue.

Jake walked down the steps to stand on the same level as the four rails. His eyes traced the tracks to where they vanished inside the tunnel leading to Camden Town. Inside, more wall lights receded into the distance.

Pulse quickening, he stared at the gaping circle of the tunnel mouth, its edge smeared with soot and filth.

It pulled at Jake's eyes. The emptiness of it.

That aching tingle came again. In his guts, his belly.

A cousin to hunger.

*"Ye-es!"* He jumped at Disclaimer's shout, as he and Subverse came rattling down the steps behind him like gatecrashers to a party, with Deak following. There were flashes from Subverse's camera as he eagerly took shots.

"ECHO!" bellowed Disclaimer. The cavernous station obliged, making him laugh.

"Keep it down!" hissed Subverse. "There could still be workers in the tunnel."

Jake knew this was a prudent suggestion. There were several types of staff they might run into: fluffers collecting garbage from the tracks, maintenance crews repairing failed signals, or even one of the tunnel-walkers who routinely strode the Underground lines at night, looking for problems. The Tube wasn't always completely empty even when it was shut down.

Disclaimer shrugged off his concern. "Nah, this

194

time of the morning, they'll have knocked off by now. Guys, here we are! We've bloody well cracked it! What do you think, Deak? A good one to add to your list, right?"

"You haven't cracked anything," said Deak softly.

"What?"

A nod toward Jake. *"He's* the one who got you down here. It wasn't your skills, it was his knowledge. Whatever's going on here," Deak added, "it isn't urban infiltration."

"See! I told you, that's what I said!" barked Subverse. He had the air of a kid ganging up against the playground loser. "It's not the same if someone just *knows* how to get in, that goes against our whole culture of discovery and – "

"Oh, come on, Sub!" Disclaimer looked as close to annoyed as Jake had ever seen. "Does it really matter? We've been talking about getting into this place for ages, and now we're here! So what if the kid knows a few shortcuts, what's wrong with that? We're the lucky ones!"

"You're not lucky," said Deak. "You were chosen. We all were."

"What do you mean, 'chosen'?"

"We're Jake's recruits. We're his troops."

Jake wasn't looking at any of them during this. He wasn't even really listening. Instead he had placed his rucksack on the ground and was rummaging through it, eventually bringing out the UV lamp. The black glass tube gave off a purple haze when he switched it on.

"Oh balls," moaned Subverse, "not this again…"

Jake swivelled in place, holding out the lamp as he ran it up and down the tiled wall.

"Mate," said Disclaimer kindly, "if you tell us what you're looking for, maybe we can help, yeah?" When Jake gave him no answer, he ran a hand through his ginger hair and turned to Deak. "Don't suppose you know what this is all about, the whole ultraviolet thing? It's like when the cops are looking for clues on the telly!"

In the corner of his eye, Jake glimpsed Deak holding up a hand. His fingernails now gave off a blueish-white glow, as did everyone's.

"More here than meets the eye," murmured Deak.

Subverse let out a string of extreme swearing under his breath as he stomped back up the stairs. Disclaimer went after him, trying to get him to calm down. Their voices shrank into the distance, absorbed by the emptiness of the station.

After a while, Deak said "He's right, you are looking for clues. You're treating this place like a crime scene." He held aloft Jake's phone. "You're picking up where Mike Thames left off. You think you can succeed where he failed. Yes?"

Jake didn't look up. "What makes you think he failed?"

He sensed, rather than saw, the questioning frown on Deak's face. He was too busy walking slowly along what was once South Kentish Town's northbound platform, sweeping the UV lamp across every surface he could reach.

Behind him, Deak sat on the concrete steps with Jake's phone and continued reading.

# Chapter 9

Sunday 19th October 2008

Eight years. Christ, it's been eight years since I last wrote anything in this article. My laptop didn't even understand the type of file it was in, I had to convert it.

Eight years since I've read my own words or even thought properly about any of this. About my dad, and what I found, what happened at York Road and Chalk Farm.

But now it's different. As of yesterday, everything's different. Now I know. I *know*.

He came back from the dead.

That's what it feels like. That Dad's come back into my life. In a way he has, and he's telling me so much, there's so much!

I have to sort my head out. Get it all down. That's what this is for. Writing this helped me a lot back then, it laid a lot of demons to rest, so maybe it can still help me. Put my thoughts into some kind of order.

Lord knows who I'm actually writing this for anymore. I remember at the start thinking this would be a proper article but there's no way any magazine or paper would touch this with a bargepole now, it's so bloody crazy. I probably sound like some rambling lunatic. I suppose it should be for my family, but just imagining Julia's face reading this... no. The kids when they're older? No. I can't burden them with all this. It's more than burden, it's damage. No Mike, you're doing this for yourself, you can't inflict it on anybody.

Okay. Get it down properly.

It happened yesterday, at my mum's funeral.

If I'm honest, I'm surprised she made it to seventy-four. The doctors told us years ago the chronic liver failure would be how she went, and they were right. But Mum hadn't really been with us for a very long time. Not since 1975, really.

To be fair, she perked up a bit when I first introduced her to Julia, but that didn't last. Even when I brought down her grandchildren to visit, she didn't do much more than put on a show of her old self. I'd hoped those little monkeys might bring Mum out of her shell, but then realised that the shell was all that was left. I even had her checked for Alzheimer's because she became so distant in recent years, and barely seemed to know me on my last few visits. But I knew it wasn't illness. It was loss. When he vanished, Dad took most of her with him.

Mum never moved out of our little house in Connaught Crescent, despite me constantly nagging her to do so. Perhaps if she had, and lived in a place without so many memories of her lost husband, she might have made a fresh start for herself. But there she stayed, looked after by neighbours and my Aunt Claire, right till the end.

Naturally, the funeral took place at Brookwood Cemetery. Its days as the London Necropolis were long gone but there was no question that Mum would be laid to rest anywhere else.

I drove down to Brookwood with Julia, leaving the kids to stay with her parents. Julia had never actually seen the cemetery and was astonished at its size. I didn't bother mentioning the Railway.

There were around thirty people at the service in the chapel. I shook hands with a few surviving Winchmores from Mum's family and some of her old friends, but although they all addressed me by name, I'd long forgotten theirs. London was my home, had been home for too long. This tiny, rural world didn't mean much to me anymore.

We accompanied the cortège to a place in the cemetery's south area called Woking Ground, which had plots set aside specifically for locals. Everyone gathered around the graveside as the coffin was lowered in. There were some sniffles. Julia was weeping softly into a tissue beside me, rubbing my back and leaning her head on my shoulder.

I simply watched, dry-eyed, as Mum was put in the ground.

People drifted away once the service was finished, some heading for the wake at a nearby church hall. That was when I felt Aunt Claire's hand fasten briefly upon my arm – a signal. I told Julia to go on ahead and that I'd join her soon. She gave me a sad but encouraging smile, perhaps assuming I'd want to do my grieving in private.

I stood in front of the grave beside Aunt Claire. Despite being eighty-three and moving slower than she once did, she seemed as sharp as ever. Even now she was almost my height, with the same angled nose and curly hair as both me and my dad, albeit grey rather than black. She was always the more serious one. 'Bossy big sister', Dad used to call her. But without her, Mum would probably have died thirty years earlier. I've learned to listen when she wants to talk.

Once we were alone, she said "I know you feel like you should be saying some meaningful words about your old mum, but you can't."

Yes I can, I wanted to say, but my open mouth was silent.

"It feels like burying someone who died years ago, doesn't it."

These were statements, not questions. Unarguable.

"Angela never did know what to do with herself without Robert around. They'd been together since school... you probably know that. Childhood sweethearts. She used to talk about the two of them ending up here," she gestured at the green fields all around, "side by side."

I stared at the granite tombstone: *Angela Dorothy Thames née Winchmore 28th January 1934 – 10th October 2008*. No grave beside it. Not for a man who left no body to bury.

We stood and listened to the wind in the trees.

"But one thing you should know," Aunt Claire said suddenly, "is that she always tried to protect you from the worst of him."

I jerked round to face her. "Who? You mean Dad?"

She nodded, still looking at the grave.

"What do you mean, the worst of him?" I demanded. That sounded so wrong, like I'd had an abusive father.

"I mean she tried to keep you away from his *business* in London." There was a curt sweep of one hand. "Your mother was trying to shield you from all that. She never wanted you to go the same way as Robert, and be infected with... to let him get inside your head so much. Especially after Moorgate, after he'd gone under."

I caught my breath, bloodrush thumping inside my ears.

She knew. She'd known all along!

"Now listen, Michael," she went on. "There's no reason for me to stay in Brookwood any longer. I'm moving down to Cornwall, I've bought a place near the coast in Falmouth. I've got a removal company coming first thing tomorrow to clean the house out, and an estate agent will be putting it on the market on Monday. Once all their fees and the solicitors and whatnot are dealt with, you and I will share the money fifty-fifty. I'm sure you see that as fair?"

I didn't have time to respond before she reached into her coat pocket and handed me a folded piece of notepaper. "That's my new address. There's no telephone. Give this to your wife and tell her she can visit me any time she likes. When she needs to get out of London. Make sure you tell her."

She left without another word, striding away from her sister-in-law's open grave with the air of someone whose work was finished.

I stared at the paper in my hand and felt oddly

bruised. An invitation for Julia, who she'd met maybe three times, to come all the way down to Falmouth. But not me, her own nephew.

I looked again at Mum's headstone and thought of how little I'd seen her, ever since I moved to London. It wasn't me who had looked after her. A pit of guilt opened in my stomach. The way Aunt Claire spoke was… what's the word I'm looking for… matriarchal? As if it were her role to look after the women in the Thames family. Maybe even protect them from the men – although that was so stupid, that whole protecting thing, what was she going on about? Dad never did anything bad to me, even if he was clearly losing the plot a bit in those last few letters, it wasn't like he ever…

That was when it properly dawned on me what Aunt Claire had said: *"Especially after Moorgate, after he'd gone under."*

After Moorgate?

There had been no word from Dad, no trace of him, following the Moorgate disaster. Only that single envelope with his final scrawled letter, and I never told a soul about that, never shared it with anybody. So how could Mum have wanted to protect me from Dad after Moorgate? There'd been absolutely no contact with him ever again.

That I knew of.

I turned from my mother's resting place and started walking. Along the path through fields of gravestones and memorials, past the Anglican church and the wide patch of blackened ground where South Bar once stood before my schoolmates set fire to it, across the strip of yellowed scrubland where the Necropolis Railway tracks had been removed, striding out of Brookwood Cemetery and into the village streets. I didn't stop walking until I reached the familiar little two-storey house on Connaught Crescent, where I let myself in the front door using the very same key Mum gave me when I left for London in 1980.

Inside the Thames family home, I stood still for a minute. A thousand memories hung suspended in the air, like the dust in the shafts of light slanting between closed curtains.

I ignored them all, and turned the entire place upside down. I yanked open drawers, swept out cupboards, pulled books off shelves, lifted sofa cushions and mattresses, rummaged through bedside cabinets. There had to be something that had been kept from me, I knew it!

Eventually I affixed the portable ladder and barged up into the attic, a place I knew my mum could not have reached for over ten years. Squatting under the roof beams, I ripped open damp cardboard boxes, upturned plastic bags, then suddenly saw what I had been desperate to find while simultaneously praying it never existed.

The large, translucent plastic box in the attic's corner was clearly full of something. A dust cloud detonated as I peeled off its lid and looked inside… at a huge pile of envelopes. Some of them were small, some were A4 manila, and there were several bulging jiffy bags. But all of them had one thing in common – the same word written on the front:

God only knows what I must have looked like, crouched in the dark and inhaling the woody smell of old paper. I stroked the envelopes, with tears finally escaping and running down my face. It felt like Dad had walked through the door, picked me up and given me a big hug.

He *hadn't* vanished after Moorgate. He hadn't cut off contact. He kept writing letters to me!

And Mum had hidden every single one.

What had he been trying to tell me? What was in these? I noticed that all of the envelopes were still sealed and none had postmarks or stamps. They'd been hand-delivered. Surely Dad wasn't lurking in Brookwood back then? Or maybe he'd hired someone to drop them off at this house. Not trusting anyone. Only me.

I wiped my face and tried to think. My impulse was to grab the first one, rip it open and read his words again, after all this time… but I knew that once I'd started, I wouldn't be able to stop. I'd be up there in that attic till sundown. And Julia was waiting for me, at the wake. Already my mobile phone was beeping with text messages that I knew would be from her, asking if I was all right.

There was no way I could tell Julia about this. I knew that much. No way.

She stopped me once before. I'm not making that mistake again.

It took a while to lug the box down from the attic, then tidy up the house as much as I could. Hopefully Aunt Claire wouldn't come back and notice the disarray before the removal men arrived to do their work. I covered the plastic box with my coat and left our old house for the last time. It was a short walk to the car park near Brookwood train station, where I put the box in the boot of my car and hid it under an old blanket.

I rejoined everyone in the church hall, helping myself to cheese sandwiches, sausage rolls and orange squash. I shook hands and thanked everyone for being so kind to my mum all these years. Julia gave me a hug, looking worried. I knew she'd be the only one to spot signs of crying on my face. I assured her I was fine, that I'd just needed a bit of time to say goodbye.

The rest of the day was a blur, my mind's eye focused entirely on what I'd found. I drove home along the M3 with my hands clenched round the wheel, feeling like there was an explosive device in the boot that only I could hear ticking.

I didn't sleep at all last night. I can't risk opening the box while Julia and the kids are around. I will need time, to read and process whatever Dad's written… assuming it isn't just some insane gibberish, right now I can't imagine what the hell it is. But I'm not rushing it. He's waited all these years, a couple more days won't hurt.

I'm also worried about Aunt Claire. Will she know that the box has gone? Does she know about it at all? I doubt it, otherwise she'd probably have burned the envelopes herself long ago, judging by the way she was talking. Mum obviously hadn't told her that she kept them all.

I wonder why she did that. Perhaps she couldn't bear to get rid of this evidence that her husband was still alive… or perhaps she planned to show them to me one day.

I'll never know now. Mum's gone.

But Dad's back.


Wednesday 22nd October 2008

My God, I don't know where to start. There's so much stuff. How long was Dad sending these things to me – weeks, months after Moorgate? Maybe even years? How come I never saw any of them? Was Mum sitting by the letterbox every morning? How obsessed must she have been to intercept every single damn thing? I could have seen all this when I was a teenager, not an old man coming up to fifty. She robbed me of so much!

Stop. Have to stop. My emotions have been all over the place the last few days. Need to get my thoughts down.

I've got the box in the garage. I've been spending a lot of time in there, going through it all. Can't really deal with Julia and the kids right now. She is keeping her distance though and not complaining – I think she thinks I'm having a reaction to the funeral, that I need to be left alone for a while. Good.

I've found what I think is the first 'new' letter that arrived after what I always assumed was the last. It's different from both the normal letters and that last one. Kind of halfway between. There's none of his old humour but he seems less manic, and his writing has become almost child-like in its simplicity as if he were trying to remember how to put words to the page. I'm finding it hard to hear Dad's voice in my head when I read it, unlike the old days when it felt as if he were talking right beside me.

I'll have to clean up the text a bit, space the words out properly and add capital letters so it isn't too confusing. His handwriting is scrawled and hurried with lots of spelling mistakes, as if he were running out of time… or maybe doing something wrong and expecting to get caught. That's the sense I get. Desperation stains these pages as much as ink.

*Mike*

*I'm sorry I can't see you or come back up but I want you to know everything. I can't tell you but can write it down.*

*This is between us YOU CAN NOT TELL ANYONE and none of this can ever be public but you deserve to know because it is about your family.*

*First you need to know why I went to London in the first place before you were born. You know I was following in your Grandpa Albert's footsteps but you need to know why.*

*He said something to me before he left that last time. I was only seven and he was different serious broken and couldn't stop all these words coming out. He said*

208

*he took more than just corpses on the Necropolis*
*trains, he was disposing of different bodies that had*
*to be moved without anyone seeing them. He said*
*they were brought up from the Tube to Waterloo and*
*stored under the arches then he would take the bodies*
*out to the cemetery at night or if they couldn't do*
*that then hide them with normal runs but nobody*
*could see the bodies and nobody knew*

Before I go on… there's something about this that
gets my skin crawling. Not just the idea that my
grandfather might have been using the Necropolis
Railway to do something secretive – it's that I think I
can prove it.

Here's what Aunt Claire told me, about seeing
what she called the 'stiff express' arrive at Brookwood
when she was a little girl. I've copied it from earlier:

*She said you could almost set your watch by it, always*
*arriving at about quarter to one in the afternoon and*
*heading back to London an hour later. Although, she swore*
*that a couple of times she heard the train in the early hours*
*of the morning, when everyone was asleep and the stations*
*were empty, despite being told by Grandpa Albert that she*
*must have dreamt it.*

Now, if it was anyone other than Aunt Claire, I'd
have assumed Albert was right and it was a kid's
dream or imagination. But something tells me she was
at least as sharp then as she is today. If she said she
heard the Necropolis train in the middle of the night,
then it was there.

I've looked it up. (The internet makes this sort of
thing so easy now. There wasn't anywhere near as

209

much information online when I started this article.) The very last run of the Railway was on 11th April 1941 for the funeral of a man called Edward Irish, but the records also state that there was an unidentified body on the train too. Somebody must have spotted what they were not meant to see – an unauthorised cargo being quietly shipped to Brookwood under everyone's noses.

This also answers a question that has been on my mind for years. Why was Grandpa Albert even at Necropolis Station on the night it was bombed, five days after the last run? Now it makes sense, if he was planning to perform one of the late-night journeys that Aunt Claire heard.

As to what they were actually transporting:

> *I asked him why it was a secret and he said the bodies had to be kept apart from the normal dead, they were the London dead and they had to be taken out from under ground and sent on.*

I feel like this is a phrase I've heard before, because it's giving me a weird tingle of recognition, even though I have no idea what Dad is referring to. What exactly are the 'London dead'?

It certainly can't just mean people who died in London – there'd be no reason to keep them separate from those who died elsewhere. Why the secrecy?

I'm wondering if perhaps 'taken out from under ground' is a reference to exhumation. Perhaps these were bodies that had already been buried in London's cemeteries, and for some reason – lack of space? –

were being disinterred and moved to Brookwood. There might be good reason to keep that quiet, especially from the families of the deceased, maybe even the churches themselves.

That's it. I think I've cracked it! No wonder Grandpa Albert didn't want anyone to know he was employed to ferry the 'London dead' from one grave to another. Imagine the uproar about how sacrilegious and disrespectful it was, especially back then. And transporting coffins whose contents had been decomposing for years couldn't be done during a normal funeral service, with all those mourners on the train. Imagine the smell! Midnight runs were the only way. It makes perfect sense.

But of course my dad was only seven when Albert revealed this (perhaps worn down by the stress of keeping it secret?), and the effect it had on him was huge:

> *So that's why when I was eighteen I got work on the Tube, the Necropolis was gone but they were getting the London dead from there so they had to know something about it and I had to find out what my dad was doing and what got him killed and somebody on the Tube had to know.*
>
> *Mike I will send more soon love you*

Reading those last words brought on a massive surge of emotions for me, too many to break down. He loved me even then, even through all this.

But more than that. My dad did precisely what I did. He went to London in 1950 or 1951 to find out why he lost his own father. Just like I went to London in 1980 to find out what happened to Dad.

We had exactly the same mission – thirty years apart.


Thursday 23rd October 2008


I've been digging through the box to find the next letter Dad sent, and I've come to realise that there aren't many actual letters from him at all. Most of it is… well, Secrets.

I wrote earlier about how Dad used to send me all sorts of bits and pieces in the Seventies. But that's nothing compared to what he sent after Moorgate. Great wodges of material, stuffed inside envelopes and jiffy bags. Everything from actual blueprints of running tunnels and station layouts – some of which look a hundred years old – to official maps, with arrows and circles drawn on in biro. Plus, several pages of notes. His handwriting varies wildly, from super-neat to barely legible scribbles.

There are also a couple of enormous folded-up Tube maps with ripped edges, which I suspect were once on display. They're old but otherwise there's nothing special about them, although of course I'd have loved them as a kid and would have put them straight up on my bedroom wall. Maybe he'd planned to give them to me at Christmas, the one he missed all those years ago.

I get the feeling that all this was in my dad's

possession for years. Like he'd been building a collection of Secrets, then sent the entire lot to me.

I've spent hours poring over these, down in the garage. I can't work out some of them but in most cases, these explain ways of getting into the staff-only areas of the London Underground, enter disused stations, even get down into the tunnels themselves. Dad was collecting ways to go behind the scenes.

I have to say, some of these are fascinating. For example:

A concealed door on a Northern Line platform at Euston that leads into a range of abandoned passenger corridors.

Doors at either end of a platform at Angel, one leading to an old lift shaft going up to the original station building, the other to tunnels left behind when they changed one central platform into two.

A bizarre way to get onto the Central Line tracks by going down to the lowest basement level of the Cumberland Hotel on Mayfair.

Another basement, in the Regis House building in the City where a door leads into King William Street, the very oldest abandoned station.

A emergency staircase down into South Kentish Town, tucked away in an alleyway behind a Camden housing estate.

And more. Tons more!

It looks like most of these Secrets are about getting onto ghost stations, or the closed-off parts of active stations. With the information here, you could get almost anywhere on the whole Tube network. I can only wonder how long it took my dad to amass all this. Maybe he started looking for these 'cracks' as soon as he started working on the Underground. There could be two decades' worth of information here.

But why? And what has all this got to do with Grandpa Albert?

Friday 24th October 2008

Back in 1975 after Dad vanished, I became convinced there was a conspiracy at London Transport, as it was called then. No matter who I phoned or how many enquiries I made, there didn't seem to be any records of Robert Thames working with them. They were hiding all trace of him, which meant they were up to something. Then as I got older, I started to realise how crazy that was. Why would they go to such trouble to delete all records of one of their staff? I must have just called the wrong offices, spoke to the wrong people, and the rest was my young imagination going into overdrive.

Now, though… now it's clear that I was on the right track.

This, I think, is the letter Dad sent to me after the last one, although there's no way of knowing if it was days, weeks or months later.

*Mike I need to explain what I was doing in London*
*I'm so sorry that it affects you too it's our family we*

*all did the same job I was doing the same work as*
*your Grandpa and Great-grandpa it's in our family.*

Before I go on… this mention of 'Great-grandpa' has made me wonder about Jacob Thames, Albert's father. Did he used to work on the Necropolis Railway as well?

It strikes me now that I know almost nothing about him. I've never seen a picture, and Dad only mentioned him a couple of times. There's that weird story Albert told my dad which he then told me, so I know Jacob died of cholera in 1906, but otherwise I haven't got a clue. I don't even know if there were other members of the Thames family back then, or who Jacob's parents were. I've never heard any other names.

Maybe Aunt Claire knows? Not that she'd be likely to talk to me, judging by how frosty she was at the funeral.

Anyway:

> *They found me after I went looking for something to do with my dad I went everywhere to Waterloo and round the old station and under the arches and even the other Necropolis line out of King's Cross and then down on the Tube I went to the ghost stations and the old places and platforms where no trains ever stopped and*
>
> *I don't remember when but I was on a train late at night when it came for me, our train stopped in the tunnel and the lights went off and all the doors opened and I think it*

*can't remember*

*[unreadable]*

*Then I was working for them I did what your Grandpa did every night we checked the maps to see if a line was shining for us that's how we found out if we had a route to take the London dead through*

*Not to Brookwood that way didn't work any more it couldn't run above ground the Necropolis line has <u>gone under</u> ground nobody can see it any more it's <u>under the Underground</u>*

*Mike you can't [unreadable]*

*Just <u>mind the gap</u> I will send more*


It's taken me a while to think it through, process it, and try not to imagine what state my dad was in when his obviously-trembling hand wrote these words. Probably the same state as me – I was shuddering when I came to the end of this letter.

This is the main thing: I was right! There was, and maybe still is, a conspiracy at work. They deleted Dad from their records because he was involved in something that's been kept secret from the public for decades!

The Necropolis Railway *never stopped running*.

Or at least, part of it didn't. Whatever those late-night runs were all about, the secret journeys to Brookwood, that part of the Railway didn't come to an end in 1941 with the Blitz. It just went underground – *literally* Underground, into the Tube lines – and became even more secret. And my dad started working for them, just like his father once did.

So I wasn't crazy, I knew I wasn't crazy, I knew it! Those bastards *were* hiding things from me, back when I was harassing them for some trace of Dad. There's no way the upper management don't know about all this. In fact it must be a government thing, surely? Something they've been keeping out of sight for years – like the Q-Whitehall tunnels that officially don't exist either, even though there's photos of them.

I wonder… could this be the reason why my dad had so much knowledge of all the ghost stations? Maybe they even *used* them somehow. Handy if you need a platform away from prying eyes. And maybe those hidden routes into the network were how they moved around, without normal staff or passengers seeing them.

God, what a story. Secret train runs, sealed records, government cover-ups… this is what I got into journalism for! Ironic that none of it will ever get published. No way am I risking that.

So was Dad also disposing of exhumed coffins from London's cemeteries? It's bizarre that they had to develop this hush-hush Tube service just for that. And he makes it sound like this happened not long after he started working for the Underground, in the early Fifties. Hard to believe he was still secretly driving trains full of the 'London dead' over twenty years later.

There's got to be more to it. I still have a lot of envelopes to look through. Dad must have left the answer in one of them for me. He must have.

But I have to stop now. Julia and I are taking the kids away for the weekend. I can't even remember where we're going. The sooner it's out of the way and I can get back to working on this, the better.

Monday 27th October 2008

Thank Christ I'm back in the garage. I've brought everything down from the attic here as well, to keep it all in one place. It's been a bloody awful weekend with the kids acting up and Julia being properly moody with me for some reason. Why the hell did I agree to take them to Southampton, of all the crappy shitholes? What a waste of my time!

But I found something fascinating today. I re-read the letter where Dad talked about looking for some sign of Grandpa Albert in the Fifties. Naturally enough he checked the old Necropolis Station in Waterloo where he once worked, but also:

> *and even the other Necropolis line out of King's Cross*

It didn't take much searching on the internet to discover that this isn't some random nonsense, like I originally thought. Turns out the Brookwood trains weren't unique after all. There was *another* Necropolis Railway!

Great Northern Cemetery Station was opened in 1861, situated behind King's Cross. It was basically just like Necropolis Station in Waterloo, being a combined mortuary and train departure point. In this case the trains went to a cemetery in New Southgate that was outside city limits at the time.

The principle was exactly the same – steam trains taking both the deceased and mourners to a burial. By then the Brookwood service had been running for seven years so it must have been seen as following a successful model, although it didn't pan out that way. Normal trains from King's Cross apparently got to New Southgate faster than the funeral trains, so in 1873 they closed the whole service down.

I'm fascinated by this mini-Necropolis Railway, especially since Dad clearly knew about it. Strange that he never once mentioned it to me. Not even as a kid.

And now I'm wondering... did this Great Northern Cemetery line transport the 'London dead' as well? It seems logical. The Metropolitan Railway, the very first underground train line, opened in 1863 and went through King's Cross. Right next door to the GNC Station. Handy if you were smuggling out exhumed coffins from churchyards around the city.

It probably became harder to conceal those late-night runs as the line fell into disuse. It's easy to imagine them moving the whole operation over to the more successful London Necropolis Company in the 1870s.

Obviously that's pure speculation, but if it's true it suggests the secret railway was running for a lot longer than I thought... decades before Grandpa Albert was even born! How far back does this thing go?

Tuesday 28th October 2008

Big breakthrough. Huge!

Today I went through everything again. I've cancelled the freelance writing jobs I had lined up, so I can concentrate on what really matters. Julia is starting to develop that scowly look and the kids are whining about how I'm never around, but to be honest I just don't have time right now, they'll just have to sort themselves out for once, I can't bloody be everywhere.

Anyway, I discovered something at the bottom of the box, which must have fallen out of one of the padded envelopes. It was a tiny torch, the type you have on your key ring. When I tried it, I realised it was one of those ultraviolet lights, the type people use to show up markings written on their property in fluorescent ink in case it gets stolen.

What was it doing there? Had my mum left it in the box by mistake? I couldn't imagine why Dad would want to send one of these to me.

It was a couple of hours later, while re-reading the most recent letter, that I found a line I'd almost skipped over:

> *every night we checked the maps to see if a line was shining for us that's how we found out if we had a route to take the London dead through*

I grabbed one of the huge Tube maps and unfolded

it on the garage floor, using paint pots and other bits and pieces to hold down the corners. On my hands and knees, I turned on the UV key-light and waved it like a magic wand.

Within seconds… I felt stupid. What was I expecting to see? Some hidden message appear before my eyes, as if by magic? A secret code written in invisible ink? All that glittered back at me were dust particles and greasy smudges of fingerprints.

I wondered where this Tube map came from, and when it had been ripped down from a platform wall. It was less complex than the modern version, and without numbered zones. There was no orange Overground or silver-grey Jubilee Line, and the Piccadilly Line didn't yet reach as far as Heathrow. Plus, both Strand and Trafalgar Square stations were still there so it was prior to the Charing Cross rebuild. A mid-1970s map, then. Like the pocket one I had as a kid, on which I used to draw little X symbols for the ghost stations.

Imagine how it felt, while having that very thought, to suddenly see an X glow up at me.

I recoiled from the map like it was alive, scuttling across the garage floor on my hands and knees. For a moment I wondered if I was hallucinating, before realising what it was. I went back and held the small UV light close, running it along the horizontal red bar of the Central Line.

It shone out of the dull plastic with a white glow. A line curving down between Marble Arch and Bond Street, terminating in a circle with a flattened cross over it.

I pulled the torch away. The glowing line vanished. I brought it closer, and there it appeared… yes, as if by magic. It didn't seem to be hand-drawn with a fluorescent marker, more like it was printed onto the plastic itself, as 'official' as all the visible lines.

My face was almost against the floor, gazing at this discovery. A Tube line where no line existed! And a station – if that's what the X symbol was meant to be – in a blank space on the map. This was what Dad was referring to: a 'route to take the London dead through'. Instructions left for the Motormen in plain sight but hidden unless you knew to check for ultra-violet markings, and who would think of doing that?

Unlike all the other stations, there was no name printed beside the glowing X. Did they even have names?

Straight away, I remembered all those non-existent places that Dad mentioned on and off for years. Was this one of them? Not a ghost station like the ones I marked as a kid, but a… what… a Necropolis station? God, an Underground Necropolis station!

"Tyburn Cross."

The words fell out of me by themselves. Given to me by Otieno in a depot canteen all those years ago. And now look, there it was in 1970s London, shining away close to Marble Arch… once the site of public executions at those infamous gallows, the Tyburn Tree.

I spent ages running the little UV torch over every single line on that map, searching for more additions. But there were none. I grabbed and unfolded the second Tube map. This one was even older, lacking a

222

Victoria Line. I noticed a tiny green curve coming off the District Line to South Acton, where I knew a one-car shuttle service ran until 1959. That meant this map was from the Fifties. Again, I methodically passed the key-light over the entire thing.

Another circle with an X! Another glowing bar, jutting out from the vertical brown strip of the Bakerloo Line between Queen's Park and Kensal Green.

What was this one called? Was it Shroud Lane perhaps, or maybe Wakebridge?

My mind was racing – is still racing – at finding evidence that all those weird station names weren't just flights of fantasy from my dad. They were actual places he knew about, had maybe even been to, and let slip by accident.

If it *was* an accident. I'm starting to think that telling me might have been a safety valve for the pressure of keeping these secrets.

And there's no doubt in my mind now that these are Necropolis stations of some kind. The names alone just feel right. Instead of the boring North and South Stations in Brookwood Cemetery, these have more evocative London-like names to suggest some kind of history… albeit a grim, funereal history. It's clear what the shroud in Shroud Lane and the wake of Wakebridge refer to, both perfectly fitting for places where exhumed corpses were being delivered. And 'taking a ride to Tyburn' meant the same thing to Londoners many centuries before Tyburn Cross existed – a journey to your final resting place.

I've been pacing the garage back and forth for ages,

jabbering away to myself, excited as hell and feeling vindicated, to be honest, about all that time I spent trying to find out what happened to Dad, and suspecting a conspiracy. I was right, I was bloody right from the start, I knew it!

I keep going back to the maps and shining the UV light on them, watching the mini-lines blaze into existence from nowhere. Such an incredible idea. To leave secret instructions for Motormen who worked on this service, telling them where to go and…

Hang on.

Are they still there?

Christ – I should have thought of this sooner. *This might still be going on!* For all I know, these ultraviolet markings might still be in use on the maps in Tube stations. Nobody would ever know.

But now I know. I can go and find them. I can get the proof I need that everything I've been writing about is true. Never mind all this history, I can see where the Necropolis stations are right now, here in 21st Century London, I can do it!

I'm going X hunting.


Wednesday 29th October 2008


I've spent the entire day on the Underground. Didn't go to bed last night, too energised to even leave the garage, so I managed to get to Golders Green early. The staff opening the gates looked a bit surprised at how keen I was to get in. Both platforms were empty

224

and silent as I ran the UV key-light over the big Tube maps on the walls. But nothing shone back at me.

So I got on the first train and tried the next station. And the next, and the next, all the way down the Northern Line.

Only once I'd started did it occur to me how much easier this would have been in the past. They didn't have CCTV cameras back then, for a start. When you start paying attention to those and noticing where they've been placed, you realise just how many there are. It's proper Big Brother down there now.

I know they'll say it's because of terrorism, especially after 7/7, but now I realise there's other reasons, aren't there? TfL and the government have a little secret, don't they? With all those cracks in the system, you need to keep a close eye on your staff and passengers, make sure none of them stumble across a way in, or find some trace of the Necropolis service running right under everybody's noses. That's what the cameras are for, I can see that now. To catch people like me. People who might find out.

It's too late for that, you bastards. I know now.

It also became difficult to check the maps without other people noticing. Many times I had to wait for them to move away before I could get near one. Sometimes I'd be scanning a map and someone would just appear out of nowhere right beside me, and I'd have to immediately jump away. They always made a big act of looking at the map as if actually trying to work out a route, ooh, where am I going, which line is that, where's such-and-such. Then there'd be the sideways looks, keeping tabs on me as I glared at them, slimy bunch of spies, protecting their secrets.

I changed lines a few times and checked maps on Piccadilly, Central and Victoria platforms, but with no luck. All those security cameras, they must have seen me coming, mustn't they? Someone noticed and sent the word along the line, to replace those maps with ultraviolet lines on them, the special ones, quick, take them down before he gets to that station.

I bet that's it. That's where I went wrong, doing it methodically, station after station. I need to be more random next time, start moving around like normal passengers do, so they don't notice that someone has cracked their code. Yes, that's the answer. I'll try that tomorrow.

I got one of the last northbound trains back, and was convinced that the train would stop in the tunnel again after Chalk Farm, another 'signal failure'. But it didn't. Not this time.

I pressed my face up against the window as the train went through North End (or Bull & Bush as it's sometimes called, after a nearby pub). A ghost station that wasn't completed. It doesn't even have an old surface building, just platforms that have never felt the tread of passengers. I've known about it for years, of course, but hadn't realised how close it is to my home. Really close. Surely I didn't choose a house on Hampstead Way because there's a Tube station a hundred metres below it? I don't remember thinking that when we bought it but... I've been living on top of a Secret all this time.

After I got off the train, I stood on the platform at Golders Green. Those tracks ran right through North

End, and if I jumped down off the platform and walked into that tunnel, eventually I would come to it, I'd be standing inside one of the old crosses on my map.

Looking into that big dark circle in the wall, it was like standing close to a hole in the ground that you could fall into. There was this feeling like a vacuum waiting to be filled, like a hunger.

Bloody staff made me leave. Two of them came out of nowhere from behind one of their secret doors and told me to go home. Spying on me again through their little cameras in the roof, tracking my movements wherever I went.

They probably followed me home as well. Who knows what they're capable of, if they can hide the entire Necropolis Railway? Good thing I'm out here in the garage. I'm keeping the light off, just using the emergency torch from the boot of my car, they won't know I'm in here.

I can hear them, though. When I press my ear to the concrete floor, I can hear the trains. That distant wind-rush, it's constant. I can hear their secret trains running underneath the ground all night, back and forth.

They never stop. All night. They never stop.


Thursday 30th October 2008

I feel weird. Kind of detached. Everything feels like it's behind glass and out of reach.

I woke up with morning light seeping through the crack beneath the garage door, so intense it was like a laser cutting across my eyes. I must have fallen asleep on the ground. I was only awake for a few seconds before I started coughing heavily, one of those dry coughs that just won't go away, even now. My head is still pounding as well.

I haven't touched booze for years but I don't remember hangovers being like this, even when I couldn't recall what I'd got up to the night before. This is more like someone's punched me and knocked some memories out of my head.

I've read back on what I wrote yesterday and frankly I don't remember writing half of it, even though I clearly did. And I can only vaguely remember being on trains and checking maps… did I spend the entire day doing that? I think I was waiting for the Tubes to start running again when I fell asleep.

I feel empty but not hungry, although I didn't eat anything all day. I started wondering why Julia wasn't texting me and then realised I left my phone in the house. Do they even know I'm here? I need to go in and clean up, talk to her, see the kids.

I'm going to do that in a minute. But first I have to write about something important.

I think I've found Dad's last letter.

It wasn't in its own envelope like the others. It was inside one of the jiffy bags, one I had only briefly examined because it didn't seem to have much in it except a couple of old travelcards, the sort of salvaged leftovers he used to send to me as a kid. But as I was putting them back in, my fingers touched a single sheet of paper, not folded but scrunched up almost into a ball.

The handwriting is barely my dad's at all, slanted and rough. I've cleaned up the text as best I can:

> *Mike don't [unreadable]*
> *I can't remember any more*
> *I'm sorry son I couldn't*
> *look where it glows that where the [unreadable]*
> *the gap*
> *lives intunnels*
> *gap the mind the gap mindthe gap thegap please god mind thegap*

I've read this over and over and it still feels like both nothing and everything. Like Dad was trying desperately to communicate but there was some barrier stopping him. A barrier in his own mind, maybe.

And after he wrote this… where did he go? What happened to him? There was still not one hint of where he actually went after Moorgate.

Beneath those few lines, the rest of the piece of paper is covered with drawings, all overlapping, some large and some small. It took me a while to realise they were wonky, uneven sketches of the same thing: the London Underground symbol. Except all the roundels had *two* bars across them instead of one, forming a flattened X.

This is…

I've seen this before. It's obviously similar to the

circle-and-cross icons that glow on the old Tube maps, but I feel like I've seen this larger version before too. I'm sure I have. Can't think where but something about this is making my flesh crawl. I'm actually shivering.

It has to be associated with the secret runs of the 'London dead', or else Dad wouldn't have drawn it. But why is it ringing a bell?

I've just looked at my research and found the official seal of the London Necropolis and Mausoleum Company, which was set up in 1852 to run the Necropolis Railway. It's a typically over-the-top Victorian design, encircled by a snake eating its own tail, featuring a Latin inscription and an hourglass with all the sand run out. Right in the centre is a classic skull and crossbones.

Looking back and forth between that and the crossed roundels that Dad drew, it seems obvious what's happened. In my mind's eye I can see the overcomplicated LNC seal simplifying over time, the serpent becoming a circle, the crossbones in the centre becoming two overlapping bars…

Yes! It has to be. This is a modern-day Necropolis logo, evolved into something more stark and modern, but it's the same thing!

I've taken a closer look at what else was in this last package, and they confirm my theory. There are two old-style season tickets, made from mauve-coloured card. Instead of issue dates and journey details, they have *LONDON TRANSPORT STAFF PASS* printed on them with the year – in this case 1973 and 1974 – which normally is also a background watermark. I had several of Dad's old staff passes in my collection so I'd assumed these two were no different.

But when I look closely, I see that where they would normally have Mr R. Thames printed in red above his signature, those spaces are blank. His five-digit staff number has been replaced by 00000. And instead of the year, the watermark is a symbol: the crossed roundel.

Special passes for a special service. These must be how Dad and others made their way around. Passing in and out of stations in broad daylight, then using their knowledge to slip into the ghost stations and unused areas, away from the prying eyes and cameras.

I'm tempted to go straight down Golders Green and see if they still work. Could I open the ticket barriers by feeding in one of these? But they're from years ago. They probably have something more sophisticated now, like a special Oyster card or something.

I really should go indoors. My cough isn't going away and those shivers haven't stopped either. I wonder if I've picked up something from all the time on the Tube yesterday. It only takes someone to sneeze and everyone in the whole car gets it. Germs spread like wildfire underground.

But I can't stop looking at all the symbols Dad drew across the letter. So weird. It's like he ran out of words... or the ability to write them... and just resorted to drawing something he must have seen hundreds of times over the years.

Crosses. Always crosses. I wonder why. Crosses

for stations glowing on the old maps. Crossed bars over the roundel. Crossbones on the old LNC seal. Tyburn Cross, whatever the hell that place is. Crosses on the

Wait, what if

Crosses on the doors of

No that can't be right. Coincidence. Just because they used to paint

No no no no no

Please oh God

I'm dead

I'm dead


Can't go out. I can't. Julia has been banging on the garage doors for hours shouting my name trying to get me to come out or talk to her but I can't. I can't go near her can't risk it not now I know. I can't risk infecting her.

She says she can hear me coughing my guts out and she's right I can't stop myself. The shivers have got worse too and it aches under my arms and my head is throbbing. Have to keep my back to the door as the sunlight is making my eyes water. Trying to keep typing to focus, block out her voice and crying and just keep going.

I know what they are now I've worked it out what the trains were for what my Dad did.

London dead.

Plague dead.

Plague trains.

232

They took the dead away not just any dead but the dead from plague still there never gone away must be little pockets of it underground still living down there in the dark wet earth

They used to paint a cross on the doors of houses where one of the family had caught the Black Death telling everyone to keep away putting the house under quarantine

And now they use the crossed roundel to mark the secret trains taking away people dead from plague can't let everyone know it will cause panic and spread it further have to keep it quiet

Stop it Julia stop screaming

Dad talked about plague pits all the time I should have seen what he was trying to do warning me what he did and what was really down there all those mass graves from the middle ages that the tunnels were built around Dad told me he's been telling me all along

Can hear the kids shouting my name asking what's wrong with Dad, Julia telling them to get inside, my head is hurting so much symptoms are getting worse I know it starts with fever then my glands will swell and sores across my skin then vomiting and

Stay away for the love of God please Julia keep away from me

I get it now why Dad vanished and couldn't come near us and why Albert did the same and abandoned his family, they were like me they got too close they couldn't risk exposing them to the sickness still under the ground

Going under

Going under with the bubonic plague

Go away all of you please I love you go away so you can live

# Chapter 10

Friday 13th August 2010
5.02am

Jake coughed once as he emerged from the crossover passage, walking from South Kentish Town's northbound platform onto the southbound. It was almost identical. The filthy walls were covered with decaying tiles and strewn with cables, with lamps spaced along its length illuminating the whole area.

There was another burst of coughing. He paused for a moment before taking a deep breath of the muggy, dusty, foul-smelling air, like a holidaymaker arriving at the beach.

And then he got back to work.

He had scoured the whole northbound side of the abandoned station, sweeping it with the UV lamp. Nothing shone back at him other than twinkling clouds of dirt swirling through the air and the now-familiar smears of mouse urine, staining the ground a luminous yellow. Since first discovering these, he had found out that rodents could actually see in the ultraviolet range, so such traces were like territorial markers for them.

Tiny fluttering silhouettes also began to appear: Tube mosquitoes. Like all insects, they were attracted to ultraviolet light and so his UV lamp drew them out of the crevices. They circled him wherever he went, like bloodsucking paparazzi pursuing a celebrity.

Over on the northbound side, he had leaned into each tunnel with the lamp held outright, but it revealed nothing but emptiness dotted with lights. At each opening, Jake had to physically push himself away from the tunnels, resisting the urge to go in…

…*go in*…

…no. No, not yet.

He'd done the same on the station's upper level, at least those parts he could reach. He even stood at the bottom of the emergency stairwell that had been capped. Looking up, it was like standing at the bottom of a deep well. Imprisoned beneath the earth. The thought didn't make him feel anything.

What did make him feel something was the fact that this place-hack was as fruitless as the others.

Jake didn't want to deal with that just yet, but still the thought was lodged in his mind like a splinter, painfully stabbing a tiny bit harder with every step he took. Little pangs of 'there's nothing here' and 'got it wrong' and 'waste of time' and 'you're stupid' and 'you're crazy', step after step.

He ground his teeth as he walked down the stairs from where the platform had been removed. A lot more railway equipment was being stored here on the southbound side: various lengths of track, large iron bolts and heaps of plastic sacks. There were also several thick tarpaulins covering yet more junk, shoved against the wall. Jake had to step around them and occasionally on them. He was irritated by the way the builders and engineers had just dumped their unused crap here over the years, as if South Kentish Town were nothing but a nameless storeroom.

236

Disclaimer and Subverse were there too. Both were visibly sweating and had taken off their outer layers, their faces now grimy. Jake could sense the closeness of the air but it didn't feel especially hot or anything. In fact, it was only now that he realised he wasn't shivering any more. He'd got used to the constant shudders wracking his body. They'd been there for... was it weeks or months? But now they seemed to have gone.

Subverse was ignoring him, clearly still pissed off with his cavalier attitude to exploring. Not so pissed off that he wasn't making the most of being there, Jake noticed. He was busy setting up a huge-lens camera on a tripod to take more pictures of all this glorious subterranean desolation, which would surely impress a lot of people on the explorers' forum.

Disclaimer, on the other hand, was just larking about and making a lot of noise, getting a kick out of being somewhere he shouldn't. Occasionally he would pose for one of the pictures and be reprimanded by Subverse for sticking his tongue out or doing handstands on the live rail. They all knew there was no current going through the tracks during engineering hours, but that didn't stop Disclaimer pretending to be electrocuted for the sake of a comedy photo.

Tuning them both out, Jake stepped around all the covered heaps of material toward the headwall on his right. The tunnel mouth yawned beside him, four rails protruding out like steel tongues. He spent a moment looking at it...

...looking *into* it...

…and found that looking away took serious effort, like turning into a hurricane.

With another deep breath, Jake switched on the black light and directed it at the rotting walls. He became so focused on this that he barely heard the footsteps echoing in the crossover tunnel, and then rattling down the steps.

"Jake!"

He looked up in surprise. Deak's voice was hushed and urgent, and his normally placid face was twisted with… Jake wasn't sure what. He wasn't very good at reading emotions any more.

Deak threw a look over his shoulder at the other two, to make sure they weren't in earshot. He held out Jake's mobile phone. "Is this true? Do you have it?"

"Is what true?"

"You know!"

Behind his spectacles, Deak's eyes were wider than Jake had ever seen them. Not with fear exactly, but certainly some kind of anxiety.

"What are you talking about?"

"The plague!" Deak hissed.

Now it made sense. Jake nodded in understanding and stepped forward – making Deak jump back, holding out the phone like it was a shield. His voice rose as he retreated toward the stairs. "You *do* have it. Jesus!"

Jake glanced down the empty platform in the direction of Disclaimer and Subverse, who had paused and were obviously aware something was going on. He had to take care of this before they also got the wrong idea and abandoned him.

"You obviously haven't read – "

"I knew something was wrong with you, you haven't stopped coughing all night and you look like shit! And we've been with you for hours, you could easily have passed it on – "

"Listen to me, Spatial Deconstruction."

Jake wasn't sure why he chose to use the full version of that ridiculous name, but it seemed to remind Deak of who he was, or at least of his reputation.

"I know why you think this but I don't have the plague. There's no Black Death anymore."

Saying it like that made it sound absurd to both of them. The anxiety melted away from Deak, although now he seemed confused. "But I read… Mike Thames, he worked it out. These plague trains, they're getting rid of people who – "

"Mike Thames," said Jake through gritted teeth, "was a stupid, raving, conspiracy theorist and a lunatic. Okay?"

"What?"

"They're not plague trains! He wasn't infected, he was just mad. He drove himself mad and then he wrote it all down, like mad people do. There. Is. No. Plague. Got it?"

Deak looked from him to the phone and back again, and Jake knew he was about to ask the obvious question. "If that's the case, what are we doing here?"

The UV lamp was suddenly too heavy to lift. His arm dropped to his side.

"I don't know," he mumbled. "I thought... it's the right day, so when I found something at Camden, I thought it meant..."

"The right day?"

Jake squeezed his eyes tight. "Doesn't matter."

For a long moment he just stood there. The rucksack on his back felt twice as heavy, filled with equipment and expectation. He floated in the blackness behind his eyelids, with the emptiness of the station ringing in his ears.

"Jake."

"We can go," he sighed. "Tell the others – "

"*Jake.*"

He opened his eyes. Deak had his back to him, facing the nearby wall.

Part of which shone.

Jake's eyes narrowed, trying to make sense of it. Something on the rectangular tiles was giving off a faint light. He glanced down at the UV lamp in his hand, hanging limp by his side, and saw it was pointing toward the wall. He brought it up, moved it across...

...and there it was. A large pattern stencilled across the wall, radiating a blueish-white glow with a faint violet outline. It was the same size, the same shape and in the same position as an ordinary London Underground sign, the ones spaced along the length of ordinary platforms with station names printed on them. Except instead of a single horizontal bar, this circle had two angled bars that met in the centre to form a flattened cross.

240

X marks the spot.

They both stared as if it might be a mirage. A lazy cloud of mosquitoes drifted in front of the symbol and around the black light.

Deak slowly took off his glasses, the way a gentleman removes his hat when a hearse passes by.

"Necropolis," he murmured. "You found it."

Jake felt a numbness creeping from head to toe. He couldn't move, couldn't speak, wasn't even sure his heart was beating.

Beside him, Deak seemed to be reciting the thoughts spiralling round Jake's own head. "This is what Mike Thames was looking for, isn't it? The... the crossed roundel. He was right all along! What else was he right about? Maybe he was right about the plague trains too?"

Jake said nothing. He tilted his hand to move the UV lamp aside, and the glowing symbol vanished. Nothing but soot-covered wall tiles. He had a horrible notion that it was gone forever, that he'd wished it into existence. But as soon as he aimed the lamp back, it materialised from nowhere. There were imperfect splashes of fluorescent paint at its edges and a few spatters and drips down the wall, all giving off the same unearthly glow.

"Take a picture," he croaked.

Deak obliged, using Jake's phone to capture the ultraviolet sign. "Evidence. Yes?" he said. "Is that what you're doing? Looking for proof to go public with his article?"

"There's got to be more." Jake almost tripped over

the tarpaulins as he finally made his legs work. He held the UV lamp with both hands, running it up and down the walls.

For a minute or two he did this in a kind of trance, not thinking about anything except what else might shine in the gloom if he got close enough. There had to be more than just the one symbol. Instructions of some kind, maybe. Directional arrows, like the emergency exits. TfL loved their signage, the Tube was riddled with them, surely this would be no different...

"That sign could be old," Deak was saying as he followed him. "They might have left that there a long time ago."

"No." Jake knew that wasn't the case. The fluorescent ink they'd used to stencil that symbol onto the wall wasn't flaking away or flecked with dirt – it was fresh. It had been placed there recently. Plus, today *was* the day, he knew that.

What if they were too late? Perhaps if they'd got down here an hour or two earlier? If it wasn't for being stuck in the housing estate hiding from the police, or he hadn't made them wait for so long at Camden Town...

"Hey guys!" Disclaimer's voice rang out. "We've found a door!"

Jake and Deak looked down to where he stood, by the headwall beside the entrance tunnel. There was a big grin on his face as he rapped his fist against what sounded like heavy wood. "I almost missed it, it's covered in dust."

"Probably just a permanent way storeroom," said

an unimpressed Subverse. Jake knew this was a collective term for lengths of rail, sleepers, bolts and other equipment used to construct the train tracks. "Looks like they're keeping a load of it down here."

Deak raised his eyebrows at Jake. "Worth a look?"

Everything suddenly went black. The lamps along the platform wall simultaneously switched off, plunging the four of them into total darkness.

Jake didn't jump, didn't make a noise in surprise, didn't react in any way. If anything, some of his muscles relaxed. The ache behind his eyes eased.

There was an excited whoop from Disclaimer, his voice carrying through the blackness. "Time for bed, children!"

Beside Jake, a beam of light sprang on as Deak fished out his torch. The others turned theirs on too. Despite their intensity, all three beams were swallowed up by the dense nothingness filling the space around them like oil. Even the lights inside the tunnels were now off. The circular opening in the headwall was so black it was like a heavy curtain had been draped across it.

The darkness brought an instant change in atmosphere. A sense of truly being below ground, buried inside the earth. Buried alive. But the thought still didn't alarm Jake, or the seasoned urban explorers with him.

"The power's been turned back on!" called Subverse, not because he'd forgotten that they all knew this but because he had to be the one to announce it. "Keep away from the third rail, it'll be live now. The trains will start running again in about an hour. We should get moving."

Disclaimer beat out a rapid drumbeat on the wooden door. "Before we go... what about this, then?"

"What about it?"

"Let's bust it open!"

Subverse threw his hands in the air. "Jesus, what's wrong with you? Criminal damage isn't part of our ethos and never has been!"

"I don't want to nick anything, just see what's inside. Hey Jake! Bring your kit down here, let's, uh, let's see if... if we can..." His voice seemed to fade.

Jake slowed to a stop. He lowered the UV lamp, switched it off.

Something was wrong.

He could feel it. The fine hairs on his arms and neck were prickling.

And – he realised that he couldn't hear anything.

He turned to Deak, who was talking but his voice was muffled, as if underwater. The echoing ambience of the station seemed to be dampened too. It almost felt like he had gone deaf, because he couldn't properly hear a thing.

Nothing but his own heartbeats and breathing and...

...and a sort of absence of noise, like a vacuum sucking at his ears.

"Can you..." he began, but his own voice also sounded muted.

His heart started pounding. This was it, wasn't it? After all this time –

A scream sliced open the silence.

Jake and Deak jumped. They spun, Deak's torch beam whipping back and forth.

Another scream, raw and strangled, echoed through the dark.

The circle of light from Deak's torch fell upon the shape of Disclaimer, down by the headwall. His huge frame was huddled in the corner and he was scrabbling at it, as if trying to dig through the wall with his hands. His eyes bulged out of his face. He was making howling, whining screams with each breath, like a panicked dog: *"Aaaaah! Aaaaah! Aaaaah! Aaaaah!"*

"Oh my God – GLEN!"

There was a crash as Subverse shoved aside the camera tripod and bolted along the platform. He approached with hands out, shouting "Glen, it's me, what's wrong, what's wrong!"

If Disclaimer heard him, there was no sign. Throat-ripping screams rasped out of him. His body was shuddering wildly, his jeans darkening around the crotch. Subverse tried to lift him but couldn't get near the whirling frenzy of arms and legs as he tried to burrow into the filthy corner.

"We have to go!" yelled Subverse, although it still sounded muted. Panic lanced through his voice, driving it higher. "Glen, we have to get out of here, Christ's sake come on, please God come on fuck fuck fuck *we have to goooo!"*

Jake stared at the two experienced place-hackers as they regressed into bawling, terrified children.

He felt nailed to the spot. Beside him, Deak also

245

seemed paralysed, mouth hanging open. His teeth were shining white.

Jake shot a glance at the UV lamp, knowing that he'd turned it off, and noticed that his own fingernails were shining too. He looked up as…

Without warning, it emerged from the tunnel.

No wind.

No noise.

No headlights.

No colours.

It edged out of the tunnel mouth, just as wide and just as black.

Disclaimer's screams and Subverse's babbling cut off. The circle of torchlight around them vanished.

It kept coming along the raised tracks, towering above them.

Jake squinted as if being blinded by a sudden intense light, even though he could see that there were no lights at all. It was a black hole moulded into something the size and shape of a moving train. Its silence filled his skull. The absence of noise deepened to a hum, a bass note that he felt in the hollows of his guts, a vibration along every bone –

Sudden movement. A shift, a thump, a painful impact.

He realised Deak had pulled him roughly to one side, into one of the crossover passages. The weight of their rucksacks had sent them both tumbling to the ground.

Deak was scrambling to his feet and about to shout something. Instantly, Jake slapped his hand across his mouth and pulled him back down. He snatched the torch out of his hand, switching it off.

Crouched awkwardly in sudden darkness, they both froze.

And Jake thought: It's come for me.

It's found me, I knew it would, *it's come for me!*

He shuffled his body around by degrees, trying not to make any noise, until he was looking out of the crossover passage. He couldn't see anything but knew that in front of him were the four rails, heading into the other tunnel on his left.

Jake peered into absolute blackness. Would he be able to tell if it was sitting right there on the rails in front of him?

The sound of Deak's rapid breathing reached him. The soft scraping of his knees and boots on concrete. He could hear again. That un-noise pressing into his ears had gone.

But he couldn't hear Disclaimer's screams, or Subverse's howls.

What he could hear was a sound he instantly recognised: the whoosh-rumble-clunk of train doors sliding open.

Then… other noises that also seemed familiar. Rustling and shuffling movement of some kind, mixed in with what could have been footsteps. And the metallic noise of locks being opened.

Jake edged forward on his knees, trying to peer around the lip of the corridor entrance. He felt Deak pull him back. His fingers remained fastened on Jake's shoulder, clearly telling him not to go out there.

Soft sounds of movement drifted out of the darkness. If those were footsteps, they were being made with such care as to be almost inaudible.

More familiar train sounds – a pneumatic hiss, then double doors shuddering together with a thump.

For a while, Jake heard nothing but his own heart whacking against his ribs. He gazed ahead, willing himself not to jump or cry out if it came gliding past… but how would he know if it did? The entire platform was totally dark, as dark as *it* was.

He glanced down at his hands. His fingernails were no longer glowing.

Jake covered his torch with one hand and switched it on. In the flesh-muted light, he could just about see the nearby tracks gleaming dully. There was nothing on them.

Deak finally let go of his shoulder. He eased his head around the corner, allowing more light to escape between his fingers. He made out the shape of the station, the tiled walls, the heaps of junk on the floor, the elevated rails vanishing into the tunnel… but that was it. Nothing black, nothing train-shaped.

Jake stood up, gradually letting go of his torch. Behind him, Deak switched on his own. They peered out and shone their lights down the length of the platform.

The empty platform.

No Disclaimer. No Subverse.

"Where… where are they?" whispered Deak.

A worried frown settled on Jake's face as he walked out. They were definitely alone. No sounds except the echoes of their footsteps.

"What happened? What *was* that?" Deak's voice was unusually high and trembling. His head darted back and forth. "What… I don't…"

"Check the other side," Jake said quietly. "Make sure they're not hiding over there."

"What? We need to get out of here!"

"Do it. They might need help."

"But what was that thing? I don't – "

"Just do it!"

Deak hesitated, then went back through the crossover. Jake trod around the equipment on the floor while sweeping torchlight in every direction. He found his UV lamp and picked it up, and also pocketed his own mobile phone. Deak must have dropped it, but its moulded rubber case had protected it from damage. Subverse's camera and tripod lay where they'd been shoved aside, with broken bits of glass from a shattered lens.

He glimpsed the bobbing light of Deak's torch moving along the northbound platform. At the last crossover passage, Deak walked back across and rejoined Jake. That made it clear that they were alone in the station.

From where they stood, both could see the door that Disclaimer had discovered. It was built inside the headwall, meaning the room behind it was alongside the tunnel. Unlike most internal doors on Tube stations, it wasn't brown and covered with colourful warning stickers. It was painted the exact same dark grey as the dusty concrete it was set into and had no markings whatsoever. Camouflaged. You had to be right on top of it to see it.

They shared a look. Tense and ready to bolt, they lifted their torches toward the void of the tunnel opening.

Deak exhaled with relief at the sight of the soot-grey inner wall, lined with wires and cables. Empty.

Jake scowled. He didn't understand. It didn't make any sense. But Disclaimer and Subverse were both gone without trace.

"Jake, what the hell just happened? Wh… where did those guys go?"

He stared into the tunnel. "It took them."

And he thought: But it didn't take *me.*

"What?" Deak ran a hand over his goatee as his eyes flicked from side to side. "When you say 'it'… that was just a train, right? With people on it. Right?"

There was nothing Jake could do but shrug.

"There had to be a driver at least… it must have been, like, a maintenance train or something," Deak convinced himself. "So maybe he thought those two had got trapped down here, and picked them up to rescue them…"

His voice tailed off as he turned this way and that, trying to make sense of it. "I don't get it. Why was I so scared? Jeez, I nearly crapped myself. I've never felt like that, *never!* And those guys went totally crazy! I mean, we were freaking out, but they just lost their minds."

Jake didn't correct him. He'd been shocked, yes. But scared?

There was no fear this time. His heart had been pounding with excitement.

"It's because of the infrasound," he said.

"Infrasound?"

"Sound too low for humans to hear."

"Right, right, it didn't make any noise at all, we never heard it coming…"

Jake nodded. "Whatever kind of engine it's got is pitched at a frequency lower than twenty hertz. It seems silent but it's noisy as hell, just outside our range of hearing… like dog whistles, but too low rather than too high."

"But why would that make us – "

"It affects people, because our bodies feel the vibrations. Triggers the fight or flight response. That's what makes people so scared around it."

Deak listened intently as his breathing slowed. He was still anxious but, Jake noted, keeping his head and not panicking. Which was one of the reasons why he'd recruited the Canadian in the first place. And the other two as well. The two it had taken.

"Hang on. You're saying, what, that it's actually designed to go sneaking around like that? So it's like a stealth bomber, except on rails?"

"If you like."

"Stealth trains! Are you kidding me?" He shook his head. "All right, screw this. We need to go back up right now. Whoever was driving it will have reported seeing us, for sure. They might send down the cops or close the way we came in."

"I'm not going anywhere."

"Listen, Jake, whatever the hell this is about, I didn't – "

"You know what it's about. You've read the article."

"You said Mike Thames was a lunatic!"

"He was. But he wasn't a liar."

Deak scowled. "You can't think… you don't think that was the same thing he wrote about? That was years ago, it can't be the same, that was back in the Eighties. What's it doing here, why would it come in and out again?"

Because of me, Jake wanted to say, because it was looking for me, it came for me like I knew it would!

Except it *hadn't* come for him. Which meant he knew why it was there.

"There's only one purpose for a Necropolis Railway," he said as he switched on the UV lamp.

Deak didn't jump, but he certainly twitched, when another crossed roundel symbol materialised on the grey door. Like the first one, it glowed blueish-white with a purple haze around its edges. Streaks of fluorescent paint had hardened below it.

He threw a questioning look at Jake, then peered more closely at the door. There were no handles, only a keyhole, but he tried to prise it open anyway. It remained sealed. "I thought this was just a place to store permanent way?"

"Sort of. At Waterloo, they used to stack the coffins under the viaduct arches, out of sight. Before they were transferred to Necropolis Station."

"God." Deak backed away from the door and

wiped his hands down his jeans. "So in there they kept…?"

"They're using the ghost stations to hide their cargo before it gets taken away. It's like a staging area." He switched off the black light, and the luminous symbol on the door disappeared.

"But *why?* Why would they keep stiffs down here and shunt them around on secret trains for years and years, what's the point? And why would they have taken our guys? They sure weren't corpses!"

"Not yet."

"Jesus. You don't think they're…"

Jake revolved again and shone his light at the tunnel entrance. "We have to follow the train."

Deak let out a laugh, the first time Jake had heard him do this, but it was drained of humour. He started shaking his head and walking away. "No way. No chance. This is not what I signed up for."

"This is exactly what you signed up for. You came here to find out how I knew so much. My 'gift'."

"Yeah, but I didn't know it would mean – "

"Well now you know!" snapped Jake. "We have to find out where it comes from. And it took our friends, remember. We have to try and get them back."

"They're not my friends. I hardly know them."

Jake looked at the world-renowned urban explorer and understood how such a man might see other people: as nothing more than resources, assistants, opportunities. But following that thought came the reminder that he'd been using Disclaimer and Subverse to get what he wanted too. And now they

253

were gone.

"They're not mine either," he admitted quietly. "But I'm not leaving them down here."

With the torch in one hand and the UV lamp in the other, he walked to the circular lip of the tunnel mouth. That strange ache surged back again… to go in, *go in*… sharpened by knowing that this time he would succumb to it.

He waited for a full minute before Deak finally came to stand beside him. "You think it reversed back in there?"

"Nowhere else it could have gone."

"This is the southbound side though, so that's going against the flow. If any trains come, they're going to run right over us."

Jake checked his watch. "Northern Line won't start up again for about an hour. If we do see a train, it'll be… that one."

He stepped forward, walking with the nearest rail between him and the live central track. Dirt-encrusted brickwork swallowed him up. Coiling above his head were the steel and concrete struts that supported the tunnel, making a concentric series of rings stretching ahead. It was like walking through a giant serpent's ribcage. Various signs and numbers were affixed to the walls alongside the cables. On the tunnel floor, the four elevated rails extended into nothingness.

Jake inhaled deeply. The air tasted of metal and soil, even dryer and hotter than in the station. He expected to start coughing but didn't. As with the shivers and headache, the coughs had stopped.

Deak stepped behind him, torch in hand. His hushed voice rang off the tubular walls. "Listen, if this isn't a plague train, then what's it for? If the... what did he call them, the 'London dead'... if they're not plague victims then what are they?"

Jake pulled his phone from his pocket and handed it over.

Deak raised an eyebrow as he accepted the device. As absurd as it looked, he held the phone up so its glow painted his face in the gloom. It crossed Jake's mind that only someone with as much experience as Deak could even consider reading while walking along a subterranean passage at the same time. But then it wouldn't be long until he knew everything that Jake knew.

With careful steps, he led the way deeper into the tunnel.

# Chapter 11

I'm writing this again. I have to. I have to. Someone should read it.

I've started writing a dozen times but found the words wouldn't come, or what did come was… not me. And sometimes staring at this laptop screen felt like looking into the sun. But things have got better and I can think more clearly. I've got my routines now and it's helped.

I'm living in my car, mostly. Driving from place to place. I've found I have to sleep during the day on the back seat with the blankets over my head. I must look like a bloody vampire, but it's being out in the daytime that makes me… not me. I found myself losing control of the car, getting blinding headaches and shivers, like having the flu all the time. It gets easier at night. So I've become kind of nocturnal. I've been keeping away from people as much as possible, avoiding crowds and waiting till the early hours before buying food or whatever I need from the empty late-night places, and I

And I haven't been home for weeks.

Can't risk it. I'm not going to go anywhere near them. The idea of giving this to Julia, of the kids being sick, just makes me want to crawl into a corner and die. I'm not going to do that to them.

I can't remember properly but I think I was

shouting out to them from inside the garage, before I left. Something about changing... about me changing? It's all hazy. Doesn't feel like that screeching voice in my memory was mine at all. I don't want to think about how I must have sounded to them. The kids must have been so frightened to hear me – no I cannot think about it.

I don't know anymore if this is the plague. Some days I'm convinced, totally convinced I've got only hours left. Other times, like today, I realise that I'd probably be dead by now if I had somehow contracted bubonic plague. I feel like death for sure, I feel strange as hell, but as far as I can tell there's no sign of the classic Black Death symptoms – marks on the skin, buboes, vomiting, there's none of that.

But there's something going on with me, and until I know what it is, I can't go back.

The thing is, even if I haven't caught the plague, I know it's down there, because that's what my dad and grandad did, it's the whole bloody point of my family. We take away the ones who caught it.

That's what Dad was doing, driving trains full of people dead or dying from plague, taking them away before they could infect others. It must have survived in little pockets underground, all the burial pits filled with bones, lingering after hundreds of years. Leaking out of the soil, reaching out to touch people... a commuter here, a tourist there... death's bony finger tapping them on the shoulder while they waited for a Tube. And the Necropolis trains doing what they've always done, taking away what was left in the night.

Sometimes I want to stand in the road and scream

all this at people. Tell them what I know. What nobody knows because it's been kept quiet for what, a hundred years, more? I see all the crowds passing outside my car windscreen, walking on pavement without seeing all the bones below their feet and I just want to… grab them, shout at them, tell them everything.

They'd think I was insane. Of course they would. So I keep it from them, keep it buried. Because that's what we do in my family. We bury things.


Wednesday 19th November 2008

I went X hunting again last night, this time on the District Line. I've been looking for weeks now. Not the above-ground stations, I don't care about them, it's only proper Underground places that count.

It's difficult though. Every station has several big maps on their walls, and it takes so long to check them all with my little key-light. Sometimes I have to stop and walk away if there are too many people, getting close, too close. And there's cameras, cameras all over, so staff keep coming and asking what I'm doing or telling me to leave. Last week at Oxford Circus I spotted a couple of transport police heading my way along the platform, but I managed to get out through another exit first.

They don't want me to find the maps, I know they don't. Got to keep the Necropolis a secret, haven't they?

258

And the ghost stations too, they've got those locked up tight. I've tried to get into a few of them and it's hard as hell, even with all the routes and blueprints. Some of the ways in that my dad knew about have been sealed off and others have now got security cameras sticking right over them, Big Bastard Brother's always watching.

Some ghost stations are simply impossible to tackle on my own – you need two or more people, and a load of equipment, if you want to get through without breaking your neck or having a chance of getting back out again. But there's only me. Who else could I trust with this?

I need to go back through everything Dad sent me again. The whole lot. I can't do that in the car, I need space. There's got to be more clues in there that I've missed, got to be something. I can't stop until I find it. I can't go home again until I find it.

Thursday 20th November 2008

I managed to find a place to work. It doesn't look like anybody's been in this warehouse for a long time. I thought there'd be alarms or dogs or something when I broke the window, but nothing happened and nobody came. The whole building is one big emptiness full of dust and cobwebs. There are lots of rectangular marks on the floor where machinery once stood. There's also a constant dripping noise from somewhere and a weird chemical smell that makes me queasy, but it doesn't matter. I've got a second torch now so the dark doesn't matter either, I just need the space.

I unpacked everything and laid it all out on the ground, unrolled all the maps, took all the letters out of their envelopes, everything, surrounding myself with it. And I spent ages shuffling round on my knees going from piece to piece, looking at every single scrap Dad sent me. Looking looking looking. But not finding anything new.

I had to get up to ease the agony in my knees, and went walking around the warehouse for a while, then I walked back and looked down at all the letters at my feet and saw it straight away.

It was right there. It's been right there all along, staring me in the face ever since I was a child, so obvious!

The underlines.

The <u>underlines</u>.

I'd never given much thought to the way that my dad used to draw a line below some words or sentences in his letters. That's how people used to emphasise things back then.

It wasn't until I had every letter in front of me that the underlined words jumped out. I brought them all together and put them in order, from the 1971 letters to those pushed through my front door and hidden by my mum.

Now I can see it. He was using the underlines to write messages within messages!

He was telling me about Necropolis.

*you won't see those on any map!*
*only in the early hours of the 13th of each month*
*All change!*
*there's meant to be nothing there but empty tunnel*
*secret station*
*not allowed in without a staff pass*
*It's not true that once you're dead then everyone's the same.*
*It's us who knows where the bodies are buried.*
*a false wall and the tunnel carries on behind it*
*between the lines*
*gone under*

I'm missing some, I know I am. I never kept the earliest letters and must have thrown some away, so there are things missing, but still I can see how it all connects together. Sometimes it looked like he was underlining things at random, but he wasn't, he wasn't, he knew what he was doing! Dad was talking to me in code. All I had to do was read between the lines, look under the words, it was all there, it's always been there!

I can sort of feel my head clearing even as I type this, like some of the fog has been lifted. I feel like a journalist again, piecing together all my sources and finally seeing the shape of the story.

Firstly, this tells me that whoever Dad worked for, he didn't trust them. He suspected they might intercept his letters to me. If they could inspect his correspondence then they probably kept tabs on him wherever he went. Or maybe he was just paranoid that someone might be reading his letters, or he didn't want Mum to know, or... there must have been some reason for it.

Secondly, now I know why I haven't been able to find any ultraviolet lines on Tube maps. I've been looking on the wrong date! *The 13th of each month*! I thought that was part of a stupid ghost story but Dad put it in there for a reason, just to sneak in the fact that the Necropolis lines only appear once a month, on the thirteenth.

It makes sense! All railways run on a timetable, don't they? There has to be a regular schedule of some kind, even for secret trains. So I'll have to wait until 13th December to go searching with my UV light again. Need to think about which stations to go to, can't do them all in one night, but anyway...

Most importantly, now I know how they've kept these Necropolis stations hidden all this time. An *empty tunnel* with a *secret station* hidden behind *a false wall* and *between the lines*, it's all there! They must have concealed tunnels and fake walls all over the Underground, you just need to know which ones have been activated. And I will when the thirteenth rolls around, I'll find them!

Those underlines were all from letters Dad sent before Moorgate. When I look at the few he sent afterwards, I find these:

*he took more than just corpses on the Necropolis trains*
*nobody could see the bodies and nobody knew*

*gone under*
*under the Underground*


This doesn't tell me much more than I already know, but again I don't know what's missing – there might have been lots more letters from him that Mum never kept or didn't even receive.

And there's that phrase – *under the Underground*. That's what these trains are, I can see that now. The Necropolis Railway didn't stop but went underground, literally Underground, underneath all the other lines on the map.

The Under Line. That's what it is, and that's why Dad drew all those lines below anything relating to it, because that's its name. The Under Line.

Then there's *Mind the Gap!* – which is always underlined. As far back as I can remember, it was one of those little rituals we had in our letters, and I used to write it as a postscript on mine too. On Dad's later letters he seemed to lose control and became obsessed with writing that, like some kind of warning... But I can't see what it refers to. Obviously there's more to it than the signs they have on the platforms to warn people away from the edge, but what? What was he trying to tell me ever since I was a child?

Ever since I was a child. My God! Dad's been trying to tell me about all this since I was just a little boy. It's like he was preparing me for knowing about the Under Line all along, without scaring me away from it, and without whoever was monitoring him realising what he was up to.

Can't stop remembering. It's not just the letters, is it? It's everything he ever did. Taking me to South Bar in Brookwood where they once offloaded coffins, showing me the old Necropolis Station at Waterloo, all the ghost stories, all the Secrets… all designed to prepare me for this.

Oh. And the little crosses I used to draw on my pocket Tube map. Can't be a coincidence that I used to draw tiny crossed roundels for the ghost stations. I thought that was my idea, but maybe Dad suggested it and I forgot.

Maybe nothing has ever been my idea.

I feel like I've been groomed. Changed to be who he wanted me to be. Like Grandpa Albert did to him. Moulded along the same lines.

The sun is up. It's sliding beneath the warehouse shutters and through the broken windows, and I'm in the corner under a rusting staircase, typing this in whatever darkness I can find. I know I should sleep, but I can't, I can't stop thinking about it all, I can't stop wondering…

Sunday 23rd November 2008

I haven't left this warehouse for three days. Will have to soon, the batteries on my laptop and phone are low, and it's starting to stink worse than it did when I broke in, thanks to me.

I've been using the camera on my phone to take pictures of everything that Dad ever sent me, all the

264

maps, blueprints, letters. It's my proof that the Under Line exists. Should have thought of this before, but some days it feels like I'm barely thinking at all. I need a record of it all, a digital record, not just scraps of paper that can get lost or damaged. It all needs to be saved forever.

I know who I'm writing this for now. My kids. Right now I have to keep away from them and can't risk getting close, but I know they'll read this one day, and read everything that my dad – their Grandpa Robert – sent me too.

My son has an email address so I'm going to scan everything and send him the lot, get him to share with his sister. Not Julia, she can't see this, she won't feel what we feel, it has to be one of us. Only another Thames will really understand. I want them to know, not keep them in the dark their whole lives.

It's not everything, I know that. Too much is guesswork and there's still a lot that doesn't make sense. Must do better. Drip-feeding bits and pieces of our history is what my dad did to me, and I need to do better with my own children. I need to tell them the whole story.

Dad's told me everything he can. There's only one other person still alive who might know more.


Friday 28th November 2008

I'm in Falmouth. I drove down here two days ago.

Aunt Claire didn't answer the door at first. I knew

she was in there. It took over an hour for her to make an appearance. She looked me up and down with proper disgust – didn't even try to hide it. But then she's never been one for pretence or sugar-coating. I told her I needed to talk to her and ask some questions about our family, that it was important.

"It'll do you no good," she said, and then finally swung the door wide to let me in.

I hadn't realised how bad I looked until I saw myself in her bathroom mirror. That pale-skinned tramp with slitted eyes peering back at me.

It took a whole day to clean myself up. I left a ring of scum around her bathtub so dark it was like spray paint. Aunt Claire stomped about opening all the windows and spraying air freshener everywhere. She fed me fruit and packaged sandwiches from a nearby shop, but hasn't made me anything herself, not even a cup of tea. Before we had a chance to talk, I collapsed on her living room sofa and slept for almost an entire day. When I woke up I found a pile of second-hand clothes on the floor beside me, bought from the local charity shop. She destroyed everything I was wearing.

I'm writing this in her living room with my recharged laptop on my knees. Through the window I can see the ocean. I can hear the whisper-crash of waves, and the air has that salty clean taste to it. It makes me shudder. It's too big, too open. I keep closing the curtains.

Even though she's now eighty-four, there's no sign that Aunt Claire has changed. Still the same efficiency-machine as always. She's looking after me the same way she looked after my mum for decades –

briskly, unsentimentally. Her little home is spotless with only a few decorations, none of the floral wallpaper or ceramic poodles you might expect from a lady of her years. No family photographs, either. I spotted their absence instantly.

She's let me into her home out of duty, not love. I know that. But maybe duty is enough to get me what I need.


Sunday 30th November 2008

Yesterday I asked her. I still can't believe

I didn't

God! She tried to

Tell it. Get it down.

I recorded her. On my phone. She didn't know but I had to do it. It's not enough to rely on paper and words, I need proof, something permanent. So I set my phone to record and left it on the sideboard.

At first, Aunt Claire just sat there and let me ask questions. I got the sense that she always expected to be doing this one day. Like a prisoner knows sooner or later there's going to be an interrogation.

I'm going to transcribe what we talked about, so there's a record of it. Like I used to in my newspaper days. Maybe doing that will help me wrap my head around it as well. There's a lot to take in, things I never

She actually tried to

Write it down. Write it down. I need to record it all.

MT: So, I think you know why I came here. I need to ask you some things about our family, and you're the only one who might –

AC: It won't help you, Michael. I told you that. You're too far gone, from the looks of things.

MT: What?

AC: [sighs] Go on then. Say what you've got to say.

MT: All right, well for starters I want to ask about Jacob. Not my boy, I mean Grandpa Albert's… your grandfather, I guess.

AC: I never met him. He died before I was born.

MT: So he did die?

AC: A man born in the 1800s? Yes, he did die.

MT: I mean, I know he must have died, I just wondered if the death certificate in 1906 was… okay, so what do you know about him? Did he work on the railways as well?

AC: Yes, he did. He was an engineer I think, and then became a train driver later.

MT: Did Albert tell you this – your dad?

AC: Mmm. I remember father saying that he was following in his old man's footsteps when he first started working for London and South Western. He would always remind me and Robert that he… this was if we weren't pulling our weight or were being lazy… he would tell us that at the age of fourteen, he was shovelling coal into fireboxes on the locomotives all day.

MT: At fourteen?

AC: Because of the war. First World War. All the

trains were being run by children and old men, because everyone else had been drafted or signed up.

MT: And this was still in London?

AC: When he started, yes. We didn't move out to Brookwood until a couple of years after I was born.

MT: Right, because Albert was working on the Necropolis Railway. Did Jacob work on it too, before him?

AC: No, he never left London his whole life, or so father said.

MT: Pretty much the only thing I know about Jacob is a story that my dad told me in a letter, about a story that your dad told him.

AC: Oh?

MT: Albert said he was taken from home in the middle of the night when he was a little boy, and that Jacob took him to some hospital which, he said, had a train running through it. He tried to take Albert onboard but he…

I went a bit quiet here because I was remembering something that made me shiver: Otieno, down in York Road Station, forcing me toward something that looked like a train but wasn't, something blacker than the tunnel. He tried to take me into it, and I got away because I…

Had that happened before? To my great-grandfather?

I hope I'm wrong. I hope to God the same thing didn't happen to Albert when he was just a child. Dragged screaming in front of that… whatever the hell it was.

MT: He got free and ran away, said some nurses found him and took him home. I think he said that was the last time he saw Jacob. I don't know how true any of it is, but my –

AC: It's totally true. Nanny Pat told us the same story a couple of years after father died, and Robert said he'd already heard it. That was the train that Jacob was driving, the Dead Body Train.

MT: Who – what? The…?

AC: That's the silly name they gave it, at any rate. It went back and forth from Whitechapel Station to London Hospital. That was where Nanny Pat worked, she was a matron there... I think it's the Royal London Hospital now. There was a stairwell in the hospital's basement that led down to a special platform. Steam engine it was, not electric. It wasn't for proper passengers, just dead bodies.

MT: Wait, so… the hospital had its own train line? Taking corpses to the Underground?

AC: No, no. Other way around. It took bodies to the hospital, so they could be taken up to the morgue… to be cremated, I suppose.

MT: And it just went to Whitechapel? Why there?

AC: Well, back then trains ran into Whitechapel from all over. That whole area has always had a lot of railways. I suppose they were bringing in bodies one by one from across London to Whitechapel, then Jacob was getting rid of them.

MT: Bloody hell. So this was a… it was the first Necropolis Railway!

AC: Not properly, not like Brookwood. These weren't funeral trains with mourners and priests and all that. It was just a way of disposing of cadavers without people seeing.

MT: But I've never heard of this Dead Body Train. They must have kept that –

AC: Buried. Yes.

MT: Right, because it wasn't just getting rid of ordinary corpses, was it? It was taking them from all over London… they were getting rid of people who'd caught the plague, weren't they? The 'London dead'. That's why they had to keep the whole thing quiet!

AC: [said nothing but sort of squinted at me]

MT: So how come you know about it? And who's 'Nanny Pat'?

AC: Patricia Thames. She was my gran. Jacob's wife. Like I said, she worked at the London Hospital.

MT: She was part of it?

AC: Mmm. She was in charge of bringing all the bodies up from Jacob's train to the morgue. Probably where they met, I expect. [long pause] We used to visit her, Robert and me. After the war ended and we could go to London again, this was. She had a lovely place near Primrose Hill, lots of beautiful flowers in the window boxes, I remember that, you could make out her house from streets away, all the colours. She'd always talk about father and grandfather. Well, she told me more than she told Robert, I don't think she doted on your dad as much as on me. Once a year we used to visit her, until she passed away in… '49, I think it was. She was a strong woman, right till the end. All the Thames women have had to be strong.

271

I felt a little ashamed, listening to this. I suppose I've always thought of my family history as being about the men: Jacob, Albert, my dad, me. I must have logically assumed that Jacob had a wife, otherwise Grandpa Albert would never have been born, but I didn't give her any thought. So it came as a surprise to hear Aunt Claire talking about her as a living, breathing person she once knew, as sweet old Nanny Pat from Primrose Hill who loved her flowers. As someone who actually worked on the Dead Body Train.

MT: The Thames women… was Patricia the first? Who was before Jacob?

AC: There is no 'before Jacob'.

MT: But where did he come from?

AC: He was born in the Thames Tunnel.

MT: The… Thames Tunnel?

AC: You've never heard of it? That surprises me. It's where we get our name from.

MT: An Underground tunnel?

AC: No – well, it probably is now, but it's older than the Underground. Pedestrian tunnel it was, not a train tunnel, going under the river. Like the one at Greenwich but much bigger, they had market stalls and all sorts down there, it was like a high street but under the ground.

I've done a quick search for the Thames Tunnel and cannot believe I never came across it before.

Maybe that's because it's now an unremarkable part of London Overground network, a section that used to be called the East London Line on all my old maps. Nothing but a vertical stripe between Wapping and Rotherhithe stations, crossing the horizontal blue lines that represent the River Thames.

But it didn't start out as being for trains – it was meant for people. There's a hell of a lot of history behind it. When it opened in 1843 (Aunt Claire was right, it pre-dated the Underground by twenty years) it was one of Britain's great engineering triumphs, although it took many years and many lives, with men digging through the earth by hand and suffering in horrific conditions. But eventually it became a monument to Victorian ingenuity: the first habitable tunnel beneath a river.

The descriptions of the Thames Tunnel in its heyday make it sound incredible! There were two enormous thoroughfares lit by gas lamps, both having a road in the centre for horses and carts, with pedestrian pavements either side. Rows of arches were cut into the tunnel walls, and inside them market traders would ply their wares onto visitors, along with entertainers of all kinds – 'from Egyptian necromancers and fortune-tellers to dancing monkeys' as one visitor back then put it. Like Aunt Claire said, it was as much a subterranean marketplace as a way for Londoners to get from one side of the river to the other.

By all accounts, the Thames Tunnel soon became one of London's darkest underbellies. Pomp and finery gave way to decay and squalor, like it always does. Travellers were lucky to reach the other side without falling foul of thieves. The shadowy recesses became a haven for whatever seediness people could get away with eighty feet below ground.

It reminds me of how scary King's Cross was in the Eighties – a city within a city, lawless and depraved. There have always been boroughs and streets that people know to avoid at night. Down in the Thames Tunnel, it was *always* night.

Eventually they cleared out both tunnels and sold them to the railway companies. But before then:

AC: A policeman found Jacob there. Just a baby in a crib, hidden away in one of the arches. Abandoned. He'd never seen daylight.

MT: A baby? Whose?

AC: Oh, almost certainly a prostitute's. There was a lot of that going on, apparently. Plenty of men sneaking down into the tunnels for a… how did Nanny Pat put it… a four-penny knee-trembler. So Lord only knows who the baby's parents were. They brought him up to the surface and took him to a church foster home. He was named after the policeman who discovered him… presumably Jacob someone, or perhaps Officer Jacobs, I don't know. And they gave him the surname Thames because of where he'd been found.

MT: So we're not named after the river, we're named after the tunnel!

AC: Yes.

MT: And Jacob was actually *born* down there? Christ.

We're all descended from a… a troglodyte!

AC: Suppose that's one way of putting it. That's why my dad and brother were immune. For a while, anyway, it doesn't last forever. [She looked me up and down at this point.]

MT: Hang on, what? They were 'immune'? What do you –

AC: Michael, why are you asking all this now? What's this for?

MT: Well, I… I want to share it.

AC: Oh no. No, you cannot share this. I won't let you. I know you're a journalist but this isn't some scandalous story you can sell –

MT: Not share with the public, just with my family. My dad – your brother – he tried to tell me all about the secret Necropolis trains and everything, and I want my kids to know the truth too. They need to understand where they came from.

AC: *No*, Michael. Good Lord, no. You can't tell your children, of all people. You can't tell anyone!

MT: I have to! I'm sorry, but this has all been buried for too long.

AC: They're just children! You can't contaminate them with –

MT: They deserve to know why I left and what's been going on, it's their family too! It's too important, I'm sorry, I'm going to tell them the whole story no matter what.

AC: [stared at me for a minute with a face like thunder] Let me get you a cup of tea.

I had no choice but to sit there while Aunt Claire got up and went into her small kitchen. My phone recorded the faint sounds of her opening cupboards and boiling a kettle, and me shifting impatiently in the chair. I felt energised at having learned so much about our past. But I was also shivering with tension at what else she might be about to reveal. Eventually she came back and laid a cup and saucer on the small table beside me.


MT: Listen, when you said Albert and my dad were immune, you don't mean… immune from the bubonic plague?

AC: [rolled her eyes] You should know better than that by now.

MT: But my dad was always going on about plague pits, and that's what the Under Line is for, isn't it?

AC: The what?

MT: The Under Line, the… the secret Tube trains, the Brookwood trains at night, the Dead Body Train, all of them! If it's not for plague victims then what were they all for?

AC: That's what they were *officially* for.

MT: Officially?

AC: That's what all the high-ups think, in London Transport or whatever it's called now, and the government. We told… they were told it was to quietly dispose of Underground workers, or anyone else, who'd come into contact with active bacterial spores containing the Black Death.

MT: You know about this! So the whole plague thing

is just a, what, a cover story?

AC: Mmm. Drink your tea, it's getting cold.

MT: How can they believe that, though? Surely if the government thought that the plague was still floating around down there, they'd never allow that sort of health risk. They'd remove all the plague pits and properly disinfect the Tube and –

AC: Too expensive. You can't shut down the whole Underground now, London relies on it. And the rest of the country relies on London.

This seemed impossible to believe at the time, but when I think about it, it's obvious that Aunt Claire was right. Imagine if people thought there was a chance, even a small one, of catching a fatal disease while travelling on the London Underground. A disease they might then transmit to their own families and friends, to hundreds of others. The entire system would have to be closed down. And would anyone risk travelling on it ever again?

Even when there's a one-day Tube strike, it costs millions to the economy. If it were permanent, without all those trains pumping people around the city, London would seize up. Markets would collapse, trade would slow, livelihoods would be ruined. The loss would be measured in billions. Far cheaper to quietly finance a clean-up operation that took away all evidence and kept the whole thing quiet. Acceptable losses, right? What are a few 'London dead' compared to the economic stability of the entire UK?

The more I think about this, the more believable it becomes. Yet another clandestine department kept from the public eye for decades, officially non-existent like Q-Whitehall and all the other black ops they run behind the scenes. Employing – maybe conscripting? – ordinary Tube workers like my dad. No wonder he could only tell me about the Under Line in code. They must have been taking care of all his mail, seeing as I was addressing my replies to 23 Leinster Gardens, and he knew that even hinting at his real work would be breaking the Official Secrets Act or something.

MT: All right, look, if what you're saying is true and –
AC: Don't forget your tea.
MT: What? In a sec. So look, if there really isn't any plague down there, then what were the trains actually for?
AC: Drink up and I'll tell you.
MT: [long pause] Why don't you just tell me anyway?
AC: Just drink your fucking tea, Michael.

There's a lot of silence on the recording after this, which is when I stared back and forth between the cup of tea on the table and Aunt Claire. Her eyes seemed to be watering.

MT: Jesus Christ.
AC: Michael… please, it won't… there won't be any pain, please just –
MT: Oh Jesus *Christ!* [loud crash of the cup hitting the wall]
AC: I'm sorry… I'm sorry but you can't, you just can't tell them, it's too late for you now Michael, you're

going under, I can see it, and you –

MT: I can't, oh God, I can't believe you… you tried to… I'm your *nephew* for God's sake, and you…

AC: You can't go back, please listen to me! You can't tell your children about all this, for their sake, you'll drag them under too! Please, Michael! Michael!

That's where the recording ends. I grabbed my phone and got out of her house as fast as I could, not letting her touch me and not looking at the tears running down her face. I didn't look back, just stormed out to my car and drove away.

It's night now. I can finally get back on the road properly. Can't drive during the day anymore. I can still hear the ocean waves from where I'm parked and it's like acid against my skin, slowly eating into my nerve endings. Just the thought of all the open sky above my head makes me want to burrow down into the footwell of the driver's seat and curl up into a ball and

London. I need to get back to London.

Wednesday 10th December 2008

I'm not the same anymore.

It's hard to write but I have to don't think I've got long

When you know and you are part of it then you change

I think that's what the 'London dead' are. The

plague was just a cover story, I see that now, but there's some kind of infection maybe, some kind of disease, it gets inside you when you're down in the tunnels and it makes you part of them, makes you part of what's under London.

Londoners, but different from everyone else, a different type of Londoner.

Immune, she said they were immune to it, my dad and Albert, and Jacob too, that's why they could work on the Under Line, of course! So obvious now! Dad and Grandad drove trains full of 'London dead' without becoming one of them because our family was *born* underground, under the river, we already belong down there.

And me, I must be immune too but

I've changed, I can feel it. I think I know now why my dad always underlined *Mind the gap* right from the start because he knew that there was a gap between him and other people. The tunnels take something from you, something human and normal and what's missing is the gap you fall into.

*The mind gap*

And the gap gets bigger and that's why I had to leave can't go back now and it's why Dad left, I can see that now

It's an act of love to stay away from your family when the gaps become too great I can't pull Julia and the kids into it with me I have to keep away and I'm so sorry but

Only a few days to go I need to go down there again check all the maps it will be there somewhere

Friday 12th December 2008

It's tonight. After midnight. It'll be running tonight, has to be tonight.

*only on the 13th of each month*

I know exactly where to go, I saw it glowing on the map, *there's meant to be nothing there but empty tunnel* but I can see the Under Line now, I can finally see it!

I'm sending this to my son so he will have everything I've found, all of my work and all his grandfather's letters and knowledge. I have sent it all over the last few days and now I'm going to send this article so he can read the full story, read *between the lines* and see what my dad was and what I am and what he will be

No, no he can't be like this, he has to understand what the Thames family is but he can't be like us

Jake you have to keep away from the Underground don't go down there and don't come looking for me, I will be back soon I promise I will see you soon

Let me succeed where my dad failed and stop you from being like us, stop you from becoming what I've become, stop you from *going under*

# Chapter 12

Friday 13th August 2010

5.49am

"You're Jacob Thames."

Deak's voice echoed along the tunnel. His footsteps came to a scraping halt. The beam from his torch made Jake's shadow stretch ahead.

He stopped walking too, and turned into the light.

"Shit. I'm right, aren't I?" Deak looked at the phone in his hand and back up again, eyes huge behind his spectacles. "You're the one he sent this to. Jake is short for Jacob. You're Mike Thames's son!"

Jake nodded.

"Holy Christ, this is... why didn't you tell me? That explains everything, you're one of them, you're a Thames!" He waved the phone. "So this is your own father who wrote all this? I thought you said he was a lunatic?"

"He was."

Deak's expression softened. "So when he vanished a couple of years ago and left his family... that was *your* family."

Jake swivelled away and resumed walking alongside the metal rail, sweeping both his torch and the UV lamp along the walls. He said nothing. He felt nothing.

He remembered everything.

It seemed to come from nowhere, his dad's madness. Almost. Jake had noticed him becoming a little withdrawn over the space of a few weeks, prone to staring into space and not hearing whatever he or his little sister were saying.

Suddenly Dad locked himself in the garage, ignoring his mum banging on the door demanding that he came out, ignoring her screams and then responding with screams of his own, words that made no sense. Even more suddenly, a day or two later, he was gone. Just gone.

Naturally there had been visits from the police, men in suits drinking tea in the living room, trying to get Mum to talk in-between her messy sobs. He could remember his sister's tears too, a child's pure and uncomprehending tears at the sky falling in. Her daddy had gone away.

Did Jake also cry? He had no memory of it. He might have been too numb, even then. He could remember going down to the empty garage by himself, walking through the space where the family car usually was, and trying to work out why his dad had hidden from them. The couple of scraps he picked up from the garage floor – an ancient cardboard ticket, and a piece of paper with weird symbols drawn on it – gave no clue.

The consensus, from detectives and doctors and friends, was that Michael Thames had suffered a bout of chronic depression following the death of his mother. It was certainly true that he hadn't been acting normally since coming back from Brookwood, so that diagnosis felt very believable and rational to everyone. It followed that he would either return home of his own accord, or be located by the police at some point and brought to safety. A little psychiatry, a dose of antidepressants plus lots of TLC and he'd soon be back to his old self.

The three of them had clung to this lifeboat until it gradually broke apart in the steady current of time, leaving them adrift.

Dad never came back. He was never found.

The children went to school, their mother went to work and they all staggered on, trying not to mention the Dad-shaped hole in their lives. It seemed their family would always have this massive gap in it.

Then the emails arrived, and Jake started falling into the gap himself.

It only took moments to veer from overjoyed surprise – mouth opening to bellow the good news, that Dad had got in touch, *Dad was still alive!* – to silent horror, as he read the fractured, desperate words in the email.

For a long time, Jake was too scared to read any more. He ignored the emails, not mentioning them to anybody. For months he actually kept a distance from his laptop, like it was an undomesticated pet that might bite him. This was worse than Missing Dad, maybe worse than Dead Dad. This was Mad Dad. How was he meant to cope with that?

Gradually Jake started dipping into the emails, looking at the scanned images of maps and drawings. He did definitely have tears in his eyes when he started reading the document, hearing his dad's old voice and mannerisms, reminded of how he used to be. That almost frightened him off, but he kept reading… kept falling. Changing from scared to intrigued to fascinated.

He read everything: every word of the document, every letter his dad's own dad sent during the 1970s, every story told about Albert Thames and the Necropolis Railway, and all the revelations from Great-Aunt Claire. He learned about the first Jacob Thames, the child born underground who gave his family their name – and who gave Jake his. That came as a shock, to discover he was named after a great great-grandfather he'd never heard of before.

And he fell deeper and deeper.

He studied all the blueprints and information from Robert Thames. He did his own research, online and in libraries, digging into London's history, looking for connections, looking for evidence. Every time he entered a Tube station, he noticed all the sealed doors, side passages and blocked-off areas. He went hunting for them, noting them down and crafting his own maps.

Soon, it was like the Under Line had always been the only thing that mattered.

Jake kept all this from his mum and sister, who only noticed how he stopped going out with friends, stopped going to college, and soon stopped leaving his room. All they could see was the distance between them and him, widening with each day.

At the start of 2010, Jake had slipped out of the house in the night and never looked back. For their sake, more than his. By that time, he understood what his dad meant at the end of his document: *'It's an act of love to stay away from your family when the gaps become too great.'*

Deak's voice, reverberating around the tunnel, drew Jake back to the present. "What happened to Mike – to your father? Did you ever hear from him again?"

Jake shook his head, not trusting his voice.

"You don't think he's… is that what you're doing all this for? Are you trying to find – "

The act of switching off his torch also cut off Deak. Jake gestured to where, about half a dozen metres ahead, the tunnel ended in a shining circle. Deak turned off his own torch, and both pulled their hoods over their heads. Together they trod slowly toward the light, making as little noise as possible.

Jake bent down into a crouch as he approached the tunnel mouth. He peered round the lip to gaze at the bright sparseness of Archway Station's platform, making him wince. There was no sign of any staff, and no sound other than the buzz of lights and hum of air conditioning.

It had been the same at Kentish Town and Tufnell Park, the two stations they'd already passed through. Both were just as empty and eerie as this one. Jake was well aware that despite it being five in the morning, they were lucky not to run into somebody. But it seemed Disclaimer had been right – at this time of night, the Tube was properly empty. Perhaps all those earlier delays had worked in their favour.

Without saying a word, Jake and Deak removed their rucksacks and carried them, then crouched down as much as they could. They shuffled forward, crab-walking in the gap between the platform edge and the first rail, beside the suicide pits. Neither looked up, not taking the chance that someone might wander onto the platform and spot two heads bobbing along past the yellow lines and *MIND THE GAP* signs.

It seemed to take forever, but finally they hobbled the full length of Archway's southbound platform and back into the tunnel. Deak stood up and yanked his hood down with a gasp of relief, massaging his legs. Jake supposed his thighs should have been burning in agony, but felt nothing as he too rose to his feet. There were no aches and pains as he retrieved his UV lamp and torch, no strain as he slipped the rucksack back on. Not out of breath, not flushed and sweating, not doing any of the things the experienced urban explorer behind him was doing. Jake simply kept walking.

Minutes passed by, measured in footsteps. The tunnel floor had been steadily veering upward ever since they left South Kentish Town, but was now at a noticeably steep angle. This branch of the Northern Line headed up a natural hill, at the top of which was the Highgate area. As they trod on, they found their bodies leaning forward against the incline.

"Now I know why you were so insistent that we got down here today," said Deak casually, as though they were wandering along a high street. "Had to be the thirteenth, right?"

Jake made a short noise of agreement. He continued sweeping the black light left and right across the dust-caked walls.

"Did you pick the same date on your previous place-hacks? With those guys?"

"Yes."

"Did they ever realise?"

He hesitated, taken by surprise by memories of meeting up with Disclaimer and Subverse over the last six months. He would discuss which ghost station he wanted to explore, explain their route, and talk them through the infiltration plan – the 'script' as Subverse called it. They never noticed the dates he picked, or that they were exactly a month apart. All they cared about was that on a regular basis, he laid out an exciting opportunity before them.

And they went along with his plans willingly. Trusted him to get them inside. Trusted him to get them back out.

"…No. They didn't."

There was a pause before Deak said "What if they're gone for good? I mean – "

"They're not gone," Jake insisted. "We'll find them."

In truth, he wasn't filled with doubt or confidence one way or the other – he didn't know if Disclaimer and Subverse were still alive or not. All he really felt was the wrongness of them being taken. It wasn't supposed to happen that way.

A couple of mice zipped out from a crack in the ground and vanished, startled by their approach. It crossed Jake's mind that what scared Disclaimer and Subverse half to death wouldn't have bothered these mice at all. They could hear ultrasound but not infrasound. Only terrifying to humans, Jake mused. To surface people.

Deak began talking about them again, and Jake wondered if he might have to order him to shut up, when abruptly they both saw the same thing. *"There!"*

It shone through the dark, on the wall to their left: a circle with two overlapping bars in its centre. The symbol of the Under Line.

Carefully, lifting their feet high and stepping over the rails, they both moved closer to it. Like the ones in South Kentish Town, it had been stencilled onto the tunnel interior using UV-sensitive fluorescent paint. This one wasn't fresh, Jake noticed, it was smeared with grime and flaking off in places. But it still gave off an intense glow in the black light.

He reached out and touched the symbol, his fingernails shining. No doubt his eyes were shining too as he gazed at it.

"This makes no sense." Beside him, Deak aimed his torch in all directions. "There's nothing here. Why have they marked this part? There's nowhere the train could have gone."

Jake tilted his head. "Shut up."

"Look, I think you've found the proof you wanted, why don't we – "

"Listen!"

Deak's expression became more raw as he heard the same thing Jake could.

A screeching sound was drifting through the tunnel.

At first it was impossible to tell whether it was

nearby or far away. They both swivelled, trying to focus on it. Gradually they realised it was distant and growing steadily louder.

"The trains have started running," murmured Deak.

Jake checked his watch and shook his head. It was still a little early for that.

Also: "That's not a normal train."

He knew every noise made by ordinary rolling stock, and this was nothing like them. It was harsher, more aggressive. A combination of deep rumble and high-pitched whine. Like a mechanical scream.

And it was coming their way.

Deak drew an unsteady breath. "Is that… is it the same train as…?"

"No." Jake knew that much at least. At South Kentish Town, it had emerged from nowhere with heart-stopping suddenness. Whatever it was, you never heard or saw it coming. This was something different.

Jake switched off his torch, leaving the UV lamp on, and turned to face the direction they had been walking, north up the hill. The tunnel bent to the left as it continued on into darkness – except it wasn't quite darkness. There was a faint glow outlining the circular ribs of the wall. It was almost like a fire, flickering yellow in the night, growing brighter with every second.

Deak saw it too. "What the hell's that?"

"I have no idea."

"It's getting closer. We need to go back!"

290

"We won't make it in time," replied Jake calmly. He knew Archway was about a kilometre away, and this – whatever it was – was approaching quickly. It would be on them before they got halfway there.

He could see Deak's normally placid face wrestling with his emotions. Almost anyone else would have ignored Jake and gone bolting down the southbound tunnel, but the Canadian visibly resisted that urge and asked "So what's your plan?"

"We kill the power."

Jake put down his torches and turned to face the side of the tunnel. The thick grey cables were bound together and fixed solidly in place, but alongside these were two unfixed copper-coloured wires. They were stretched taut about ten centimetres apart. Jake had never noticed these before reading the letter from Robert Thames that described his experience in the Kennington Loop. These were tunnel telephone wires, once used by Motormen to contact their controllers by hooking a portable handset onto them. And they had one other important purpose.

He took a wire in each hand and brought them close, rubbing them together. After a few seconds, everything lit up. The lozenge-shaped lights along one side of the tunnel all sprang on, giving out a steady glow. Jake and Deak screwed their eyes tight as the shadows were thrown back.

Jake nodded, satisfied. Connecting the wires had tripped a circuit and cut off track power to this section. Now there was no electric current passing along the live rail for a train to use, so –

"It's still coming!"

Deak's shout made him spin round. That shrill screech hadn't stopped. It grew louder.

Whatever was coming down the tunnel didn't need electricity.

Jake whirled, feeling the urge to sprint for his life, to try and outrun whatever was bearing down on them, but then his brain processed what Deak was bellowing.

"…fake! Look at the wall, it's fake!"

He followed Deak's pointing finger to the crossed roundel symbol. That part of tunnel wall had *two* sets of cables and telephone wires. The ones on either side of the symbol had been shunted upwards and were bolted to the ceiling. There was a space about three metres wide where duplicate cables and wires weren't connected to anything – weren't real. Only because of the tunnel lights was this now noticeable.

Just like the house facades at Leinster Gardens, thought Jake, even as the ear-splitting squeal began driving proper thoughts out of his head.

Deak pounded the false section of wall, then ran his hands along the edges. He let out a cry when he pulled cobwebs away from a very recognisable sight: a grey metal post, with a slot in the front below the yellow dial of an Oyster card reader. Its ordinariness was almost comical. It looked for all the world like the stanchion of a passenger gate, but buried in the tunnel wall rather than standing in a Tube station ticket hall.

Deak was shouting above the noise, but Jake was already moving, his body knowing the answer before his mind could work it out. He unzipped his jacket, reached into an inner pocket and brought out a small rectangle of card. The meaningless scrap he'd found on the floor of the family garage, printed with *LONDON TRANSPORT STAFF PASS 1974.* Only after reading his dad's document did he realise what the card offered him.

*A way in!*

Jake fed the card into the slot on the stanchion. There was a second or two of feeling ridiculous – and then he and Deak jumped as several things happened at once.

A split appeared right down the middle of the fake section of wall. Slowly, the two halves folded inward with a grind of rusty gears. There was solid blackness on the other side.

With a equally creaky whirr, the roof of the tunnel seemed to move by itself. Jake watched a curved length of metal descend from the very centre of the tunnel. It was like a train track but with large clamps spaced along it. Its bent shape made it look as if it were snaking along the ceiling into the opening.

Despite being startled, Deak wasted no time in jumping through the space where the fake wall had been. Jake grabbed his UV lamp and torch from the floor and followed, as the screech from whatever was approaching grew even louder.

They found themselves in another tunnel, a little narrower than the Northern Line one, and simpler – Deak's torchlight bounced back from blank walls. Jake looked around, quickly finding another stanchion, out of which poked the staff pass.

He snatched the piece of card. Instantly the two halves of fake wall revolved back toward their original positions, like a closing door. In the ceiling, the curved metal track – a suspension railway, Jake realised – was pulled upward. It vanished completely just as the sections of wall thudded back into place, cutting off the light from outside.

Jake looked at Deak who was still not panicking, but breathing hard and aiming his torch around wildly. There was no other source of light, except for a very thin line where the edges of the wall-doors met in the middle.

Deak started to speak, but Jake gestured him to be silent, and then to switch off his torch. He pressed his face to the narrow gap of light, peering through to see…

Something huge, yellow and metallic, that missed them by mere seconds.

It heaved past, slower than a normal Tube train but of similar size. He heard the heavy growl of a diesel engine. That explained why cutting off the track current hadn't stopped it – it was running on its own power. The hideous screeching rose in volume as the first car passed, and Jake had to look away as intense yellow-orange sparks filled his vision.

"It's a rail grinding unit!" he called out above the noise.

Deak's nod and look of relief made it clear that he also knew about these specialist engines. Every railway and subway system used them to keep the metal rails smooth and polished, and London Underground was no different. Of course it made sense that they would perform this maintenance during the early hours.

The bright flares from the RGU's grinders continued blazing through the narrow gap as its second and third car went by. Jake and Deak remained motionless, waiting to see if it would stop… if whoever was driving it had spotted two figures in the tunnel…

Both of them relaxed as the rail grinder passed by on the other side of the wall. It continued along the southbound tunnel, its screeching slowly fading with distance.

Deak's torch came back on. "Where the hell are we?"

They stood in a circular tunnel leading straight ahead. There were no lights, no cables, no telephone wires, no warning signs and no white plaques with serial numbers – just grey concrete. The only thing they could see was a pair of steel tracks that began a few metres in front of them. The lack of ceramic posts suggested they were not electrified, resembling old-fashioned steam railway tracks. They stretched on into pure dark.

Jake whispered "We're on the Under Line."

He stood straight and drew in a lungful of thick, stale air. He could see roiling clouds of dust in the torch beam. There was sweat running down Deak's face and fogging his glasses, but to Jake it felt as cool as a forest.

"I don't believe this," Deak was muttering. "This is crazy… that they could have a set up like this, it's..."

"Come on." Jake stowed his own torch in his rucksack and turned on the UV lamp, making the dust glitter as he walked through it. He stopped after a few paces when he realised that Deak hadn't budged. He had the look of someone who just couldn't make his own limbs move, no matter how hard he tried.

Jake offered a thin smile. "Don't you want to be the first to explore a hidden underground railway?"

It took a minute, but eventually Deak made himself follow Jake. Their footsteps echoed off the walls as they walked between the two elevated rails. In front of them, the tunnel shrank into the distance.

In a near-whisper, Deak asked "Where did you get that… whatever it was, to open the doors?"

"Staff pass. My dad left it behind."

"For you to find?"

He frowned. "No… I don't think so." That had never occurred to him before. In the document Dad warned Jake away from following him, so surely he hadn't left it there deliberately.

"Do you still have it? Can we use it to get out?"

He patted his jacket pocket reassuringly. Deliberate or not, there was a sense of rightness that he now owned the same cardboard key that Robert Thames used in the Seventies, to pass in and out of concealed doorways like that one.

"Jake," began Deak after a while, "what are we doing here?"

Jake glanced at him as if to say *Really?*

"I mean, what are you expecting to find? Okay, it's a train that disposes of dead bodies, whether they're plague victims or whatever, but what's the point of seeing it if you already – "

"You know there's no plague," Jake told him. "And

you know they're not dead bodies."

"What else could they be? All that stuff your dad was saying at the end, about the 'London dead', I mean, he made them sound like they were almost, I dunno… warped or something. But he was crazy by that point, you said that yourself. So you can't believe any of that stuff, right?"

Jake was silent for a while. The only sound was their footsteps, echoing into the dark. Then he raised the UV lamp in his hand and pointed out the tiny fluttering shapes hovering around it. "You see these?"

"The mosquitoes?"

"There was a story in the news, a few years ago, about the mosquitoes that live in the Underground tunnels. They're not the same as normal ones any more. If you put them with above-ground mosquitoes, they refuse to mate. Won't go near them."

"So?"

"They've evolved into a different subspecies. Genetically they're a different breed, even though that sort of speciation normally takes thousands of years. With Tube mosquitoes, it's happened in about a hundred."

The disbelief was thick in Deak's voice. "That's mosquitoes! They're just insects, they're much simpler creatures than human beings! It's not like people spend a hundred years underground – "

"But we have," said Jake. "People have been travelling and living underground for centuries. Especially here. London's been around for two thousand years, and that's just recorded history. There were tribal settlements in the Thames Basin area a

297

thousand years before Londinium was built, there's proof of that. And maybe thousands more years before then, right back to the Stone Age."

"Jesus, it's not like they had the Tube back then!"

"No, but there were always tunnels of some kind. Early Britons built long barrows into hillsides, huge burial chambers for their dead. Then came ditches, wells, mines, the Romans with their sewers and drains... proper graves, mausoleums, cemeteries. There's always been some sort of underground, especially in London. Here more than anywhere else."

His voice was gravelly, unused to speaking so much. He found himself saying words he had never spoken aloud, about research he had never explained to another living soul.

"And there have always been different subspecies of human, different tribes and Homo Whatevers. We think we're all the same now, but we're not, because we're always changing. The environment you live in changes you, it changes your genes, like with these mosquitoes. The mice too, they're not the same down here as above. Mice can see ultraviolet light, did you know that? Nocturnal species like rodents evolve to see in low-light environments – "

"Wait, stop! So you're saying the 'London dead' aren't actually dead bodies at all, they're..."

"People," Jake nodded. "Living people. Londoners. They're what London *does* to people, if they're under-ground long enough. If they go through the wrong tunnels too often, if they breathe in all the particles of rust and dust and... bones, germs, bacteria, all of it! All compressed down by the city, building on top of

298

itself year after year."

He glanced up at the ceiling and licked dry lips, his voice even croakier. "All the old Londons are still down here, you know. All the streets and buildings and tombs from medieval times, Saxon times, Roman times, Celtic times… back to when it was Lundenburh and Londuniu and Lundein… all sunk into the clay and forgotten. Dead Londons. Down here are all the dead Londons."

Without looking back, he could tell that Deak was shaking his head. He must think I'm insane, Jake thought, as insane as Dad was.

"Er right, so, the Under Line…"

"Must have started with the Victorians," Jake went on, "when they built the Thames Tunnel and the Underground, started noticing the changed people… they wouldn't have known what they were dealing with. Back then a lot of people were worried that all the tunnelling might get too close to hell and disturb the devil, so they probably thought people were being possessed by demons. Or just being driven mad. They hushed it all up and quietly got rid of them, bundled them away in secret trains to cemeteries outside London, burying them in hallowed ground so they wouldn't rise again. But the more Tube lines they built, the more it happened, and it got harder to make them vanish. They brought the trains fully underground, set up the Under Line so that now…"

"Now what?"

Jake increased his pace, eyes narrowing, staring up ahead.

*"What?"* demanded Deak. His voice had grown

shrill. "What's the Under Line *for?*"

"They're death trains."

"Like the Necropolis – "

"No. Like the trains at death camps."

"What do you mean, death camps?"

Jake raised the UV lamp at what was now directly in front of them. "They're Auschwitz for my people."

Deak stopped dead. He lifted his torch, throwing a circle of light on the solid object only a few metres ahead. *"Fuck!"*

It sat there on the rails, facing them.

Something black.

Something train-shaped.

The cabin and door windows gave the impression of a three-eyed beast glaring down, or of looking through the arches of a church, it was monstrous and holy at the same time, or so it felt to Jake who was gazing up at it with an urge to fall to his knees and beg for his life or pray or something, something, it was here, *it was really here!*

Deak seemed frozen solid, but he wasn't babbling in terror or running away. The fact that Jake could hear his gasps, that there wasn't a vacuum in his ears or buzzing in his head, told him the train wasn't generating infrasound. Engines off, it sat motionless on the rails.

Like it was waiting for them.

Jake's eyes roved over its outline. Its modern shape surprised him. Based on his dad's description of what he'd seen at York Road, he'd expected the train to be a classic 1938 Stock. But with its broad front windows, twin headlamps and destination indicator at the top, it resembled rolling stock from the Eighties or Nineties. And yet it felt more basic than ordinary trains, simpler, like a prototype design.

At the top in the centre was some kind of raised metal spine, which seemed to run down the length of the train. He remembered the suspension rail and clamps that descended from the tunnel ceiling – the spine must be what they hooked onto, to carry it through the concealed door. His eyes dropped to its front wheels, which were nothing at all like a Tube train's. Instead of steel they were large industrial tyres, with solid rubber guards on either side designed to grip onto the rails.

It struck him how much customisation there'd been: every centimetre painted a non-reflective matt black, no running lights, wheels engineered to move as quietly as possible, and powered by something outside the range of human hearing. It was, as Deak had said, a stealth train.

A Dead Body Train, like the one Jacob Thames drove to the morgue beneath London Hospital.

A Necropolis train, like the steam engine Albert Thames drove to Brookwood Cemetery in the middle of the night.

An Under Line train, like those Robert Thames drove through the tunnels of the London Underground.

And now here it was, the 2010 model, waiting for Jake.

The front cabin was empty, its interior looking ordinary in the torchlight. He noticed a short set of

301

steps built into the side of the concrete tunnel, leading up to the left of the train. He started heading to it.

Deak grabbed his arm. "What the hell is this! What's it doing here?"

"It's stopped at a platform," he replied as though explaining to a child. "This is where the passengers get off."

"Passengers?" Deak's face was white. "Oh God, you mean…"

Jake felt a humourless smile settle briefly on his face. "Last stop for the 'London dead'."

He walked up the steps alongside the berthed train, past the edge of the tunnel mouth and out into…

…a huge, dark space that was part station and part tomb.

It was a circular chamber at least ten times larger than any normal platform. The floor beneath his feet wasn't concrete but white marble riddled with tiny cracks. Enormous arches and columns stretched up to a domed ceiling like a cathedral roof. Ornate sculptures could be glimpsed among the shadows – angels, gargoyles and things between – all thick with dust. It looked, felt, smelled, tasted like the sepulchre of a medieval church.

Yet the impression was of a bloated Tube station, swollen to enormous size. The walls were covered with overlapping rectangular tiles, exactly the same as those used on Underground platforms. These had faded to a sickly yellow colour and were coated with mould, with many cracked or fallen off entirely.

There was a crossed roundel symbol fixed to the tiles, made from rusting metal. The ring was the same dark red as a normal London Underground sign, but printed onto it was a circular snake, eating its own tail. The overlapping bars were black rather than blue. Carved into their centre were two symbols: a skull and crossbones and an empty hourglass.

Hanging below the roundel was a separate sign made from white enamel. A name was printed on it.

# CRYPTGATE

Jake let out a slow breath, knowing he had finally found what his dad was searching for: a Necropolis station.

He took a few more steps. The air swarmed with mosquitoes, whisper-buzzing through a cloying, soupy atmosphere. The air was somehow both dank but also dust-dry. The entire chamber would have been pitch black if not for weak sunlight slanting down through an archway on the far right wall. It was covered by a rusting gate, beyond which was a wide stone stairway.

What was up there? Could there be a station building above?

For a moment he tried to picture what might be on the surface, striving to recall if there was a disused station in this area. He thought how the concealed tunnel had slanted off between Archway and Highgate… and suddenly it was obvious.

"Highgate Cemetery." He glanced back at Deak. "We're underneath Highgate Cemetery!"

Deak was still crouched on the steps from the tunnel floor. He peered over the platform edge like a terrified animal, eyes enormous behind his glasses.

Jake took in all the Gothic sculpting, so similar to all the mausoleums and tombs in the cemetery above. The chamber felt equally Victorian, as if it had been built around the same time. But of course there was no Underground back then.

*The stations came first*, he thought. Before the trains! Maybe beneath every cemetery in London –

"Jake!" called Deak in a choked voice. "What is this place?"

Only distantly was Jake aware of how terrified Deak sounded, and couldn't quite understand why. Perhaps it was because all Deak saw was a vast black pit filled with clouds of buzzing insects, whereas for Jake…

It dawned on him then how much he could see, even in the dark. Every detail was outlined in a blue-white sheen. The stone arches spaced around the walls were faintly glowing with the same light. He couldn't make out what was inside them, whether they were rooms or…

No. Not rooms. Shelves.

This was where they interred the coffins. Like in the catacombs of Highgate Cemetery up above. This was where they buried the 'London dead'.

At last, he started to feel something. A deep, slow anger.

He stared at the luminous archways and imagined all the bodies stacked inside. The bodies of all those people who had gone under. All *his* people, mesmerised by black lights and lured aboard the Dead Body Trains, transported quietly to the Necropolis stations, buried in consecrated earth but without gravestones, without hymns or prayers or mourners, without trace.

"Dad," he whispered.

Was he in there? Had his father been sealed within a casket? And Robert Thames too, when he finally changed too much?

How many of the Thames family ended up here, in the death camps they helped to run?

Jake dropped to his knees, as if in worship, as if crushed.

His palms pressed on the cold marble floor and the heavy rucksack slipped from his shoulders. What use was it now? It didn't contain a flamethrower to burn this place to ash, or a bomb to blow it to pieces and finally free all those people dragged there on an ultraviolet leash to be put down like dogs, like subhuman monsters…

Deak was calling his name, grabbing his shoulders and trying to get him to stand. He felt himself be pulled round, toward the platform where the train sat. There was another tunnel mouth at the far end, and the twin tracks continued into darkness.

Jake could see the full length of the train now. There were only two cars, each with driver cabins on the end so it could travel in either direction. It should have been almost invisible in the darkness, with no lights on inside, but... it was *blazing!* Apart from the cabs, every window along its length was shining with blue-white fire, making him wince as though staring at stadium floodlights.

The UV lamp rolled away from his fingers. He didn't need it anymore. He hadn't needed it for quite some time.

Jake's eyes narrowed as he strained to see... was that... movement?

Yes, there were shapes through the windows. Hazy silhouettes, drifting from side to side.

"Still onboard," murmured Jake, "they're still onboard..."

"What? What are you talking about?"

He stood up, shrugging off Deak's grip, and walked toward the train. Like all the other doors, the driver's entrance was closed. Crouching, he searched for a small panel and pressed one of the two square buttons on it. The cab door hissed open, sliding backward over the train's black hull.

Jake stepped into the cabin. To his right were the huge front windows, and to his left the sealed internal door. In front of him was a single chair where the driver sat, facing forward. It looked like any Tube cab except the controls were simpler than a modern train's should be, with fewer buttons and switches, and no screens showing camera feeds or digital information. Maybe the Under Line trains were all run automatically now. No need for Motormen anymore.

His eyes swept across the moulded plastic dashboard. Two buttons, red and black, were labelled 'Saloon Lights A'. Instantly, Jake reached out and pushed the black one.

He heard Deak's voice from outside. "Oh my God."

Jake stepped out from the cab and back onto the marble platform. The train's windows were now dark, smeared with years of grime – the intense ultraviolet glow from inside was gone.

He glanced at Deak, whose mouth hung open, and then spun back when he heard a sudden *thump* sound.

A hand was now pressed against the inside of a window.

*Thump.* And another.

*Thump thump thump.* More palms appeared, squashed onto glass.

Jake and Deak watched as – *thump-thump-thump-thump-thump* – a dozen hands slapped against the windows, fingers splayed, moving, sliding.

The sealed doors began shuddering. From inside came the sound of banging on metal.

Deak grabbed Jake's arm. "What is this, what, *what the fuck's going on!*"

"They're free now," Jake told him.

A few fingertips squeezed between the rubber-lined edges of the nearest double doors.

"They want to get out."

More fingers appeared, straining to pull the doors open. They probed through the gap from top to bottom, wriggling like thick worms. Some were white. Some were brown or black. Some wore rings or wedding bands. Some had painted fingernails.

"They want to go under, where they belong."

He felt Deak grab his arm again. His yells echoed, bouncing off the domed ceiling. "Give me the staff pass, we have to go! Jake, give me the ticket!"

"Of course we have to go. That's what I'm here for."

"Wh-what?"

He began walking back to the open door of the train's cabin.

"Oh no... no no no, you can't... you can't let them out! Jesus, *stop!*"

Jake didn't feel the fist slam into his face, so he kept walking.

He didn't feel the second or third punch either. Or the solid impact that jarred every bone in his body as he was thrown to the ground. No pain reached him.

But he was aware of Deak's hands rummaging through his jacket pockets. He heard more words that didn't really sink in, and then sensed him stand up and race down the short flight of steps.

Jake staggered back to his feet, blood streaming down his jaw, pitter-pattering onto white marble. There should have been pain in his face and along his limbs. Those sensations were becoming more and more distant, fading like Deak's footsteps.

Slowly, he approached the train and went back inside the front cabin. The upholstered seat welcomed his body. Through the window he could just about make out a dwindling pool of torchlight shrinking down the tunnel.

The internal door behind him vibrated with more thumping sounds.

Jake looked at the panel of buttons, knowing one of them would open all the car doors… but also knowing that this would only mean detraining them into a Necropolis station. Into the death camp.

On his left was what looked like a master switch set to a position marked 'ATO'. He pulled the switch down. The whole train shuddered and he instantly felt a kind of absence of noise, like a vacuum sucking at his ears, and a buzzing inside his head. Unlike before, this wasn't an overwhelming sensation. It was modulating up and down, almost singsong, almost like music.

The pounding noises stopped. He could feel a strange easing of pressure, a calming. Mollified by the infrasound from the train's motors, they settled down the way ordinary Tube passengers would. Taking their seats, waiting for the train to depart… trusting the driver to do his job.

Jake pressed another button and the side door whirred shut, enclosing him in the cabin's narrow space. His right forearm leaned on the shiny black armrest alongside the chair, and he gripped a large red lever – the traction brake controller. The dead-man's handle. He twisted it down and pushed forward.

The Dead Body Train pulled away from the station without making a sound.

The melodic pulsing inside Jake's skull intensified as the lever moved forward in his hand, notch by notch. He didn't feel the sensation of movement – he hardly felt a thing now – but he saw the circular walls and twin rails passing by outside the cab's windows.

A couple of lights flashed on the panel. He heard a clunking sound from above the cabin. Up ahead, the two halves of the concealed door were wide open, and the rails came to an end in front of it. The train rolled right off them and through thin air, suspended by the clamps now hooked onto its metal spine. It curved through the wall and out into the Northern Line's southbound tunnel, where its rubber tyres slotted atop the electrified rails. Once both cars were settled onto their wheels, the suspension grips detached from the spine.

Jake eased the controller forward and felt the train increase speed, snaking out from the Necropolis toward the metropolis –

– and straight into the back of another train.

He barely had time to notice it before it filled the cabin's windows: a dirty yellow lump of metal on the tracks. He didn't let go of the dead-man's handle, didn't react in the slightest, as it rushed at him.

There was a loud metallic bang, and a shriek of escaping gas. The yellow vehicle was slammed forward a couple of metres. Now he recognised it as the rail grinding unit that had almost run them down earlier. But it wasn't running, there were no orange sparks, and something else was different – a figure clung onto its side. A pair of massive eyes, a howling mouth.

Jake saw the RGU continue onward with a screech of wheels, rolling ahead… rolling downhill. It was downhill all the way from Highgate. All the way down into the heart of the city where the citizens were now beginning their early-morning Friday commute, where the stations were filling with people, where the normal trains had started running.

The runaway train with the screaming man on it fell toward the waking world.

In the cabin, Jake watched it vanish into the distance. He saw the circular ribs of the Northern Line tunnel pass by as he kept the dead-man's handle pressed forward, following the RGU as if it were a herald announcing his approach.

His eyes refocused onto his own reflection, bent by the curved glass. Spiky blonde hair, paper-white skin, staring blue eyes, bloody red mouth. He hardly recognised that face anymore. But he could tell it was smiling.

The train whispered through the tunnel, carrying Jake deeper into London.

# Chapter 13

Saturday 12th March 2022

10.25pm

"You left him down there."

She stared at the man cowering on the floor in front of her. He was wearing multiple layers of grubby clothes and gave off a sour stink. Long, greying hair hung lank beside a bearded face that was smeared with dirt. He wore a pair of rounded spectacles with one lens badly cracked.

He gaped up at her in panic. One of his wrists was handcuffed to a pipe that ran from floor to ceiling. He held up his other hand as if to ward her off.

"No," he gabbled, "no I didn't, listen – "

"You attacked him. Abandoned him."

"Please, look, that's not what happened, I – "

She raised the Browning 9mm semi-automatic and aimed it at his face.

*"You left him there to die!"*

Her voice rang around the windowless room. She was a dark figure in boots, black jeans and padded camouflage jacket, her hands in tight leather gloves and her hair swept up beneath a baseball cap. Neon lights suspended from a low ceiling threw her shadow onto the plain floor. Dense clouds of dust were all that filled the empty space. There was nobody else down there. Nobody to witness what she came to do.

The gun in her rock-steady grip pointed down at the man.

"No! Please, please listen, I didn't, I swear!" He was crouching on a filthy bare mattress, surrounded by boxes, sheets, cans of food, old clothes and a range of equipment, like a human nest.

She glared at him, finger rigid around the pistol's trigger.

"Jake's still alive!" he squealed. "I saw him, I can prove it!"

"You saw him? When?"

"Right after! He – he was inside the…"

His gaze drifted away from the gun, as if distracted by something worse.

"…Inside the train."

Her fierce expression didn't budge a millimetre, but the gun was lowered toward the floor.

She stared at the shivering man kneeling before her, handcuffed and helpless, pleading and pathetic, filthy and foul-smelling. It was difficult to match this sight to the pictures of that cool and confident figure she had seen, known only by the absurd name of Spatial Deconstruction, or 'Deak' to those who knew him. He had a calm and smug air in all those snaps of him climbing fences, scaling walls, squeezing through sewer pipes and standing on scaffolding high above city lights. Now he looked gaunt rather than lean, terrified rather than cool. Only the overgrown, matted goatee and glasses echoed his former self.

"Tell me what happened," she said, "after you left him."

He shuffled on the mattress as much as he could with one arm chained in place. There was a tremor constantly running through his body which, she had noticed during the last hour or so, occasionally got worse. It juddered through him now as he gazed into the near-distance, back through the years.

"I ran... I ran back the way we'd come," he began in a strained voice. "To where the wall opened. I put the ticket in the machine and it opened like before, and I just ran back out into the tunnel. There was a train just sitting there, the rail grinder. I could hear voices from up front... I think the drivers were talking to, you know, to the control room, asking why the power had been turned off. I climbed onto the side of it. I must have thought... it'll start moving again and it would carry me out of there."

Deak took a series of short breaths, as if preparing to duck his head under water, then muttered "It came after me."

The handgun lowered further, suddenly heavier in her grip. "The black train?"

"I didn't hear it coming. You *couldn't* hear it. There was just this crash, something hitting the back of the grinder. I nearly fell off and when I looked back there it was, it was right there, right there behind me, it..." He shook his head, eyes wide.

"What happened!" she snapped.

"It... the grinding train, it started moving by itself. The air brakes must have been damaged or something, but it started moving without the engine being on. I could hear the drivers up in the cabin freaking and trying to stop it, and next thing I knew it was rolling right through a station, and they… I saw them dive out. They just jumped onto a platform and left it, and it just got faster and faster."

"Rolling down Highgate Hill."

He nodded, looking up at her. "It wouldn't stop, it wasn't going to stop. I was hanging on tight and saw a couple more platforms go by and I knew sooner or later it was going to hit another train, so when it went through the old station I made myself jump off… and it carried on, with nobody driving it. It was broken, out of control."

"So you were back in South Kentish Town? But what about the black train?"

"It stopped there."

"What?"

"I was looking round for the way out and then one second the tunnel was empty and the next it just, it just, it was there, came along the rails like a ghost, and then it stopped… I jumped into one of the side passages but I couldn't run. I couldn't take my eyes off it. It just sat there right in front of me. It was so black. I only had my torch and I could hardly see it, it was all so black…"

After a moment, he added "And then its doors all opened and they got out."

Tremors went through him again, but this time they rippled across her skin as well. For some reason that image – *the doors all opening at once* – was giving her goosebumps.

"What… who got out?" she asked in a near-whisper.

315

"They did. The two of them. The two guys, Subverse and…"

"Disclaimer? You're saying they were actually *on* the train? You saw them get off?"

"Yes, they just kind of jumped down and – "

"Didn't you say something to them? Find out what had happened, where they'd been?"

"I tried. I tried to grab them and talk to them, but it was like they didn't see me. They didn't say anything, they just walked right past me. But I never saw them again. I guess they must have gone back up to the street."

"What did they look like, I mean, what state were they in? Were they hurt?"

"No. They were just kind of staring. Like they were sleepwalking."

She glanced away, mulling this over, then back to Deak. "And then what?"

"The doors all closed, but there were still… people… on the train."

"How do you – "

"I saw them, I saw them, I saw their faces! They came up against the windows all at the same time, they were just *there!* All these faces and hands… all pressing on the glass. They didn't make any noise, they were just looking out. Staring at me. All staring at me."

Imagining this brought another shudder through her body.

"That's when I saw him," said Deak.

"Jake? You saw Jake? On the train?"

"At the front. The side window. It was him. His face. Pressed against the glass like all the others, but inside the cabin. And he…"

"What? What did he do?"

"Nothing."

"He didn't get out? He didn't say anything to you?"

"No. He just looked at me. For a long time. Then he pulled away from the window and the train moved off. It didn't make a sound, it just kept moving… into the tunnel."

He peered up at her with a nervous expression. The handcuff chain clinked softly. She continued looking down at him for a moment, then half-turned away, lost in thought.

"I know about the runaway rail grinder," she said after a while. "It was in the news. It nearly hit a train, before they redirected it onto another branch of the Northern Line. Could have killed dozens."

She turned back, the gun still held at her side. "But there was no mention of any other train coming after it. I've never come across anything about a 'black train', and I've read a hell of a lot of stuff about the Underground lately, so either everything you just told me is a lie, or – "

"No! It's not, I swear, I've told you what happened. They cover it up, every time. They make up reports and fake the evidence, do whatever they have to – "

"So where did it go? Where *could* it go? It left South Kentish Town and then what, it vanished into thin air, it went into another magic door, what!"

317

He shook his head, looking helpless. "I know… I know everything I've said sounds insane, I know it does. I thought the same thing when I read what Mike Thames wrote, the whole thing sounded so crazy…"

He watched her crouch down, putting them at eye-level. She rested the 9mm pistol on her knee. His eyes flicked down to it. Its flat muzzle was pointed directly toward him.

"All I know for sure is that you were the last one to see Jake Thames alive. And for all I know, you've been in hiding all this time because you were the one who murdered him."

"What? Why would I – "

"Maybe you didn't like the competition. I'm guessing that's why you came to the UK in the first place – to get rid of Jake, stop him becoming more famous than you."

Deak didn't react with the shock or guilt she was expecting. In fact he looked almost bemused in the way he shook his head. "It's true, I only hooked up with that crew because of Jake. I guess I wanted to find out who this kid was, and maybe steal some of his secrets for myself. Back then I'd do anything to keep my edge, for sure. But I wasn't there to hurt him." He met her gaze. "I didn't kill Jake. I swear to God. I'm not a killer."

She digested this. "But you did punch him out and leave him down there."

Now there was guilt, twisting Deak's pallid face. "I was so scared, that place was… you can't imagine. You can't imagine. It was…" He licked cracked lips. "Look, if you don't believe me you should find the

318

other two guys, speak to them. They'll tell you what happened that night, they were with us. If you can find them, then they'll – "

"I already have."

"For real? You've spoken to them? Then you know I never – "

"Disclaimer is dead."

Deak sank heavily against the wall, disturbing some of the detritus around him.

"How?"

She considered what to tell him, recalling all the medical reports and police records she had read.

In late August 2010, Glen Patrick Leventhal-Tipton was registered at a private mental health clinic and remained a patient there for nearly a year. They diagnosed him with temporally graded retrograde amnesia and severe post-traumatic stress disorder, but could not identify the cause. Eventually, with a great deal of expensive therapy and medication, he was released into the care of his family. According to the subsequent doctors' reports, he remained un-communicative and withdrawn. His character had changed drastically, with little left of his former outgoing nature. He never discussed with anyone why he was found alone in Castle Court off Kentish Town Road early in the morning, and seemed to have no memory of that night. None of Glen's friends had a clue where he had been, but said he would often vanish in the early hours: "Off on an adventure!", he'd tell them.

Three years later, in April 2014...

"He threw himself under a train," she said quietly. "At Camden Town."

Deak spent a long moment looking at the floor. Then he nodded steadily. As if that somehow made sense to him.

"And Subverse? Is he…?"

"No. He's alive." But not the same man at all, she thought.

When she finally met him, Subverse – real name Neil Mackie – was hard to recognise. The tattoos and piercings were gone, the once-shaved head now covered with thinning curls, his dark eyes softened by oblong varifocals. That counter-culture creature she'd seen on the forum, whose loquacious ramblings accompanied hundreds of moody photographs of derelict places, had thrown himself into the main-stream rather than under a train. He worked in IT now. A middle-aged middle manager.

From Neil, she had learned a lot. He hadn't gone back to urban exploration, and admitted he didn't even like to think about those days anymore. But he did provide a lot of background about their 'mission' to get into South Kentish Town. A semblance of his past self had animated Subverse's now-chubby features when he talked about Jake. Even years later, he was still irritated by that "scrawny little shit". But when she asked him for details about what happened that night…

"He didn't seem to remember anything," she told Deak. "I could tell he wasn't lying to me, he just seemed kind of vacant about it all. He had no idea how he got out of the station, or what happened to any of you. He didn't even know that Disclaimer… that he was gone."

He hadn't asked about his old partner in crime, and she hadn't the heart to tell him. It was clear that Disclaimer and Subverse – Glen and Neil – were close friends for years, and yet after that night, they seemed to forget each other's existence.

As she sat in his cubicle in an open-plan company office, with photos of a wife and child on his paper-strewn desk, it was clear that Subverse had been scared back to normality. After years of living on the world's dark fringes, fascinated with subterranea and decay, he was now hiding in the light.

"It was the same for me," murmured Deak. "I didn't remember any of it for a long time. I was sick as a dog for weeks. Starving, useless, until someone got me to a hospital. Then it started coming back to me. I'd get these flashes… messed-up images, and night-mares of being in tunnels with something coming after me, chasing me… I still get them."

The words escaped her. "So do I."

Deak looked at her with interest, making her stand up and turn away. She shouldn't have said that. There was no need for him to know about what happened to her.

Whatever the hell *did* happen.

She could remember getting the Night Tube home from central London, and then… images of running through tunnels, an empty rotting station, something coming after her, something she couldn't quite see…

Like Deak, she'd been sick and useless for weeks. Followed by half-recalled images, queasy dreams and

321

crawling skin.

Since that day back in 2017, she couldn't bring herself to travel on the London Underground. She'd tried so hard. It was a struggle just to stand on a platform, rigid from head to toe. For years now, going into any kind of tunnel at all made her nervous. Even walking through pedestrian subways could bring on an anxiety attack.

"It's the train," Deak said, "the Under Line train. Jake said it emitted infrasound, outside the range of our hearing, that's why you can't hear it coming. But the infrasound affects us in different ways... triggers adrenalin, and stops our brains forming short-term memories... that's why we don't easily remember it. I thought I was going mad or hallucinating at first. Took me a long time to realise they were actually proper memories, trying to break through."

He ran his free hand down his bearded face. "I doubt I'd have remembered anything if not for the pictures. Even then, it was weeks after I got out of hospital – "

She spun back round. "What pictures?"

"The ones I took. On Jake's phone. Every now and then I used it to snap a few things, while I was reading the document. Then when we got to the... the Necropolis place... I was so scared, but I made myself take pictures. And then at the ghost station when the train came in and stopped. I was shaking so bad, thought they'd be blurred but you can just about see it sitting on the tracks, and all the... the faces against the glass..."

She shook her head. "Wait, you mean you actually

took pictures of it? And of Jake?"

Deak nodded. "Without those, I'd never have remembered a thing."

"What happened to the phone?"

"I've still got it."

"It's *here?*"

"Over there, in that corner."

Warily, she picked her way through the pile of rubbish to the left of where she'd handcuffed Deak. Her nose wrinkled as she pushed aside pizza boxes and takeaway cartons, kicked back a pile of stained sheets, rolled away a couple of broken torches. It crossed her mind that this might be a trap of some sort. Was some spring-loaded thing about to stab her or explode or… but then she pulled a torn old coat away from the corner and saw it, lying on the floor.

She picked it up. Her heartbeat fluttered.

"It ran out of power years ago," she heard Deak say as if from far away. "I mean, it's ancient now, don't know if it still works but the pictures are still on there, and all Mike Thames's stuff…"

Her gloved hand closed around the iPhone 3GS with its distinctive rubber case. She stood straight and drew a deep breath. "This is Jake's."

"Yes it is, I swear, and if you can get it working then – "

"No. I *know* it's his."

She tried to swallow down the emotion surging up her throat, wanting to push through her eyes, nose and mouth.

Her voice cracked. "I remember it."

She remembered seeing the phone on the pine coffee table in the front room, where all the remote controls lived. She remembered coming across it on a kitchen sideboard strewn with house keys, notepads and fruit bowls, and being told not to put her drink down next to it. She remembered accidentally kicking it where it lay on the floor recharging, and being shouted at every time she did. She was the reason why it had a shockproof and waterproof case.

Deak shuffled among all the rubbish so he could stare up at her. "You remember it. So you knew him. You knew Jake. Yes?"

All she could manage was a nod.

"Why didn't you say? Then you know he… wait, you're…" He looked her up and down, trying to peer past the dark clothing and baseball cap, trying to gauge her age. "Jesus, are you *her?*"

She glanced at him. "What?"

"There was a picture on the phone, of him when he was younger, in a park with a little girl. But that was years ago, so she'd be… That's you, isn't it? You're Jake's kid sister!"

She turned away again, taking a ragged breath.

He had a picture of me! Of both of us!

She assumed that he'd forgotten all about her, his annoying whiny brat of a sister. But he must have been looking at her every single day. She knew exactly which picture Deak referred to: sitting on a park bench in the sunshine, smiling big smiles, their matching blonde hair side by side. Jacob and Emily Thames.

He kept my picture.

He never forgot me.

Oh Jesus, Jake, *what happened to you!*

Clutching the phone, Emily squeezed her eyes shut. After nearly a year of searching for the missing half of her family… finally, finally.

It started with a death. Last summer her Great-Aunt Claire passed away, at the grand old age of ninety-six. For many years her mother lived with Claire in her small house in Falmouth, looking after their ageing relative… although Emily always knew this was something of an excuse, since the old girl was more than capable of looking after herself right up until her final weeks. The real reason was that Mum hated London so much. She had sold their old house in Golders Green and left the city as soon as Emily moved into student accommodation.

The funeral in Falmouth had been as efficient and no-nonsense as Great-Aunt Claire herself: a simple ceremony and the scattering of her ashes into the bay. There were few attendees, just a handful of locals. Some were surprised that Claire hadn't wanted to be buried in Brookwood Cemetery, in the village where she was born. Yet Emily knew that sentimentality wasn't in her nature. She'd always been kind to her and Jake when they were kids, but was hardly the cuddly granny type.

It was after the funeral when Emily's mother delivered the first shock. Great-Aunt Claire had left the house to Mum so she could continue living there, but bequeathed all of her savings to her only other living relative. And so Emily discovered she had just inherited around seventy thousand pounds.

Barely had she recovered from this when the second shock came. Her mum had changed her surname back to her maiden name, something easily achieved since her husband had been a missing person for twelve years. So now she was Julia Spencer again rather than Julia Thames.

Emily was enraged. It felt like being abandoned at an orphanage. She bellowed at her mother about how she never wanted to talk about Dad or Jake, never wanted to tell her what happened – it was like she was trying to forget ever having a husband and son. They'd had this argument many times over the past decade but now Emily felt like things had gone too far. "Why are you trying to forget them?" she had shouted. "Why haven't you done anything to find them!"

This time, her mother's defences cracked. With tears running down her tired face, she told Emily what she had kept from her when she was too young to understand... not that Mum really understood much, even now.

And so Emily finally learned about how her father became obsessed with letters sent to him by his own father, Robert Thames, from when he was a Tube driver in the Seventies. Mum explained how Dad started losing his grip on the world, fixated on his own family's history, and on the idea that there was something hidden in the London Underground... "Just stupid nonsense, madness," she called it.

Back then, in 2000, young Emily had been kept away from most of this. Until one night her dad took the car and left, never to return, never to be seen again.

Fresh tears poured from her mother when she told Emily that the exact same thing happened to Jake. Within a year, her brother had also become withdrawn and started heading off into the night without explanation. He vanished for hours at a time, then for days, and then… didn't come back home again.

This Emily did remember: holding her crying mother's hands over the kitchen table as, between sobs, she told her thirteen year old daughter it was just the two of them now. Emily always assumed that Jake had met up with Dad, and for some reason the two of them had gone to live elsewhere, splitting their family down the middle and leaving her to look after a broken, helpless mother.

"That's why I never told you," Mum had said, there in Great-Aunt Claire's house. "I don't know why they both went that way but there's something about it that's… I don't know… contagious." She'd stroked Emily's long blonde hair the way she used to. "Not you. I couldn't take the chance. Not you as well."

Taking the train back to London, Emily had physically ached, as if some old wounds had been stitched up and new ones sliced into her at the same time. She understood more, and yet felt like she wasn't being told anything. There was a temptation to forget all about what her mother had said and just get on with it, go back to her job and her friends, crack on with her life…

But now she was the last Thames. And the only

327

person in the world who still cared about her dad and brother.

No sooner had she resolved to find out the truth than Emily realised that there was no way she could do it herself. Where would she even start? No, she would be smart – she would get professional help.

Once the money from Great-Aunt Claire came through, she immediately went looking for the finest private detective agency she could find. After a few meetings with Global Investigations (UK) Ltd and a five-figure down payment, they took her case. The hunt was on.

The 'digital detective' assigned to work with Emily was a laser-sharp and knowledgeable woman. She was also confident that she'd get results quickly. But although she spent the rest of 2021 searching for any trace of Mike or Jake Thames, there was nothing. The frustration in the detective's voice grew as she kept reporting a lack of results, as did a trace of humility at her earlier boast. But she wasn't the type to give up, and neither was Emily.

At the start of this year, Emily instructed her to focus on the London Underground. After what Mum had said about her dad being obsessed with it, that seemed logical. On a defunct blog, the detective found a post about breaking into British Museum Station that mentioned a 'Jake'. He had been part of an urban exploration crew that was last active in 2010, which fit the timeline. Emily's excitement had spiked – they'd found a trace!

The crew's faces were all blurred in their photos, but the detective contacted the forum's old moderator and acquired pictures of three of them – all but Jake. Face-recognition software made quick work of the crew's pseudonyms. Disclaimer and Subverse were easily named and located, although only the latter was still alive for Emily to visit. The fourth member, Spatial Deconstruction, was identified as Toby Gabriel Bouchard, a Canadian national.

This man was the key. Toby, or 'Deak' as Subverse called him, was the last person to see Jake alive. But he turned out to be as hard to find as Jake himself. Deak was thought to be living in the UK, but there were no traces of him anywhere on the internet. He had no digital footprint since leaving Toronto. He was a 'nonline'.

The detective admitted that finding nonlines was exceptionally difficult these days. "However," she had said to Emily over a secure phone line, "if you're willing to stump up another, say, fifteen or twenty grand, and you don't mind bending the rules a smidgen, there might be a way…"

Emily never found out precisely what the detective did with the extra money, but assumed it involved bribing someone to access police CCTV cameras or surveillance drones or something like that. She was almost certainly risking her career at Global Investigations by doing this, not to mention criminal charges.

Some weeks later, the detective met Emily in person to tell her there was a place in central London where a man strongly resembling Toby Bouchard could be seen entering, but never leaving. There had been a proper sparkle in the detective's eyes, like she was enjoying 'bending the rules' – or to be more accurate, 'breaking the law'. She even offered to come along as backup. But Emily had already decided how to approach this confrontation, and it would be best if there were no witnesses.

Which was how Emily Thames came to be in the Charing Cross area earlier that night, with a baseball cap low over her face and a gun inside her padded jacket.

It was easy to miss the subway entrance on William IV Street, as it seemed like an unremarkable open space between shops. She had to fight off a nervous tremble at the idea of going below ground, but made herself walk down several flights of steps, each right-angling deeper and deeper.

Emily had never been through the pedestrian walkways beneath Charing Cross Station before, and was startled at what a maze they were. The walls were tiled in rows of white, yellow and orange as if the 1970s were still going on down there. Up ahead, stairs and escalators led to nearly a dozen surface exits. Small shops were shuttered for the night, and rows of advertising billboards were set into the walls – not the modern digital kind that addressed you by name as you passed, just old-fashioned hoardings for posters.

The broad passageways were empty except for a few homeless people hunkered inside sleeping bags. The sight of them made Emily feel that she was walking through hostile territory. But this was just the start.

She checked that no-one was nearby, then gripped the edge of the first advert billboard and pulled hard. Then the next, and the next, until she found one that shifted under her touch. The entire billboard moved outwards on creaking hinges, just wide enough for someone to step behind it.

The detective's hunch had been right! Since Deak was only ever seen entering the subway on CCTV, never leaving, there had to be a concealed route in there he was using. She looked around again before squeezing through the gap. It felt like she was stepping *behind* real life, somehow.

Emily had found herself standing in a cylindrical shaft lined with mould-encrusted bricks. A spiral staircase made from iron coiled around the wall, down into pitch blackness.

Her stomach rolled. The fear roared back at the idea of going down there, down into the earth, and yet... part of the bloodrush could have been excitement. She felt close to getting some answers. Her hand shook as she aimed a small torch into the shaft and forced leaden legs to move down the staircase. Behind the billboard above, the everyday sounds of traffic and people faded away. Nothing but her bootsteps and breathing, echoing in the dark.

In less than a minute, she reached the bottom of the shaft. It felt like being in a pressure cooker, making her lungs work harder to draw in air. She stood still for a long time, fighting off a rising panic, but slowly amazement took over.

She was in a cramped passageway with a brick wall on one side and a concave wall on the other, which was covered in familiar ceramic tiles. They were yellowed with coloured patterns of brown and green, all dulled by thick dust. It was unmistakably the interior of an Underground station – but only a fragment. Walled off, hidden away, forgotten.

Her torch beam shone on a rusty metal sign. A red roundel with a blue bar across it, which displayed the words *TRAFALGAR SQ.* beneath drooping cobwebs.

She felt it, then. The gut-deep curiosity that made urban explorers want to go to places where they were forbidden. Perhaps the same fascination that took root in her brother and father years ago.

That same taut ache. A cousin to hunger.

Treading forward, she saw how the passage turned into a Y-shaped junction. There were two arrow-shaped signs on the wall. One said *Strand Tube Station (Tunnel V) – 60 yds* and the other *Conference Rooms J-M + Telecoms Exchange D – 25 yds*. The left side was walled up with brighter, newer bricks. The right side led to somewhere that gave off enough light for her to switch off the torch. That, and the tread marks on the filthy floor, told her she was definitely on the right track.

Before long, Emily was exploring a series of rooms made from smooth concrete. They were laced with pipes and connected by doorless openings. A couple of them had working neon lights that buzzed and flickered, emitting a sickly haze. Also still working was a huge ventilation unit in one corner, but the air was stifling and heavy with dust. It also stank to high heaven – someone had been using one of these rooms as a toilet.

She had prowled nervously through the doorways, closing in on sounds of movement and muttering. She found a room full of old mattresses and piles of rubbish. This was where she discovered Deak, squatting in the mess and stuffing items into a ripped backpack.

And this was where Emily made him yelp with fright as she pulled a gun on him and threatened to *blow his fucking head off if he didn't tell her what she wanted to know!*

He'd told her. The whole story.

"His sister," he whispered, gaping up at her. "It's you, isn't it? And you're still looking for Jake, of course you are."

Deak's eyes dropped to the handgun by her side. "That's, that's right, isn't it? You're not... I mean, you're not here to...?"

Emily made a show of flicking the safety catch on the side of the gun and sliding it back into her jacket's inside pocket. He didn't need to know that the Browning 9mm semi-automatic was only a replica. She wouldn't have a clue where to find a real gun, and even tracking down an authentic-looking fake had been hard. She'd anticipated having to intimidate Deak into telling her the truth, hence the gun and handcuffs. But now it was clear that he was only too willing to talk.

She looked again at Jake's old phone in her hand. "You've had this all these years."

Deak nodded. "I memorised everything on it. Before the power went." He tapped the side of his head with a grubby finger.

"What for? And what the hell have you been doing all this time, living down here like a rat?" Emily glanced around. "What even *is* this place, anyway?"

"It's Q-Whitehall… part of it."

"What's that?"

"Q-Whitehall! You know! The government's secret tunnels. All the government buildings are linked up, all over the city, all over." His hands plucked the air as if drawing connections between dust motes. "They've been here for years, right under everyone's noses. Officially top secret."

Emily tilted her head. "Really."

Deak shrugged with something of his old sardonic cool. "I've been in similar tunnel networks in Russia and Germany, even France. Europe's full of Cold War relics… tunnels, bunkers, tracking stations."

She glanced around the room and admitted that it did have the look of an official facility about it: featureless, soulless. As unlikely as it sounded, maybe this Q-Whitehall thing really had been an actual place once.

She felt uneasy. If that was real… what else might be too?

"That's what you're doing down here," she guessed. "You're trying to find the Under Line again."

"Yes!" Deak's face became animated. "Yes yes yes! I'm continuing Jake's work! Oh and now you're here, now Jake's sister is with me, this is perfect, this is so perfect – "

"After everything you've told me, why would you want to go back to that place? And I thought you said it was under Highgate Cemetery?"

"Not just that place, all of them, *all* the stations!" He scrambled around in the muck on the floor, rattling the handcuffs. "I've been looking for them all, finding the ways in. I've drawn a map! I've been down in all the tunnels looking for the ultraviolet marks, the signs on the Tube maps just like Jake found, but I've found much more, much more! I've drawn a map, you should see my map!"

"You're still doing all this? For the past *twelve years?*"

"This is what I do, this is me, this is proper spatial deconstruction! Oh it's going to blow their minds when I put it up, the forums are going to explode! They'll still remember me," he nodded rapidly, "I was the best, wait till they see this, they'll see I'm still the best…"

Emily ran a hand over her mouth, feeling queasy. God, she thought, what's happened to him?

Jake. That's what happened to him. Jake happened. Jake broke him.

"And now you're here," Deak went on, "it'll be much easier, we need to go down there tonight, together."

"Tonight?"

"It's the thirteenth! Yes? Yes? I told you what Mike Thames said – your dad, I mean, what your dad said. Early hours of the thirteenth, that's when the Under Line runs. And this time I'll find it. It'll definitely come if you're there."

She frowned. "If *I'm* there? Why does – "

"Because you're a Thames! They always come for you guys. It was obvious after I saw Jake in the cabin that's where he was going to end up, that's where you

335

all end up eventually. You're all Motormen! Drivers for the Under Line. People like you don't go under the same way as everyone else, that's why you're so useful to them. You're *already* under, you were *born* under."

Despite the stifling heat and the sweat coating Emily's face, hearing these words brought a shiver.

"The black train never comes for me but it'll come for a Thames, that's why we need to go together!"

She blinked, vision blurring. All of a sudden Emily was back there, trapped on a Night Tube with all those screaming people…

…running through the dark, through a dilapidated station…

…feeling something slide up behind her in total silence, hearing nothing but her own panicked breathing and…

…and a sort of absence of noise, like a vacuum sucking at her ears.

She'd had these flashes before, and knew they were from whatever happened to her five years ago. But only now did she wonder if it hadn't been some random encounter. Perhaps that particular Night Tube had been targeted – *because she was on it.*

It came for her. That's what Deak was getting at. And as much as Emily wanted to say that was crazy and ridiculous, it felt… no, it *was* ridiculous, of course it was!

Emily opened her mouth to say as much, but Deak was digging into the pocket of his stained and ripped trousers, producing something that he held up toward her. "Look, this will get us in! The train will come for you and we can follow it and we can get in, like before!"

She took the small piece of card from his fingers. It was grubby with ragged edges, and the text on it was partially faded. But she could see the words *LONDON TRANSPORT STAFF PASS 1974* and a serial number of five zeroes. The watermark was a London Underground symbol, but with two bars instead of one, overlapping in the middle. The crossed roundel – just like Deak had described.

This is proof, she thought. Proof that everything he said is true!

Or is it all bullshit and only this card is real? Some weird misprint he's built a story around?

Emily shifted her weight from foot to foot as if trying to find her balance. She'd been down there too long, breathed too much dirt and dust, and listened to far too many of Deak's words.

And he was still talking. "…got everything we need, I've got my map, my guide, all the equipment is ready, it's all next door." With his free hand, he gestured to a doorway at the side of the room. "You'll see, go and see, we've got everything we need, we're ready to go."

Almost in a trance and full of half-memories, she walked toward the opening. She slid the staff pass into the back pocket of her jeans and pulled the small torch from her jacket. At the doorway, she swept its beam inside. It looked like one more empty concrete box of a room… the word 'bunker' now felt right, if what Deak said about this place was true. It was five or six metres square with another empty doorframe at its far end, with darkness beyond.

Emily walked in and saw it wasn't quite empty. Along one wall were racks of machinery that looked like telephone switchboards, of the type where connections were manually plugged into sockets. There were a few other pieces of equipment that had dials, knobs and fat iron keys similar to early typewriters. It brought to mind documentary programmes she'd seen about the Second World War, breaking Nazi codes and all that. Was this place really that old?

More modern equipment was piled in the corner around a battered backpack. Several torches, plus a set of industrial bolt cutters, a loop of cable and what looked like climbing gear.

"You'll see the map," called Deak from the other room, "you'll see my guide, you'll see!"

The circle of white light from Emily's torch travelled round the walls. She glimpsed a flash of colour at the edge of the beam – down on the ground. She aimed the torch at her feet and jumped, startled. "Jesus Christ!"

The floor of the room was a Tube map.

The *entire* floor.

Emily spun in place, gazing down at the ribbons of colour that stretched across the room, vanishing into the shadows. It was recognisably a huge version of the London Underground map, but created by hand.

All the lines were there, zigzagging and criss-crossing over each other in their recognisable hues: dark blue for Piccadilly Line, green for District Line, red for Central Line, light blue for Victoria Line,

338

yellow for Circle Line, brown for Bakerloo Line, purple for Elizabeth Line and all the rest. Many had been painted onto the floor with a small brush, but others had been filled in using marker pens, felt tips, crayons, biros, congealed food sauces and coloured strips of paper taped into place. It was like a schoolchild's collage, but on a gigantic scale.

The circles and stubs of Tube stations had also been added, their names sketchily handwritten. All the disused stations were there too. Emily's gaze was drawn to Brompton Road, drawn in the gap between Knightsbridge and South Kensington, a few centimetres away from the tip of her left boot.

With her jaw hanging open, she scanned the enormous map all around her. The work of years – the work of an obsessive. Or a lunatic. The lunatic next door.

She stepped backward slowly, panning her torch and trying to take it all in. As she did, the back of her boot hit something. Sitting there in the rough centre of the room was what looked like a carry-lantern of modern design, the sort of thing used when camping outdoors. Emily knelt down to turn it on, assuming it would provide more light than her own small torch. Only when she flicked the switch did she notice that the light bulb inside was oil-black.

The lantern gave off a faint purplish glow. She stood up, turning off her torch. The room was now dark except for hundreds of tiny flecks shining on the walls and ceiling, and on her own clothes and gloves. Ultraviolet light, she realised. Just like in the nightclubs… and in the story Deak told her. He must be using this lantern the way Jake had when he –

"Oh my God."

Emily revolved with a hand across her mouth. On the Northern Line, something new had appeared. A shining line between Archway and Highgate, curving toward a crudely drawn symbol – a circle with an X in it. A crossed roundel, added in UV-sensitive fluorescent paint.

There was another, glowing blue-white in the dark, coming off the Bakerloo Line. And another off the Victoria Line.

And another. And another. And another. And another.

The map was dotted with them, fifteen, twenty, twenty-five… so many. There were so many! If these were real then the Under Line had grown over the years along with the rest of the Underground and now it was, bloody hell, now it was…

"…Everywhere," Emily breathed.

Some of the Xs had names scrawled beside them in spidery handwriting, and had been underlined. Emily trod this way and that, peering down at the floor to make them out.

She saw _Still Street_ jutting out near the ghost station of York Road. _Wakebridge_ emerged close to the long-abandoned Lords. _Soulsditch_ was connected to the derelict St Mary's.

Not all were linked to stations, some branching out from the spaces between them. Flanked by the famous Earl's and Barons Courts was the unheard-of _Paupers Court_. Above Epping, beyond the uppermost tip of the

Central Line, lay _Wreath Wood_. And halfway between Marble Arch and Bond Street, hanging off the line, dangled _Tyburn Cross_.

Emily scanned the floor in all directions, finding a _Downbourne_, and a _Greybury_, and a _Hearsefield_… names that sounded like they should be actual places with histories and postcodes. But nobody on the surface knew of them. They only existed down here, aglow in the dark, ablaze beneath her feet.

She crouched lower and ran her fingertips across the hand-painted Piccadilly Line, finding Brompton Road and a luminous X snaking away from it. Its name shone in front of her, a name she'd convinced herself she had imagined or dreamt and couldn't possibly have seen for real, scrolling across the electronic display inside a Night Tube.

> **This is a Piccadilly Line service to Heathrow Terminals 1, 2, 3 and 5**
>
> **The next station is Shroud Lane**
>
> **Please mind the gap between the train and the platform**

_Shroud Lane_.

Where it had come from. Where it wanted to take her.

She stood up and stared across the floor at all the Xs, some clustered together, some spaced out, but appearing right up to the far wall with the empty doorframe, which was totally dark and oddly shaped as if there were something filling it even though it had no door, and she squinted to try and make out what she was looking at only to realise that the darkness –

*"AAAH!"*

– was looking back at her –

*"Jesus!"*

– with a pair of eyes.

*"Shit shit shit!"* Emily bolted back the way she had come, slamming her shoulder against the edge of the wall and tumbling awkwardly. She kicked her body backward, sliding into the pile of rubbish where Deak still sat with one arm handcuffed to a pipe. She gasped for air, unable to think or breathe, heart trying to punch-punch-punch through her ribs.

She turned to Deak, pointed at the doorway, tried to speak but couldn't. He just looked at her through his fractured spectacles.

"What… there's… haaa… there's someone…"

She struggled to force out the words. Her hand gripped his shoulder, as if needing some kind of anchor. "Who's in there!" she managed to say. *"Who the fuck is in there!"*

Deak brushed some of his straggly hair away from his face. "I already told you."

"Yuh-you said… your map…"

He nodded. "And my guide."

"Wh-what?"

"She's my guide. She'll be *our* guide."

Emily's panicked breathing stopped dead for a few seconds, then resumed slower. She stared at the doorway. There were no sounds from beyond and no signs of movement. In her mind she was replaying that jolt of electric panic when she'd realised that the darkness was *looking at her…*

There's someone in there, she thought, Deak's got someone down here with him! She – he called it 'she'.

With effort, Emily made herself crawl across concrete. Above her, the single neon tube in the light fittings buzzed and flickered, making the whole room stutter like an old movie reel.

She peered round the edge of the doorframe, into the room with the Tube map floor.

The walls and ceiling were speckled with tiny glowing points, reflecting ultraviolet light. Crossed roundels shone on the ground. The lantern still gave off a faint purple glow. And standing very close to it, twinkling from head to toe like a night sky filled with stars, was…

Something black.

Something human-shaped.

Emily's breath caught in her throat but she resisted the impulse to scramble away. The figure seemed bulky, saggy, misshapen. She was barely able to make out its face, which seemed so coated with dirt that the features were indistinct. All except those wide, bright eyes. They gazed back at her without blinking.

"Who is that!" she hissed. Already her imagination was coming up with horror stories like Deak kidnapping someone and keeping them down here for years, imprisoned, abused… maybe turned into something dangerous, monstrous. Her hand reached inside her jacket.

"No! Please don't!" cried Deak. He looked alarmed,

stretching out his free hand to her. "It's okay, she won't hurt you, I promise, it's fine!"

He thought she was going to draw the gun and open fire. She hadn't told him it was fake. Instead she pulled out her torch, but he shook his head at that too. "No bright light. They don't like it. It's ultraviolet light they're drawn to."

"Oh God." The story he'd told her raced through her mind. She stared again at the near-silhouette. "That's a… one of the…"

"She's one of the 'London dead'." Deak let out a cracked laugh. "Stupid name for them, but then people were stupid back then. You can see for yourself they're not dead! I'm not going to call them that when I post my work on the forum, it'll make me look ridiculous. I'm going to come up with a better name. I thought maybe 'Londonites', or even better, 'Londoneaths', which really reflects – "

"What's it doing here!"

"I found her. On the Bakerloo Line. I was tunnel-walking near Waterloo and she just kind of slid out of a gap in the wall… gave me a heart attack. But she didn't attack me or anything, just stared at my ultra-violet light."

Emily looked again at the UV lantern that seemed to have transfixed the figure. It – she? – continued to stand close to it.

"I lured her back with it," said Deak matter-of-factly. "She just followed me, staring at it the whole time. I got her up to the surface through an emergency stairwell and she started getting agitated, sort of staring up at the sky and freaking out, but once I got

344

her back down here she was fine."

"You took that... you took her through the streets?" she asked with disbelief.

"Sure. Nobody even noticed." He shrugged. "It's London."

Emily's eyes grew used to the quasi-light in the room. She realised that the figure that had struck her as freakishly shaped, perhaps even deformed, wasn't quite as strange as it seemed. That was indeed the face of a Caucasian woman in her forties. But all other traces of gender were hidden beneath a slightly baggy boiler suit, covering her from the neck down. There was a sleeveless high-visibility jacket with reflective strips dangling from her shoulders, which would have been blazing in the UV light if it weren't so caked with soot. Dangling beneath her chin was a breath mask, and most of her hair was hidden beneath a hard plastic helmet.

"She's... a cleaner?"

"A fluffer," nodded Deak. "That's what they call the Tube cleaners. I think many of those who go under are fluffers, or maintenance workers, or track walkers, you know... Underground staff who spend too long underground."

Emily suddenly felt like she was inspecting an animal at the zoo. "Can she talk? Can she understand us?"

"No. Never speaks. I don't think she understands words anymore."

"And you... you've kept her here for how long, weeks?"

"She literally just needs somewhere dark to be, that's about it. She hardly even needs to eat or drink, a few scraps seem to be enough. Otherwise she's almost totally cut off from everything."

Without looking away, Emily rose to her feet and approached the doorway. The woman didn't react to the movement, just continued staring down at the UV lamp. Literally like a rabbit in headlights.

But… there was still an awareness on her dirt-covered face. Emily could see it. This wasn't a zoo animal or some subhuman mutant. This was a normal person – someone's mum, someone's daughter. She looked shell-shocked, stunned but still functioning on some basic level. Like PTSD sufferers, Emily thought. Like soldiers coming back from war.

Deak was right. The 'London dead' weren't dead in the slightest. But they were definitely changed.

Emily felt the shock and fear ebb away, replaced by fascination. She drew closer. The woman never blinked, which by itself was enough to make her disturbing. But it seemed like her head was jerking and tilting slightly, tiny fractions of movement. It made Emily think of the way a cat's ears twitched in response to every noise. She remembered Deak talking about infrasound… was she picking up things most people couldn't hear?

She gestured to the black light lamp. "Why is she so hypnotised by that?"

"They can see ultraviolet light, I told you that already, didn't I? That's why the black train produces so much of it, to attract them, like insects. Yes?"

"People aren't insects!" she said, almost offended.

"Ha, I said something similar to Jake. But he was right, they've adapted to being underground. Rats and mice can see ultraviolet, plenty of other nocturnal animals too, but not us... the lenses in our eyes stop it reaching our retinas. So their lenses must have changed, atrophied maybe. Their hearing's changed too, so they can detect sound below twenty hertz."

Deak's voice washed over her, his words normalising this bizarre situation, making it sound almost scientific. Almost believable.

The woman's faraway gaze and expressionless face weren't even that strange, really. Emily saw this every day while walking the streets of London: all the people staring at smartphones, watching their tablets, listening to music through earpieces. Thousand-yard stares. Everyone had them. That blank look of focusing on something beyond your surroundings, that only you're experiencing.

She tried to imagine this shadowy figure as an ordinary woman. Going to work for Transport for London every night and cleaning all the crap off the tracks, but spending too long in the dark earth, crushed under the hot weight of the city... it must have been like locking yourself inside a sensory deprivation tank every night. Your eyesight and hearing becoming deadened, so that the normal world didn't reach them anymore – your perceptions gradually slipping *under* human range. Hearing the unhearable. Seeing the unseeable.

Her skin prickled. The ideas swirling round her head felt like they belonged to someone else, injected into her skull.

Emily shook herself and turned to look at Deak. "What are you going to do with her?"

"I'm going to set her free. I'm taking her down with me, with us, tonight. Then I'll turn off the lamp, see where she goes and we can follow her. She's our guide!"

She looked back at the adjacent room, with the Xs giving off their eerie glow. "You think she'll lead you to one of those places."

"Yes, and with the staff pass, we'll be able to get in. I've got proper cameras this time, we can take pictures and get evidence. We can prove the Under Line is real! Biggest piece of urban exploration this century!"

She held out a hand toward the woman. "But you can't just use her like that, like a… a bloodhound! She's still a human being. You've as good as kidnapped her."

"She's *not* a human being!" Deak jerked on the handcuff angrily. "And listen, if I hadn't rescued her when I did, then the train would have come for her. I saved her!"

Emily glared at him. "Didn't you ever think that this woman's got a family? Friends? They're all wondering what happened to her, and you've got her down here! She needs help, we need to get her to a hospital or something."

"Then she'll be dead," he snapped, "properly dead, killed, murdered. That's what the Under Line's for! Weren't you listening? That's why there was a Dead Body Train in the first place, to get rid of them without people knowing they existed! You take her to a hospital and that's the last anyone will ever see of her."

"But why would they do that? She's obviously sick! Look, whatever this 'London dead' thing is, it's like a virus or something, right, something people pick up by – "

"No no no no! The Londoneaths aren't sick, they're *different*. We see them as 'not us', we can't help it. They're like a rival species, a rival tribe. Londoners have always hunted down Londoneaths, probably before there even was a London. They would have entombed them in barrows, burned them in pyres, buried them in plague pits, hanged them at Tyburn, whatever was right for the time. Using trains to take them away in coffins was the Victorians' way of making it a bit more civilised, but it's the same thing."

"Jesus, that's…" Emily chewed her lip. "You're talking about ethnic cleansing."

Deak nodded, hair curtaining his face.

"So you think if you hadn't brought her here, the train would have taken her to one of those stations and… buried her."

"Probably cremated her, actually. The stations have always been close to cemeteries so I expect that's how it's done nowadays. No evidence that way. Yes? One way or another, they don't come back."

She looked back and forth between him and the glittering silhouette inside the room, her mind racing. "If you're right, then when Jake stole their train, he wasn't just rescuing Disclaimer and Subverse, was he? He was rescuing all of the… the ones like her." She couldn't bring herself to say his word for them.

A grin split Deak's filthy face. "Prison breakout!

Yes? I didn't realise it then but you're right, he was on a rescue mission the whole time. Jake said the stations were like death camps for his people."

Her head jerked round. "His people?"

Deak nodded toward the room. "*Your* people."

She opened her mouth as if to refute this, but something was chiming at the back of her mind. Another idea that felt pushed into her brain from the outside.

With a deep breath, Emily stepped into the room.

"What are you doing?"

Ignoring Deak, she approached the woman. Her heart was pounding again and her throat was dry, but she reminded herself that this wasn't a monster. There was an odour of dusty staleness about her but no stench of rotting flesh, no rabid foaming jaws, no evil red glare. This was a person... a different kind of person.

The staring eyes rose to meet Emily's own. They looked at each other in the twinkling dark. Londoner and Londoneath.

The woman's body sparkled with UV-reflective scraps as she shifted slightly. It crossed Emily's mind to introduce herself, or to assure her that she meant no harm. But she sensed how pointless that would be. Odd that she should be so sure of that, but she was. It felt like simultaneously discovering some unknown breed of animal and meeting someone who knew her extremely well.

"I'm... I'm looking for Jake." She cleared her throat and raised her voice. "Jacob Thames, my brother. Do you know where he is?"

"She won't understand you," came Deak's voice from the other room. "She doesn't respond to words anymore."

Emily could see that this was true – that her voice made no impact – yet she could also see that the woman was definitely responding to something. Her micro-movements became more noticeable, and she was swivelling in her direction.

An idea came to her as she glanced down at Deak's hand-made map. Emily knelt and pointed to the crossed roundel symbol with the name _Cryptgate_ scratched below it. Her finger drew a path from there to a point between Archway and Highgate Stations, and then along the painted black stripe of the Northern Line until she reached South Kentish Town. Her pointing hand turned into an open palm.

"Then where?" she said. "Show me on here. Where did it go?"

"That won't work either," called Deak, guessing what she was doing. "She doesn't care about the map."

"It's not a map," she heard herself reply, "it's an atlas of her world."

The woman stared down at her. Emily repeated the movement, drawing a path from Necropolis station to ghost station, then went back and did it again and again.

What else could she do to get through to her? Damn it, if only her brother's old phone still worked, she could show her the pictures Deak said he took of –

The woman crouched to the floor with such speed that Emily didn't have time to react. Suddenly her hand was being gripped.

She must have made some kind of noise because Deak's voice became alarmed. "What's happening?"

Emily couldn't speak or move. The crouching figure held her leather-clad hand. The woman's hand was also gloved, with a thick plastic that was dark grey with dirt.

But she wasn't looking at Emily – her head was tilted off to one side. As if something far more interesting were going on in the shadows of the room.

Without looking down, she began to pull Emily's hand across the floor, following the black line through South Kentish Town… on to Camden Town… Mornington Crescent…

She searched the woman's face, finding nothing except those eyes staring into thin air. Her head tilted to a different angle. It looked like she was straining to hear something far away… yes, Emily realised, she's listening! But to what?

To whom?

She felt her hand being firmly guided down the Northern Line, past Charing Cross and Embankment – and stopped. The woman pushed her hand against the floor, enough to hurt a little.

"Emily! What's going on!" called Deak.

She licked dry lips and replied "She's showing me… I think she's showing me where the train went. It stopped just after Embankment. But there's nothing there."

"Just after Embankment? But that's in the river!" She heard Deak's body twisting among the piles of rubbish. "Wait, wait, there's a… I remember this, it's on the blueprints. There's an old tunnel loop under the river, like the one at Kennington. It used to run from Charing Cross round to Embankment, before they extended the line. But that was a hundred years ago… Is that where she's pointing to?"

"I think so," said Emily, not actually sure what to think.

"Wait, no, it was bombed! In the Blitz, it got hit with a bomb and totally flooded. It's all been sealed off, nothing can get in or out. How could Jake have taken a train in? There's nothing there!"

Emily let out a small gasp as she felt the woman's grip tighten further. Their joined hands described a tight circle on the floor, once, twice.

The woman let go but remained crouched. Her head tilted again, as if hearing another faraway noise, then swivelled so that her unblinking eyes bored into Emily's.

And she knew. "That's where he took them."

Deak's voice was full of astonishment. "Into the river?"

She nodded – and the woman nodded too, at precisely the same time.

"That's where Jake ended up," said Emily. "Beneath the Thames."

Sunday 13th March 2022
1.14am

Emily pushed open the hatch a few centimetres and peeked through at the real world.

Lights stabbed her eyes, making her wince. She looked out at the empty pedestrian subway with its white-yellow-orange tiling. Waited. Listened. There were distant sounds of people, but nobody nearby.

Quickly, she stepped through the gap, then eased shut the advertising billboard set into the wall. She retraced her steps to the William IV Street entrance but found it blocked with a steel gate. Her boots left grimy prints on the floor as she hurried deeper through the passageways. She passed a ticket office where a fair few people were coming and going, taking the Night Tube home or coming into the West End for a late Saturday night out.

Glimpsing CCTV cameras, Emily pulled down her baseball cap and hurried up the stairs to one of the few exits still open. Her jacket felt lighter without the fake gun. She'd left it down there, along with the handcuffs. As she finally unlocked them from Deak's wrist, he had begged for her to come with him – with them – down into the Tube tunnels. But she'd left without saying another word.

Had to get out. While she could.

He was still down there, with his map and his guide, waiting for her to return. Absolutely convinced she would return. "We need you," Deak had called out as she walked away, "we'll wait for you!"

She found herself standing outside Charing Cross Station. Scores of people were passing back and forth, taxis were growling through the station gates, and buses and cars were cruising along the Strand. The night sky was invisible in the glare of streetlamps, headlights and shops.

Emily fought an urge to run back underground.

She took a deep breath. London's air, peppered with vehicle exhaust and industrial fumes, filled her lungs. The mild wind felt polar after the sweltering pressure below. And God, the unending swarms of people… was it always this crowded?

It took a while for her body to acclimatise, feeling like a deep sea diver in a pressure chamber. Eventually she pulled off the baseball cap and dropped it, letting her blonde hair fall to her shoulders. Her gloves also came off and were discarded. She started to walk.

Emily strolled along Villiers Street, which was as busy as always. Pubs and bars were still open, with many people eagerly queuing for small restaurants and street-food sellers. Fairy lights were strung along the whole length of the street, giving it a slightly carnival atmosphere. There were plenty of half-drunk revellers enjoying themselves, and groups of young people – well, her age, really – talking, walking, laughing, kissing.

There were also those who kept to themselves, even here. Only a few, but Emily's eyes were drawn to them. Men and women who didn't talk, walk, laugh, kiss. They didn't pay attention to anything, just stared into space. You saw this a lot on trains and buses: people withdrawn into themselves, secure in their private inner worlds.

At the bottom of Villiers Street was the edifice of Embankment Station, with its familiar roundels and signs. Emily hesitated before walking through the entrance. Again, she felt that impulse to turn and run down the escalators, to scurry back underground… but she crossed the ticket hall and came out the other side through an identical archway.

In front of her were the roads of Victoria Embankment, running along the north bank of the river. Several people stood near the traffic lights, waiting to cross. Just standing patiently.

The lights changed to red, and the traffic came to a slow halt. On the pedestrian crossing, the glowing red figure changed to a walking green man. Red and green, stop and go. No need to think in London, it told you what you needed to know.

Everyone looked jolted out of half-sleep by the beeping sound. And Emily's skin prickled as she watched the strangers start to walk at precisely the same moment. All crossing the road in silent unison.

All receiving the same signal.

She stood overlooking the River Thames. It was hard to see much of it with all the piers and walkways blocking her view. To her right was Hungerford Bridge, beyond which she could see Big Ben, and the equally familiar London Eye on the south bank.

Turning left, Emily walked along Victoria Embankment. The pavement was much emptier but there were still a few people wandering along. There were raised benches facing the river, some filled with the bulky shapes of homeless people in sleeping bags. Old wrought-iron streetlamps lit up rows of trees.

She stopped when she came to Cleopatra's Needle, a towering stone obelisk covered with hieroglyphs. Amazing to think that this chunk of ancient Egypt was now part of modern London, over three thousand years later. Standing sentry were two large sculptures of sphinxes, which were added when the obelisk was installed during Victorian times. One of their plinths was heavily pockmarked, damaged during the air raids of the First World War.

So much history.

She walked down into the area behind Cleopatra's Needle. It was a wide concrete space, a block of the embankment jutting out over the river. Openings on either side were guarded by overlapping railings, with stairs that led directly to the foreshore. Pale brown water lapped against muddy sand, sprinkled with stones and pebbles. She could literally step down into the Thames if she wanted. Presumably this was from the days when fishing boats or ferries were boarded here. Another outpost of yesteryear.

Emily stood alone. She leaned over the wall with the breadth of the river before her, its surface sparkling with reflected lights. She looked out at the buildings along the south bank. She listened to the rumble-squeal of trains passing along Hungerford Bridge. Unending traffic continued to growl softly behind her. Her eyes dipped to the River Thames below.

This is where I came from, she thought. If what Deak said was true – if what Great-Aunt Claire told

Dad was true. We all started here. With Jacob.

No, surely that was absurd. All that nonsense about her great-great-grandfather, if he even existed. Christ Almighty, the whole thing was ridiculous! Urban myths and made-up bullshit from a deranged obsessive who's been living in a pit for years! But…

But the woman was real.

Emily pictured the strange, silent figure who stood in the map room. Her faraway expression, withdrawn into herself, secure in her private world. Eyes wide as she followed the ultraviolet light... the way people follow the red and green lights on the surface. No need to think in London, it told you what you needed to know.

Yes, she was real. As real as anyone living on the skin of the city. And she knew, didn't she? She knew what Emily was looking for. Her unblinking eyes, her nod in perfect sync… she *knew*.

Emily stared at the water, wondering what was really down there. This part of the embankment was almost directly above the abandoned loop of the Northern Line, which Deak said had been cracked from above during the Blitz, flooded and sealed off. And this was where the woman's hand described a tight circle.

Maybe they're still there after all these years. Maybe Jake founded a colony in that sealed-off tunnel. A new Thames Tunnel for a new population. A Londoneath population.

Emily pulled Jake's old mobile phone from her jacket pocket. She held it with both hands, turning it over and over, feeling the protective rubber casing.

She could still visualise the image he'd used as its background, of them as kids, smiling together in the sunshine.

If she could get it working again, she could see it. Like the hieroglyphs carved on Cleopatra's Needle behind her, this beaten and battered device had survived intact for a long time and could still tell a story. It still had Jake inside it, and her as a little girl, and their mum and dad. Them as a family, the four of them. Not just her brother's memories but all of their memories.

Also on there were the pictures Deak said he took in 2010. Of South Kentish Town… of the faces at the windows… of Jake, staring out. The last picture of him.

And more, of course, much more. Her father's document and research. Her grandfather's letters, the smuggled-out blueprints and information. Surely she could take the phone to some technical geeky place and get them to power it up again, get it working, download everything on it? It must be possible!

I could read it all for myself, she thought. Prove that Deak was telling the truth. Know everything they knew. And then I could…

She reached into the back pocket of her jeans and pulled out Robert Thames's 1974 staff pass. She held the faded piece of card in one hand and Jake's phone in the other.

…And then I could see it for myself.

Excitement quickened her pulse. She glanced down at the river. Jake might still be there – right there, beneath the water. Her dad might even be there! Of course that's where they were, in the Thames Tunnel, of course. It's where we came from, she thought, it's our home!

Suddenly it all seemed very simple. She already had all that she needed. She had her grandfather's pass to unlock all the secret doorways. She had someone to accompany her, an experienced explorer with an actual map. She even had a guide, one of the Londoneath who knew where her people would gather. And every scrap of knowledge that her family had learned through the decades was on the phone in her hand.

Their legacy. Her birthright. Yes?

"Yes," she whispered to the wind.

Yes! She was *born* to go under.

Her blood was pounding now, there was a coppery taste in her mouth, and her eyes were fixed on the phone and the staff pass like they glowed in the dark. It all seemed obvious that this was what she should be doing, this was where she belonged. There was almost an ache inside her, filling the hollows of her torso, like some magnetic pull, like some special kind of gravity that only she could feel, drawing her under the ground, under the river, under the city, under the world –

The phone rang.

Emily jumped back with a cry. Her heart skipped as an electronic ringtone split the air.

She gaped at Jake's old phone in her hand. Is that – is he – ?

No, she realised, the ringing was coming from her

own phone. The iPhone remained dead.

"Shit!" She jammed the staff pass back into her jeans pocket then fumbled inside her jacket. Her phone was flashing the caller ID: *Peter*.

Her mouth opened to tell it to accept the call, but something made her pause. She wasn't sure she trusted her own voice to sound normal right now.

"Silent," she said to her phone. Biometrically recognising her, it obeyed and stopped ringing.

Peter's grinning face filled the display. He had cropped black hair, blue eyes and a sort of smooth baby-face, contrasting with his corded neck and broad shoulders. She could easily imagine his voice, with his hybrid Polish-Cockney accent, making some cheeky remark about her. He was very plain speaking but surprisingly witty for a scaffolder.

Emily felt a smile tug at her mouth. She'd learned to be super-cagey with men after a handful of crap boyfriends over the years. Well, some were crap and some she scared away, to be fair. But Peter didn't seem to be budging. It was only six weeks since they met, but she'd spent a lot of time with him and they spoke every day.

How did he become part of her life so quickly? As soon as they started talking, it felt as if they already knew each other. Not in a clichéd romantic way – it was literally like they'd been to the same school, or she'd forgotten a first date with him, or something like that.

Peter knew she was out tonight but had no idea where, or what she was up to. Her phone listed his previous missed calls over the past few hours, when

361

she'd had no signal below the streets. It made her feel funny. She wasn't used to anyone calling to make sure she was okay.

The phone went dark. She put it back inside her jacket… then took it out again. Leaning both elbows on top of the embankment wall, she held Jake's clunky, obsolete brick in one hand and her ultra-thin 5G device in the other.

Her eyes flicked back and forth between them. Past and present.

She tried to remember what she'd been thinking, only moments ago. Now all she could think about was… not Peter himself so much, more the change he had triggered.

He didn't make her feel special or amazing or one in a million – he made her feel *ordinary*. Just an ordinary woman, going out with an equally ordinary funny-and-quite-nice-looking bloke.

Equally ordinary was a recent visit by Alicia, one of the girls she shared a flat with while at university. During their epic five-cups-of-tea-and-two-bottles-of-wine chat, they'd discussed employment and Emily started to think about doing something other than tedious temp jobs. That Broadcast Journalism degree had taught her a lot. She always loved the idea of working as a researcher or reporter, digging up stories.

So now she was seriously considering retaking it, maybe doing an Open University refresher course. She'd already begun looking for vacancies at TV studios and online newsdesks. Funny how something as ordinary as getting a new job could be so exhilarating.

For the first time, 'ordinary' wasn't an impossible pipe dream after all.

For the first time, Emily's whole life wasn't one big bastard mess.

She had only been twelve years old when her dad lost his mind and vanished. Thirteen when her brother went the same way. Seventeen when her mother moved to Falmouth, leaving her alone. Twenty when something terrifying and inexplicable happened to her on a Night Tube, leaving her wandering around South Kensington in the early hours of the morning without knowing how she got there. She remembered being terrified on the train, and all the other passengers being terrified, so surely *something* had happened, and yet... there had been nothing in the news the next day. No social media posts from people about their experience. No record of any unusual incidents on a Night Tube. It was like she'd imagined the whole thing! Was she going insane, losing her mind like Dad did?

After that she couldn't remember her own name on some days, and couldn't pass the exams for her degree, and couldn't go out by herself anymore, and couldn't socialise with anyone, and couldn't set foot anywhere below ground without breaking into a cold sweat and wanting to cry.

All those years of wondering out loud in the middle of the night: "Why is this happening to me? Why can't I just be ordinary, for God's sake! *What's wrong with me?*"

Cold wind blew hair across her face as she nodded.

363

Now she knew what had happened to her. Now she knew why. She could never be ordinary.

She was a Thames.

Her arms stretched, holding out both phones over the water. She thought of how the river was shown on the Underground map: a jagged blue bar running beneath all the Tube lines. Like a scar across the face of London, gouged deep into its skin.

We're the same, she thought. We're a scar. We disfigure anyone who gets too close.

Emily blinked back tears, making the two phones in her hands look blurred. It was time, wasn't it? Time to let go of a life that she didn't deserve to have.

Say it. Or it's not real.

"Time to let go," breathed Emily into the wind.

Her eyes closed. She allowed one of her hands to loosen its grip.

The phone slipped through her fingers and into the empty air beyond the wall. She imagined it flipping over and over as it fell, before the sound of it splashing into the river reached her.

Shivers went through her body from head to toe.

She'd made her choice.

Emily turned away from the Thames. She strode up the steps beside Cleopatra's Needle, back onto the pavement. She moved with urgency, looking like someone on a mission.

There were still a few people passing by at this time of night, but they didn't notice her. Nobody glanced her way. The Londoners ignored her like they ignored everyone else.

364

And why shouldn't they?

She was just as ordinary as them.

That smile came again. She lifted her phone to her ear and told it to return the most recent call. As she waited to hear Peter's voice, Emily made her way home through the streets of London.

# Author's Notes

This novel is the result of a long-held fascination with the London Underground and its history.

As a native Londoner I have travelled on the Tube thousands of times, but it always feels like inhabiting a slightly different world to the city on the surface. The facts and figures of the Underground are just as fascinating as its mysteries and shadowy corners, and I hope this book does justice to both aspects.

This book is a work of fiction, but real people, locations and events have been referred to in a fictional context. Some of these events are of a tragic nature involving loss of life, but are included as a matter of historical fact to enrich the story. No disrespect is intended to anyone who may have been affected by historical events referenced within the novel.

Urban exploration is featured in this book. The practice of 'place hacking' environments that are normally out of bounds is a fascinating one. I am indebted to several real-life explorers whose writings and photographs have directly informed some locations featured in the novel.

However, I am obliged to note that **urban exploration is usually illegal and highly dangerous**. This book should not be viewed as any kind of endorsement or encouragement of such activity. None of the fictional characters or situations should be considered representative of urban exploration in general or of any specific practitioners or incidents.

## Acknowledgements

Many thanks to Tug Wilson, Kath Middleton, Julie Stacey, Manab Roy, Steve Opsblum, Eileen Gilbey, Rosemary Green, Ann Voysey and Paul Tilling for feedback, proofreading and providing information.

Additional thanks to the owners, contributors and members of these online resources:

Abandoned Tube Stations
District Dave's London Underground Forum
Disused Stations
Going Underground
Guerrilla Exploring
Ian Visits
Londonist
Railways Archive
*SQUAREWHEELS*
STC New Southgate Website
Subterranea Britannica
Tubeprune
Underground History

Thanks also to the London Transport Museum and the Hidden London tours.

# Bibliography

Many thanks to the authors of the following books, which were both inspirational and served as valuable resources.

Peter Ackroyd, *Illustrated London* (Chatto and Windus, 2003)

Peter Ackroyd, *London Under* (Vintage, 2012)

Catharine Arnold, *Necropolis: London And Its Dead* (Pocket Books, 2007)

David Brandon and Alan Brooke, *Haunted London Underground* (The History Press, 2013)

John M. Clarke, *The Brookwood Necropolis Railway* (Oakwood Press, 2006)

Bradley L. Garrett, *Explore Everything* (Verso, 2014)

Stephen Halliday, *London Underground Facts* (David and Charles Ltd, 2009)

Andrew Martin, *The Necropolis Railway* (Faber and Faber, 2009)

Ninjalicious, *Access All Areas* (Ninjalicious, 2005)

Ben Pedroche, *Do Not Alight Here* (Capital History, 2013)

Fiona Rule, *London's Labyrinth* (Ian Allen Publishing, 2013)

Stephen Smith, *Underground London* (Abacus, 2005)

Richard Trench and Ellis Hillman, *London Under London* (John Murray Publishers Ltd, 1992)

# About the Author

David Wailing writes modern fiction, a blend of mystery, thriller and humour.

At present he has six novels available as eBooks on Amazon:

**Auto**

**Auto 2**

**Bang**

**Duallists**

**Fake Kate**

**Under**

The short story **Signal Failure**, a prelude to Under, is permanently free to download in eBook format from Amazon, iTunes, Kobo and Nook.

David lives in north London on the Piccadilly Line.

www.davidwailing.com

facebook.com/davidwailing

twitter.com/davidwailing

25173241R00221

Printed in Poland
by Amazon Fulfillment
Poland Sp. z o.o., Wrocław